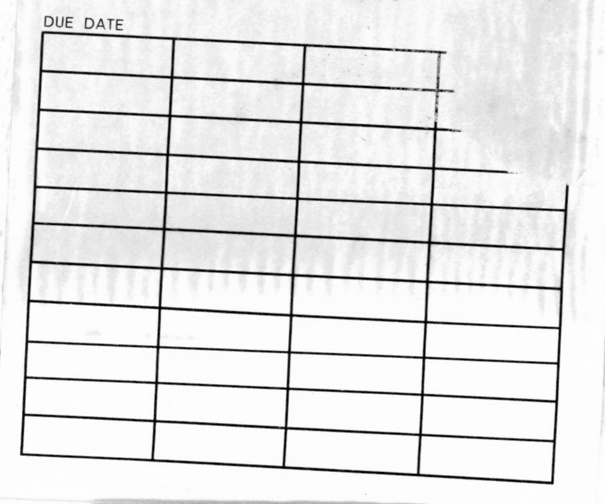

Webster

MOTH SMOKE

MOTH SMOKE

Mohsin Hamid

FARRAR, STRAUS AND GIROUX · NEW YORK

Farrar, Straus and Giroux
19 Union Square West, New York 10003

Distributed in Canada by Douglas & McIntyre Ltd.
Printed in the United States of America
Designed by Abby Kagan
First edition, 2000
Library of Congress Cataloging-in-Publication Data

Hamid, Mohsin, 1971–
Moth smoke / Mohsin Hamid. — 1st ed.
p. cm.
ISBN 0-374-21354-2 (alk. paper)
I. Title.
PS3558.A12 M68 2000
813'.54—dc21 99-045753

For

Nasim,

Naved,

and

Zebunnisa

contents

MOTH SMOKE

It is said that one evening, in the year his stomach was to fail him, the Emperor Shah Jahan asked a Sufi saint what would become of the Mughal Empire.

"Who will sit on the throne after me?" asked Shah Jahan.

"Tell me the names of your sons," replied the saint.

"Dara is my eldest son."

"The fate of Dara should be asked from Iskandar."

The Emperor's toes curled beneath him. "Shuja is my second son."

"But Shuja is not shuja."

"What about Murad?"

"Murad will not fulfill his murad."

The Emperor closed his eyes. "Aurangzeb is my youngest son."

"Yes," said the saint. "He will be aurangzeb."

The Emperor gazed across the plain at the incomplete splendor of his wife's mausoleum and commanded his workers to redouble their efforts. It would be finished before the war of succession began.

• • •

The truth of the saint's words became apparent. Aurangzeb was crowned Emperor, and he obtained from the theologians a fatwa against his defeated brother, charging Dara Shikoh with apostasy and sentencing him to death.

The Alamgirnama *records the incident thus: "The pillars of Faith apprehended disturbances from Dara Shikoh's life. The Emperor, therefore, out of necessity to protect the Holy Law, and also for reasons of state, considered it unlawful to allow him to remain alive."*

Imprisoned in his fort at Agra, staring at the Taj he had built, an aged Shah Jahan received as a gift from his youngest son the head of his eldest. Perhaps he doubted, then, the memory that his boys had once played together, far from his supervision and years ago, in Lahore.

When the uncertain future becomes the past, the past in turn becomes uncertain.

Yesterday, an ordinary man may have been roused from his sleep to sit in judgment at the midnight trial of an empire. Before him, as he blinked dreams from his lashes, sat a prince accused of the greatest of all crimes, a poet and pantheist, a possible future. None present were innocent, save perhaps the judge. And perhaps not even he.

CHAPTER 1

one

My cell is full of shadows. Hanging naked from a wire in the hall outside, a bulb casts light cut by rusted bars into thin strips that snake along the concrete floor and up the back wall. People like stains dissolve into the grayness.

I sit alone, the drying smell of a man's insides burning in my nostrils. Out of my imagination the footsteps of a guard approach, become real when a darkness silhouettes itself behind the bars and a shadow falls like blindness over the shadows in the cell. I hear the man who had been heaving scuttle into a corner, and then there is quiet.

The guard calls my name.

I hesitate before I rise to my feet and walk toward the bars, my back straight and chin up but my elbows tucked in close about the soft lower part of my rib cage. A hand slides out of the guard's silhouette, offering me something, and I reach for it slowly, expecting it to be pulled back, surprised when it is not. I take hold of it, feeling the envelope smooth and sharp against my fingers. The guard walks away, pausing only to raise his hand and pluck delicately at the wire of the bulb, sending the light into an uneasy shivering. Someone curses, and I shut my eyes against the dizziness. When I open them again, the shadows are almost still and I can make out the grime on my fingers against the white of the envelope.

My name in the handwriting of a woman I know well.

I don't read it, not even when I notice the damp imprints my fingers begin to leave in the paper.

CHAPTER 2

judgment (before intermission)

You sit behind a high desk, wearing a black robe and a white wig, tastefully powdered.

The cast begins to enter, filing into this chamber of dim tube lights and slow-turning ceiling fans. Murad Badshah, the partner in crime: remorselessly large, staggeringly, stutteringly eloquent. Aurangzeb, the best friend: righteously treacherous, impeccably dressed, unfairly sexy. And radiant, moth-burning Mumtaz: wife, mother, and lover. Three players in this trial of intimates, witnesses and liars all.

They are pursued by a pair of hawk-faced men dressed in black and white: both forbidding, both hungry, but one tall and slender, the other short and fat. Two reflections of the same soul in the cosmic house of mirrors, or uncanny coincidence? It is impossible to say. Their eyes flick about them, their lips silently voice oratories of power and emotion. To be human is to know them, to know what such beings are and must be: these two are lawyers.

A steady stream of commoners and nobles follows, their diversity the work of a skilled casting director. They take their places with a silent murmur, moving slowly, every hesitation well rehearsed. A brief but stylish crowd scene, and above it all you preside like the marble rider of some great equestrian statue.

Then a pause, a silence. All eyes turn to the door.

He enters. The accused: Darashikoh Shezad.

A hard man with shadowed eyes, manacled, cuffed, disheveled, proud, erect. A man capable of anything and afraid of nothing. Two guards accompany him, and yes, they are brutes, but they would offer scant reassurance if this man were not chained. He is the terrible almost-hero of a great story: powerful, tragic, and dangerous. He alone meets your eyes.

And then he is seated and it begins.

Your gavel falls like the hammer of God.

Perhaps a query (*Where did I get this thing?*) flashes through your mind before vanishing forever, like a firefly in the belly of a frog. But the die has been cast. There is no going back.

The case is announced.

The prosecutor rises to his feet, and his opening remarks reek of closure.

"Milord," he says (and he means you), "the court has before it today a case no less clear than the task of the executioner. The accused has stretched out his neck beneath the heavy blade of justice, and there is no question but that this blade must fall. For he has blood on his hands, Milord. Young blood. The blood of a child. He killed not out of anger, not out of scheme or plan or design. He killed as a serpent kills that which it does not intend to eat: he killed out of indifference. He killed because his nature is to kill, because the death of a child has no meaning for him.

"There can be no doubt here, Milord; no more facts exist to be found. The balancing of scales awaits, Milord; redress for wrong is come. Tender humanity screams in fear, confronted by such a monster, and conscience weeps with rage. The law licks its lips at the prospect of punishing such a one, and justice can shut its eyes today, so easy is its task."

The prosecutor pauses, his words leaping about the courtroom like shadows cast by unsheathed knives in the flickering light of some dying candle.

"For this, Milord, is his crime . . ."

CHAPTER 3

two

Steadying the steering wheel with my knees, I pull the last unbroken cigarette out of a battered pack of Flakes. There are trees by the side of the road, but only on one side, and it's the wrong side, so their shadows run away from me in long smiles that jump over boundary walls and grin at each other while I bake in my car like a snail on hot asphalt.

Knees turn the wheel left, then right, steering around an ambitious pothole, a crack aspiring to canyonhood. Fingers twist the barrel of the cigarette, loosening the tobacco, coaxing it into a sweaty palm, rubbing the Flake between thumb and forefinger until it's almost empty. Eyes flick up and down, watching the road through the arc the steering wheel cuts above the dashboard. Foot gentle on the accelerator.

Slide the ashtray out and tip half the tobacco in. Take the compass I've had longer than I've had this car, which is a long time, and spear the hash on one blackened end. Left hand holds the tobacco in its palm and the compass in its fingers, right hand grips a plastic lighter while its thumb spins the flint. Sparks, no flame. Sparks, no flame. Then a light, and when the blue fire licks the hash, a sweet smell with a suddenness that's almost eager.

Crumble the hash into the tobacco, crush it, break it, feel the heat telling nerves in fingertips to pass on the message of a little hurt. Knead it, mix it thoroughly. Hold empty Flake in mouth by its filter, suck and refill, pack against a thumbnail, tip tip tip, repeat, tip tip tip, and twist the end shut. Incisors grab a bit of filter, pull it out, gently, like a bitch lifting a pup. Tear off a strip to let the smoke through, reinsert the rest to hold open the end and keep things in their place.

I light up while rubbing the hash and tobacco residue off my hand and onto my jeans. Rolling while rolling, solo, and baking while baking in the heat. It helps kill time on long afternoons, and I haven't traveled very far, but I know that no place has afternoons longer than this place, Lahore, especially in the summertime.

Two drops of Visine and I'm set.

The sun sits down. Evening. I pull up to a big gate in a high wall that surrounds what I think is Ozi's place. His new place, that is. His old place was smaller. I'm a little nervous because it's been a few years, or maybe because my house is the same size it was when he left, so I swing my face in front of the rearview and look myself in the eye. Then I honk out a pair of security guards.

"Sir?" one says.

"I've come to meet Aurangzeb saab."

"Your name?"

"Tell him Daru is here."

Access obtained, I cruise down a driveway too short to serve as a landing strip for a getaway plane, perhaps, and pass not one but two lovely new Pajeros. Yes, God has been kind to Ozi's dad, the frequently investigated but as yet unincarcerated Federal Secretary (Retired) Khurram Shah.

The front door opens and a servant leads me inside and

upstairs. Time has ripened Ozi's face and peeled his hairline back from his temples with two smooth strokes of a fruit knife. We crouch, facing each other with our arms spread wide, and pause for a moment, grinning. Then we embrace and he lifts me off my feet. I thump him on the back and squeeze the wind out of his lungs for good measure. Neither of us says hello.

"You've gone bald," I exclaim.

"Thanks a lot, yaar," he replies.

Mumtaz steps forward and kisses me on the cheek. "Hello, Daru," she says. Hoarse voice, from intimacy's border with asthma: parched beaches, dust whipped by the wind. Very sexy but not much to drink.

I try on a welcoming, harmless smile. It gets caught on my teeth. "Hello, Mumtaz."

"And this," Ozi says, hoisting up a tired little boy, "is Muazzam."

Muazzam starts to cry, wrapping his arms around his father's neck and hiding his face.

"You certainly have a way with kids," Ozi tells me.

"He's exhausted," Mumtaz says. "You should put him to bed."

A muffled "No" comes from the boy.

We sit down on a set of low-slung sofas like black-cushioned metal spiders. Mumtaz is watching me and I look away because she's beautiful and I don't want to stare. I haven't seen her since the wedding, and I must have been more drunk than I thought because I don't remember thinking then that Ozi was such a lucky bastard.

"Scotch?" Ozi asks.

"Of course," I respond.

Ozi starts to hand Muazzam to Mumtaz, but she stands up. "I'll get it," she says.

"Do you really think I've gone bald?" Ozi asks me.

"I'm afraid so, handsome," I tell him, even though he still has hair left. Ozi's vain enough to survive a little teasing.

Mumtaz pulls an unopened bottle of Black Label out of a cabinet. My bootlegger tells me Blacks are going for four thousand apiece these days. I stick to McDowell's, smuggled in from India and, at eight-fifty, priced for those of us who make an honest living. But Ozi can afford the good stuff, and Black Label is fine by me, provided someone else is paying.

"Ozi claims he was a real heartthrob in his younger days," Mumtaz says, cracking the seal.

"He certainly was," I reply. "Lahore ran out of tissues the night you two were married."

"I still am a heartthrob," Ozi protests, touching his temples. "A little skin is sexy."

"Absolutely."

"At our age, my hirsute chum, all women care about is cash. And my bank account is hairy enough for a harem."

"Such refinement," Mumtaz says, handing me a Scotch, nicely watered and iced. "Are all Lahori men like him?"

"Certainly not," I tell her.

"Be careful, Daru," Ozi says, accepting his glass from Mumtaz. "She's trying to divide us."

Mumtaz sits down next to him. Her drink is stiffer than either of ours. "Since you're one of my husband's dearest friends," she says, "I have little hope for you."

Ozi gives me a wink.

"But a little hope," she adds, "is better than none at all."

"Cheers," I say. The three of us clink our glasses.

You know you're in trouble when you can't meet a woman's eye, particularly if the woman happens to be your best friend's wife. So I'm definitely in trouble, because I keep looking at Mumtaz and jerking my gaze away whenever she looks at me. I hope she doesn't notice, but she probably does. Then again, maybe I'm thinking too much. Stoner's paranoia.

We're well into our second round of drinks when I pull out a pack of reds. "Smoke?"

"I've quit," Ozi says.

"You can't be serious." The Ozi I knew was a half-pack-a-day man. The very fellow, in fact, who got me started on cigarettes in the first place, when we were fourteen, because he looked so cool smoking on the roof of his old house.

"I'm a father now. I have to be responsible."

"To whom?" I ask. "I feel abandoned."

"You should quit, too."

I extend the pack. "Come on. One more. For old times."

He shakes his head. "Sorry, yaar."

"Well, I haven't quit," Mumtaz says, taking one. "And I've been dying for a smoke."

Ozi gives Mumtaz a look over the head of their son.

"He's asleep," she says. "Why don't you take him to bed?"

Ozi carries the boy out and I light our cigarettes.

"I'm not allowed to smoke when he's in the room," she explains, picking a newspaper off the table. "Do you read this?"

"Sometimes. There's a story today about a missing girl in Defense. The police suspect her family killed her when they discovered she had a lover. Her lover claims the police did something with her after the two of them were caught on a date by a mobile unit and taken into the station. And her family insists she never had a lover. Strange stuff."

"I read it. By someone called Zulfikar Manto."

"That's right. I hadn't heard of him before. Good article."

She nods once, her eyes on the front page.

"Let's talk about this quitting-smoking thing," I say to Ozi when he returns, unwilling to let him off the hook so easily.

"It'll kill you," he says.

I flick some ash into the ashtray. "That's no reason to quit. You have to weigh the benefit against the loss."

"And what exactly is the benefit?"

I spread my hands and take a drag to demonstrate. "Pleasure, yaar."

"Didn't you tell me smoking ruined your stamina as a boxer?"

Mumtaz raises an eyebrow, the curved half of a slender question mark, black, in recline.

"Ruined is a strong word," I say.

"You never won."

"I won all the time. I just never won a championship."

"It takes years off your life."

"It helps fight boredom. It gives you more to do and less time to do it in."

"I must not be that bored. A wife and son do keep life interesting."

I look at Mumtaz, cigarette in hand, but refrain from pointing out that the pleasures of having a husband and son haven't eliminated her desire for the occasional puff.

"What sort of person," Mumtaz asks, exhaling, "tries to convince someone not to quit smoking?"

"Only a good friend," I respond. "Who else would care?"

"It's too late," Ozi says. "I haven't had a cigarette in three years."

"You've been away," I point out. "Surrounded by health-crazy Americans. I'll have you smoking again in a month."

"Don't corrupt him," Mumtaz says to me, pulling her legs up onto the sofa and resting her head on Ozi's shoulder.

"I've never corrupted anyone," I say.

"I don't believe you," she says.

She's finished her cigarette but hasn't put it out properly, so it's still smoking in the ashtray. I crush mine into it, grinding until both stop burning. "I never lie," I lie.

She smiles.

By the time I leave for home, I'm happily trashed. Not a bad reunion, all in all. Ozi and Mumtaz see me out, we shake hands and kiss cheeks, respectively, and I'm off, driving under the hot candle of a shadow-casting moon that's bigger and brighter and yellower than it should be. There are no clouds and no wind, and there are no stars because of the dust. The road sucks on the tires of my car. Great night for a joint, but I don't think I'm sober enough to roll one, and I should have been paying more attention because I've run into a police check post and it's too late to turn. There's nothing for it. I have to stop. I light a cigarette to cover my breath and open a window.

A flashlight shines into my eyes and I can make out a mustache but little else. "Bring your car to the side of the road," the mustache says.

I do it.

"Registration," says the mustache. "License."

I give them to him, anticipating the list of possible bribe-yielding items he'll ask me about. I hope he doesn't smell the booze.

"Get out," says the mustache.

They search my car: the dickey, the glove compartment, under the seats. Nothing. Now if I'm lucky the mustache will let me go. But I'm not lucky and he continues hunting.

"Where are you coming from?" asks the mustache.

"My parents' house." Always a safe answer.

"Where do they live?"

"In the cantonment." The police are terrified of the army.

He smiles, and I think, Damn, he's smelled the booze. He has.

"Have you been drinking?" he asks.

"What sort of question is that? I'm a good Muslim." Stupid answer. He knows I'm drunk. I should beg for mercy and throw him a bribe.

Other mustaches gather around. "Let's take this good Muslim back to the station," one says.

"Do you know the penalty for drinking?" asks the first mustache.

"Eternal hellfire?"

"No, before that. Do you know how many years you will be shut in prison?"

This has gone far enough, I think. One of these guys might be a fundo with a bad temper, so I'd better buy my way out of this fast. "Isn't there some way we can sort this out?" I ask.

"What do you mean?"

"Perhaps I could pay a fine instead," I suggest.

"Shut him in prison," one of the mustaches mutters.

The first mustache leads me a short distance away from the others. "This is a very serious crime," he says, "but I see that you're sorry for what you've done. Give me two thousand, and I'll convince them to let you go."

"I don't have two thousand," I say, relieved that we've started haggling.

"How much do you have?"

I take out my wallet and shuffle through the notes. "Seven hundred and eighty-three."

"Give it to me."

"I'm very low on petrol. Let me keep the eighty-three."

"Fine."

I drive off in a state of drunken emptiness that I know will give way to anger, because I can't afford to throw away seven hundred rupees like that. But for now I'm still buzzing, so I take swoopy turns with a grin that's so separate from my eyes it feels like my face belongs to two people. If there's a camera filming my life it moves up, higher and higher, until I'm just a pair of headlights winding my way home.

I'm huddled under the sheets in my cold bedroom when I hear, above the air conditioner's hum, a sound I don't want to hear. It's Manucci, knocking on my door.

"Saab, your breakfast is ready," he says.

Manucci only does this when I'm late. I look at my alarm clock: ten minutes to nine. I should be leaving right now. "Breakfast!" I roar. I shower and shave at the same time, cutting myself, throw on a suit, and try to gulp down the water Manucci has brought me, but it's so cold I have to drink it slowly. I have a headache and an upset stomach, signs that last night's Black Label might have been fake, and my shirt is missing a button.

I grab my briefcase, shovel some fried egg into my mouth with pieces of toast, and head out the door. A dog is lying in the middle of the driveway, just outside the gate, and he doesn't stir when I yell at him or even when I send a stone thudding into his back. I look around for a stick but can't find one, so I walk forward empty-handed to see if he's dead. He is. He can't have been dead for long because gorged ticks still cover his ears like bunches of grapes. There are a lot of dead dogs these days: the heat's killing them. I push him with my foot toward the refuse pile by the gate and notice he's already stiff, tendons like tight ropes wrapped around his bones.

Small houses hunched over shoulder-high boundary walls disgorge a few tardy inhabitants onto the narrow street. My place is plain, unlike some of the pink-painted, column-sporting mini-monstrosities nearby. A gray cement block, more or less, with rectangular windows, a couple of balconies too narrow to use, and the best bloody tree in the neighborhood: a banyan that's been around forever and covers most of the dust patch I call my front lawn.

I drive fast, belching up the taste of egg from time to time, and I'm thinking about an appointment I have at ten which I'd rather not have at all. Still, I'm not happy when my car's engine dies on me and a quick glance tells me that I'm out of fuel. I try to make it to the next petrol pump on sheer momentum, but there's too much traffic and I have to hit the brakes. I take off my jacket, roll up my sleeves, open the door, and push with one hand on the steering wheel until the car is by the side of the road. People honk at me unnecessarily as they drive past, and my white shirt is turning translucent in spots.

I walk the half-kilometer or so to the station and buy some regular, a container, and a funnel. It's 9:48. Petrol swishing beside me, I jog back, inhaling the dark smoke buses spit in my direction and feeling sweat fill my eyebrows and overflow, stinging, into my eyes. I restart my car, driving with one hand and unbuttoning my shirt with the other so I can dry myself off with a rag.

I'm in the office by eleven minutes after ten, cold because I'm soaked and the air-conditioning in the bank is always too strong. I smell like a garage on a windless day, and I'm sure I look a mess.

Raider sees me and shakes his head. Raider's real name is Haider, and his dream is to become a hostile takeover specialist on Wall Street. He's the only man at our bank who wears suspenders.

"You're in for it, yaar," he says.

"Is he here?" I ask.

"Is he ever late?"

"Is he pissed?"

"He isn't smiling."

Raider's talking about my client, Malik Jiwan, a rural landlord with half a million U.S. in his account, a seat in the Provincial Assembly, and eyebrows that meet in the middle like a second pair of whiskers. His pastimes include fighting the spread of primary education and stalling the census. Right now he's sitting behind my desk, in my chair, rotating imperiously.

"You're late," he says.

I'm in no mood for this. "Sorry, Mr. Jiwan, my car—"

"Never mind. Has my check cleared?"

"Your check?"

He strokes his beard and looks at me, saying nothing.

I remind myself why God gave bankers lips: to kiss up to our clients. "Please tell me: what check?"

"The check for thirty thousand U.S. I deposited with you."

"Let me just find out." I call customer services and give them the account number. "I'm afraid it hasn't gone through yet."

"That's ridiculous. I deposited it a week ago."

I'm enjoying his discomfort. "International checks can take some time."

"Didn't I tell you to take care of this personally?"

"I don't remember your saying that, Mr. Jiwan."

"Well, I remember saying it."

Good for you. "Next time you really ought to consider a cashier's check."

"Are you making fun of me?"

God forbid. "No," I say.

"Young man, I don't like the way you're smiling."

I'm not one of your serfs, you bastard. And I want you to get the hell out of my chair. "Mr. Jiwan, I'm not trying to be disrespectful."

"Your tone is disrespectful."

Before the Day of Judgment, as every good banker knows, will come a Night of Insolvency. And on that Night I intend to go calling on one or two of my more troublesome clients. But for now my bank is still sound, and I'm limited in my choice of responses to Mr. Jiwan's attempt to impose feudal hierarchy on my office. "Mr. Jiwan, I'm doing my best to provide you with any service you require."

"Do you know who I am?"

I'm beginning to lose my patience. "Yes, I do."

"I can have you thrown on the street."

"Don't threaten me, Mr. Jiwan. I don't work for you. You're a client of this bank, and if you don't like the service you receive here, you're free to go elsewhere."

"We'll see who goes elsewhere. I want to speak to your Branch Manager."

"Certainly." I escort him to my BM's office, outwardly calm, because I don't want him to see me squirm. But from the way my BM grabs Mr. Jiwan's hand, in both of his, and also from the way my BM bows slightly, at the waist and at the neck, a double bend, I know this is going to be unpleasant.

"Ghulam," Mr. Jiwan is saying, "this boy has just insulted me."

"Shut the door, Mr. Shezad," my BM says to me. "What happened?"

I know I need to present my case forcefully. "Sir," I begin.

"Not you," my BM says. "Malik saab, tell me what happened."

"I told this boy to take care of a deposit personally. Today, when I find out that he hasn't done so, he calls me a liar, and says that I never told him to. He's rude to me, and when I tell him I won't stand for it, he raises his voice and tells me to take my business to another bank."

My BM is looking at me with hard eyes. "This is unacceptable, Mr. Shezad."

"Please let me tell you what happened, sir."

"You told Malik saab to take his business to another bank?"

"You see, sir—"

"Mr. Shezad, this isn't the first time a client has complained about your attitude. You're on very dangerous ground. Just answer my question."

"No, sir, I didn't say that."

"Are you saying that I'm lying?" asks Mr. Jiwan.

I've had a bad day. A bad month, actually. And there's only so much nonsense a self-respecting fellow can be expected to take from these megalomaniacs. So I say it. "This is a bank, not your servant quarters, Mr. Jiwan. If you want better service, maybe you ought to learn some manners."

"Enough!" my BM yells.

I've never heard him yell before.

His voice brings me to my senses. What am I doing? Fear grabs me by the throat and makes me wave my hands like I'm erasing the wrong answer from a blackboard. "I'm very sorry, sir," I say. "I'm sorry, Mr. Jiwan."

They don't say anything.

"I don't know what came over me," I go on. "It won't happen again. I'm very sorry."

My BM says, "You're fired, Mr. Shezad."

A quick side step into unreality, like meeting your mother when you're tripping. Am I losing my job? Right now? Is it possible?

Pull yourself together.

"Please, sir," I say.

"No, Mr. Shezad."

"But please, sir. Please."

"No."

I leave my BM's office, leave them both watching me, and walk to my desk, and I look around it, and there's so much to do, so much work to do, and I can do it. I can do it. But I can't concentrate. My nose is running, and I taste it in my mouth, and my face is hot even though I'm cold.

Everyone is staring at me. How can they know already? I want to tell them it's a mistake, but I look down at my desk instead. Just act natural. Don't draw attention to yourself.

My BM is walking Mr. Jiwan out. I pick up a pen and move some papers, and they don't say anything to me. Everything will be all right.

Someone comes to stand in front of my desk. Ignore him and he'll go away.

"Mr. Shezad."

I raise my head. It's my BM. There's a security guard beside him.

"Yes, sir?"

"You're fired, Mr. Shezad."

"But, you see, sir, I'm really very sorry. Don't fire me. I'll work a month without pay."

"You have a serious psychological problem, Mr. Shezad. Your severance pay will be sent to your home by registered post. You need to stop crying, collect your personal items, and go home."

"Do you want me to fill out some form?"

"No, Mr. Shezad. Please leave."

He's watching me. I'm looking for personal items on my desk but not finding any. Pick up my briefcase. Legs move, feet go one in front of the other. Look straight ahead as the guard opens the door. Turn the key in the ignition. Drive. Drive where? Home. Give briefcase to Manucci and ignore the words that come out of his mouth because I'm going to my room, shutting the door, locking it, pulling the curtains, taking off my clothes, crawling under the sheets, and curling up in the dark dark dark.

I don't know if I've been sleeping or dreaming while I'm awake, but suddenly my eyelids snap apart under the sheets and I'm back from somewhere very different. I feel feverish and I'm covered in sweat, but I think it's because I didn't turn on the AC or even the fan. Unnh, I need to go to the bathroom.

Sitting hunched over on the toilet, I feel the wet smoothness of my skin as my belly doubles over and touches itself. My stomach is so bad that I'm passing liquid. It burns. I grab the lota and wash myself.

Walking naked to the window in my room, I pull open the curtains and see an overripe sun swelling on the horizon.

I remember that I've agreed to go to a party with Ozi and Mumtaz. When they come to pick me up, Mumtaz is wearing something black that exposes her shoulders. She kisses me on the cheek. Her smell stays near me.

"Are you all right?" she asks, concern mixed with the gravel of her voice.

"I'm not feeling well."

She smiles sympathetically. "What's wrong?"

"Upset stomach."

"Have some Immodium and let's go," Ozi says.

"I'm not going," I say.

"Come on, yaar," Ozi says, turning his hands palm up and tilting his head.

"I'm feeling really bad."

"That's how we'll all be feeling in the morning. You just have a head start."

"I'm sorry, yaar. I'm not going."

"Yes, you are. I insist."

"Look at me: I'm not dressed and I look horrible."

"You always look horrible. Throw on some clothes and let's go. We'll wait in the car."

In a daze, I put on a pair of black jeans, with a black T-shirt, black belt, and black loafers, slip some hash into a half-empty pack of cigarettes, and head out.

"You two match," Ozi says, meaning Mumtaz and me.

I sit in the back of Ozi's Pajero. I've never been in a Pajero before. Costs more than my house and moves like a bull, powerful and single-minded. Ozi drives by pointing it in one direction and stepping on the gas, trusting that everyone will get out of our way. Occasionally, when he cuts things too close and has to swerve to avoid crushing someone, the Pajero's engine grumbles with disappointment and Ozi swears.

"Stupid bastard."

"It was a red light," Mumtaz points out.

"So? He could see me coming."

"There are rules, you know."

"And the first is, bigger cars have the right of way."

A favorite line. One I haven't heard in a long, long time. I remember speeding around the city with Ozi in his '82 Corolla, feet sweating sockless in battered boat shoes, following cute girls up and down the Boulevard, memorizing their number plates and avoiding cops because neither of us had a license. Hair chopped in senior school crew cuts. Eyes pot-red behind his wayfarers and my aviators. Stickers of universities I would never attend on the back windshield. Poondi, in the days of cheap petrol and skipping class and heavy-metal cassettes recorded with too much bass and even more treble. We had some good times, Ozi and I, before he left.

I would have reached out and clapped him on the shoulder then, grinned at him in the rearview, but I don't do it now. I'm too tired.

We arrive at the party. A mostly male mob is gathered outside the gate, hoping to get in. It's summertime, after all, and parties are few and far between.

Ozi pulls up and honks, and we get some glares.

"Sorry, sir, I can't open the gate," says a security guard.

"You'll have to. I'm parking inside," says Ozi.

The Pajero must give Ozi's words added authority, because instead of laughing in his face, the guard says, "But how will we keep these people outside?"

"That's your problem. If anyone tries to get in, hit them one."

The guard disappears. Ozi inches the car forward, pushing the crowd out of his way. I hear people swearing. Suddenly the gate opens and we drive in, leaving two security guards and some servants to scuffle with the crowd.

Ozi and Mumtaz head indoors, toward the music, and I'm about to follow them when someone grabs my arm. It's Raider, taut with nervous energy. "Shit, yaar," he says.

"Let's not talk about it." The last thing I want to do just now is think about what happened today. Besides, the pity in Raider's face is making me feel unwell.

He nods and raises his hands in accommodation. "That's right," he says. "To hell with those bastards. I can't believe—"

"Leave it."

Raider shifts from foot to foot, an intensely vacant look in his eyes, and grins at me. "You're a killer, yaar. A killer. I like your style, partying tonight. I'd be a complete wreck."

I take hold of his shoulders. "Please, shut up."

He ducks his head. "Sorry." Then he starts grinning again. "But I've got the perfect thing for you."

"What?"

"Ex."

I should have guessed he was on something. "Here?"

He nods. "Great stuff, yaar. Very peppy."

I shake my head. "Not tonight."

"Especially tonight. I know what I'm talking about."

"How much?"

"Two thousand."

"I can't, yaar. It's too much."

Raider smiles. "Just take it, then. A gift."

That's the problem with Raider, why he'll never make it to Wall Street or probably even to Karachi, for that matter: he's too generous. He's the last person you want on your side in a negotiation.

"Thanks," I say. "But I can't. Another time."

"Just call," Raider says, suddenly sad. "The bank will be boring without you. All worker bees and no wasps."

I pat him on the back and walk off.

Then I'm inside. I see the familiar faces of Lahore's party crowd, and soon I'm caught up in the whole hugging, handshaking, cheek-kissing scene. Tonight's venue is a mansion with marble floors and twenty-foot ceilings. Rumor has it that the owner made his fortune as a smuggler, which is probably true but could also be social retribution for his recent ascent to wealth.

The dance floor is packed. Ozi and Mumtaz are shaking it down to "Stayin' Alive." They make a sexy pair, a welcome new addition to the scene, and I overhear the update passing like a Reuters report: "Aurangzeb and Mumtaz, back from New York, very cool." Information is key at these things: no one wants to be caught holding social stock that's about to crash.

I see Nadira glaring in my direction as she dances with some guy whose wet shirt sticks to his back. Keeping her eyes fixed on mine, she pulls closer to him and grinds her body against his, running her hands up his thighs. I've never understood why she does this to me, since she's the one who ended it. As usual, I try to ignore her.

I'm in no mood to dance and there are too many people at the bar, so I wander through the house and out to the back lawn. Finding a wrought-iron bench, I sit down to watch the party out of the darkness.

As I roll a joint, couples argue and kiss, unable to see me seeing them. Two guys are pacing about. One seems to be calming the other down, but I'm too far away to hear their words. Several people chat on their mobiles.

Then a woman walks in my direction.

"Daru?" she says.

"Here, Mumtaz."

She comes over and sits down, her body as far from mine as this narrow bench will allow.

"How did you find me?" I ask.

"I watched you go outside. What are you doing?"

"Just enjoying the night air."

She smiles and says conspiratorially, "It looks like you're rolling a jay."

"I suppose it does look like that."

"Can I have some?"

I look down. "Where's Ozi? We should all share it."

She points to the house with her chin. "He's inside, chatting it up with some old school buddies. Besides, he's stopped smoking pot."

"I can see I'm going to have to be firm with him," I say. "He's forgotten his roots."

"We used to smoke together before. I was stoned when we first met. He was dancing. Ozi's a great dancer, you know."

"I know. He's a charmer. Women love him." I finish rolling the joint. "Do you want me to go and get him?"

She shakes her head. "No, let him enjoy himself."

I light up. We share it. She takes one hit and starts coughing, but she takes another before handing it back. I don't say anything, shutting my eyes and smoking slowly as we keep passing the joint. When it's done, I flick it into a hedge.

Both of us are silent. I stare straight ahead.

"What's wrong?" asks Mumtaz.

"Nothing. I shouldn't have come."

"I'm sorry if Ozi forced you."

"It's not that. I had a bad day."

"What happened?" she asks.

The joint has made my throat burn and my eyes water. "I got fired."

Mumtaz brushes my face with her fingers. They come away wet. "I'm sorry," she says.

My stomach constricts. "I don't know what I'm going to do." I shut my eyes and bend over, coughing through my nose.

Mumtaz puts her arm around me. "It'll be okay," she says gently. "Don't be scared."

I stay bent over like that for a long time, until the coughing stops, and I wipe my face on my jeans before I sit back up. "I'm so sorry," I say. "Please go in to Ozi."

"I'd rather stay outside with you for a little bit. If you don't mind."

My coughing seems to have loosened the tightness wrapped around my chest. I take a deep breath, my lungs raw like I've been for a long run. "This bastard told my boss I was rude." I start to laugh. "I wish I'd known I was going to get fired. There are a few more things I'd have liked to say."

Mumtaz laughs with me. "I can imagine."

I love her voice. It has the soul of a whisper, meant only for the person she's speaking to, even when she isn't speaking softly. "Are you stoned?"

"You know, I'm really stoned."

I nod. "This is good hash. Courtesy of a friend of mine, Murad Badshah."

"Murad? Did he go to school with you and Ozi?"

I smile. "No. I met him while I was at Punjab University, when Ozi was off studying in the States."

"Well, his hash has certainly given me a buzz." She moves her arm back and rests both of her hands in her lap. I find my mind tracing the line her skin touched as it curved around me.

"I'm pretty stoned myself," I say.

"You look less unhappy."

"I feel completely empty."

"You'll find something to fill you."

"Such as?"

"I'm sure you'll find something."

I light a cigarette.

"May I have one?" she asks.

"I'm sorry. Of course."

I light it for her.

A bird passes overhead, invisible, the sound of agitated air.

"Did you ever study with Professor Julius Superb?" she asks me.

I grin. "Do you know where his name comes from?"

She laughs. "No, but it's fabulous."

"His great-grandfather was the batman of a Scottish officer who tried for years to get him to convert. When the Indian Mutiny broke out, the old Scot wound up with a knife in his chest. Julius's great-grandfather came to him on his deathbed and said he'd decided to become a Christian. And the last thing the Scot could croak before he died was: Superb. Julius is the fourth generation of the line."

Mumtaz is laughing so hard she has to hold her sides. "I don't believe it," she gasps.

"It's true," I say. "Professor S. told us himself."

"No." She's smiling at me and shaking her head.

"Seriously." I smile back. "But how do you know him?"

"I came across an article of his today. It's called 'The Phoenix and the Flame.' Have you read it?"

"No."

"Let me read a piece of it to you."

"You have it with you?"

"Just one page that I tore out. Do you think that's odd?"

"No."

"It is odd, isn't it? Whenever I read something interesting, I tear out a piece and keep it as a talisman until I find something new to replace it with. It's a sort of superstition. I did it once and it helped me break out of writer's block, so I've done it ever since. Librarians must hate me."

I look at her, surprised. "What do you write?"

"I can't tell you."

I shake my head. "What do you mean?"

"I'm teasing. I used to write for some magazines in New York."

"That must have been fantastic."

"Not really. I wrote boring stuff."

"And now?"

"Now I'll read you this article." She opens a little bag and takes out a folded piece of paper. "Could you keep your lighter lit so I can read this? Thanks. Here's what it says: 'My father liked to wonder aloud whether the phoenix was re-created by the fire of its funeral pyre or transformed so that what emerged was a soulless shadow of its former being, identical in appearance but without the joy in life its predecessor had had. He wondered alternatively whether the fire might be purificatory, a redemptive, rejuvenating blaze that destroyed the withered shell of the old phoenix and allowed the creature's essence to emerge stronger than it was before in a young, new body. Or, he would ask, was the fire a manifestation of entropy, slowly sapping the life-energy of the phoenix over the eons, a little death in a life that could know no beginning and no end but which could nonetheless be subject to an ever-decreasing magnitude? He asked me once if I thought the fires in our lives, the traumas, increased our fulfillment by setting up contrasts that illuminated more clearly our everyday joys; or perhaps I viewed them instead as tests that made us stronger by teaching us to endure; or did I believe, rather, that they simply amplified what we already were, in the end making the strong stronger, the weak weaker, and the dangerous deadly?' That's it."

The gas coming from my lighter hisses, suddenly audible, until I relax my thumb and extinguish the flame. Back in my pocket, the metal radiates heat into the skin below my hipbone.

"That's vintage Superb," I tell her, a little wistfully. "He teaches economics, but basically he's a freelance thinker."

"I like the image his article brought to my mind, of this old Punjab University fuddy-duddy hard at work in his office."

"He's a comrade."

"Comrade?"

"Communist."

"Are there many?"

"Not anymore. The unshaven boys are the new populists. But they leave Professor S. alone. I think they've decided he's harmless. Or irrelevant."

"What about the other Communists?"

"Most of them have become experts at couching their beliefs in religiously acceptable terms. The academic version of Sufi poets, you might call them."

"And the rest?"

"Some professors were roughed up. They left."

"How sad."

I shrug. "Good old Professor S. is still writing away. Which brings me back to you. You haven't told me what you're writing now."

"I have a question for you first."

"What?"

"Tell me about boxing."

"What do you want to know?"

"Everything. What's it like? How did you get into it?"

"Family tradition. I was an out-of-shape little kid. Very soft. One day my uncle took me aside and said, 'The time has come,' or something like that. He trained me in the evenings: jump rope, speed bag, heavy bag. He was pretty lazy, so he usually sat on a chair and smoked while I pounded away, but every so often he put on his gloves and knocked me around so I'd learn not to be scared. I boxed until the end of college."

"You said you never won a championship."

"No. But I made it to a couple. And I won more fights than I lost."

"Did your mother approve?"

"No, but she always came to watch when I asked her. She hid her face behind her hands, but she came."

"I'm sure she was terrified."

I lean back on the bench and look up at the sky. Two stars, a low-riding moon, dusty haze. Cloudless but not clear. Not very dark but dark enough. Impossible to see anything falling.

I think of my mother on a rooftop, of waking beside her, early, at first light on an almost-quiet summer morning. The flies would come later, swinging up over the walls with the rising sun, buzzing and ripe like honeybees.

Someone calls our names. It's Ozi.

"There you two are," he says. "What are you doing out here?"

"Talking," Mumtaz says. "I like this friend of yours."

Ozi smiles and puts his arm around me. "You'll get over it soon enough," he tells her.

We walk inside, Mumtaz and I on opposite sides of Ozi, and

the pounding of the music gets louder as we approach, the lights from the dance floor reflecting off the walls so that colors start to blur and change, again and again and again.

The police don't stop us on our drive home. We are in a Pajero, after all.

CHAPTER 4

opening the purple box: an interview with professor julius superb

ZULFIKAR MANTO: Good to meet you, Professor. I've read some of your work. None of the academic materials, I'm afraid. Econometrics scares the hell out of me and I can hardly even pronounce heteroscedasticity. But I enjoyed that piece you wrote a few months ago about the phoenix myth. Very witty.

JULIUS SUPERB: Yes, ah, likewise.

ZM: Your students speak highly of you. They say you're a brave man.

JS: They say I'm, ah, a man. A brave man. Do they?

ZM: Is something wrong?

JS: Wrong? No, no, of course not. Please excuse me. Never having met, you see. I was somewhat unprepared. But that's your business. I don't mean to presume. I've read all your articles. That is to say, all that I've come across. And they are top-notch. Really first-class journalism. Commendable. Ah, I've lost my train of thought. What was the question?

ZM: Actually, I asked if something was wrong. But let's begin at the beginning. How did you first meet Darashikoh Shezad?

JS: He was a student of mine. He distinguished himself by attending my lectures and taking notes. It was this second characteristic, note-taking, that really caught my eye. So one day I said, "What do you think you're doing?" To which he replied, "I'm sorry, Professor?" And I responded, "No, you're not. You've been doing it for weeks. You're taking notes."

ZM: Is that really so unusual?

JS: Not really. But I confront each and every one of them. No one takes notes in my class without explaining themselves to me personally. I hit them with an impromptu quiz, right there, one on one. And if they do well enough, I ask them to come to my discussion group. Most refuse. Daru didn't.

ZM: Discussion group?

JS: Yes. On alternate Tuesdays. From noon until two. Lunch included.

ZM: What do you discuss?

JS: Anything. Economics, development, politics, literature. Someone presents a paper and the rest of us tear it apart.

ZM: Sounds fun.

JS: It is. I soon realized Daru had potential, so I encouraged him to pursue a Ph.D. Which he did, for a while.

ZM: How long?

JS: I met him when he began his master's. So that would have been another . . . two years. Two years of dissertation work.

ZM: And what was the subject of his dissertation?

JS: Development. Microcredit, specifically. Small loans to low-income groups, guaranteed by the community. The Grameen Bank model and variations. Explaining low default rates, analyzing claims of paternalism, social critiques, that sort of thing.

ZM: What did you think?

JS: Daru? Brilliant. Though a bit of a seat-of-the-pants economist. Could have used more quant training. Liked to assert rather than prove. And not the best at handling criticism. Took methodological challenges very personally. But talented, definitely.

ZM: And his dissertation?

JS: Needed focus. But, to be fair, he was more into implementation than theory. Could have done some good work.

ZM: Why did he stop?

JS: Money, I think. His girlfriend had just left him for a textile baron's son. He got a job offer from a bank, and he couldn't resist. He told me it was impossible to make a living in academia or development. I told him he was wrong: students will pay good cash for exam questions, and multilaterals certainly make some poor people (their employees) well off. He didn't appreciate the humor. So I said he was too bright to work for a bank, which was true. And I asked him about his commitment to being someone who acts rather than complains. He said he was acting for himself so he could stop complaining. And he left.

ZM: How did you feel?

JS: I was disappointed, naturally. But more, I was worried for him. I didn't think he was choosing a path that would make him happy. It's hard to stop thinking once you've started.

ZM: Did you remain in touch afterwards?

JS: No, unfortunately. Which is another bad sign. Most of the students I bring into my discussion group don't just disappear. I suspect Daru was too dissatisfied with what he was doing to let himself look back. Actually, don't quote me on that. How would I know? As a professor I have a tendency to slip into omniscient narrative.

ZM: How did you hear he had been arrested?

JS: The same way the rest of the city did, I suppose: everyone is talking about this case.

ZM: Why do you think that is? Why has it received so much attention?

JS: I've given quite a bit of thought to that question. It can be analyzed using a three-dimensional matrix. On the X axis, that is, the horizontal axis, is the accused. On the vertical axis, Y, is the crime. And on the Z axis, rising up off the page, is the defense. And this situation is clearly in the . . . I can see I'm losing you.

ZM: I'm afraid so.

JS: Well . . . let's use a box instead of a matrix. The case is a box. In this situation, the accused is bright, well educated, and charismatic. An orphan. Extremely sympathetic. So the box is wide. The crime is violent and despicable: the needless killing of a boy. So the box is long. And the defense invokes a grand conspiracy, corruption, which is particularly resonant these days. So the box is tall.

ZM: Criminal, crime, and conspiracy. That's why everyone is talking about it?

JS: One more thing: sex, which is purple. This box is covered with it. Painted. Smeared. Naturally, if there is a big purple box lying around, people will stare. That's why everyone is talking about it.

ZM: And do you think he's guilty?

JS: That, my dear, ah, Mr. Manto, I just don't know. From my experience, Daru is completely crazy. Quick-tempered, oversensitive, inconsistent. But so am I, and I haven't killed anyone, yet.

ZM: Thank you.

JS: It has been my good fortune, I assure you.

CHAPTER 5

three

May arrives with a burst of heat that leaves nine dead in Jacobabad, but one evening a flirtatious breeze makes the trees swell and it looks just bearable enough for me to step outside with a cigarette in my mouth and another behind my ear. These are my last two smokes and I smoke them like an addict consuming all that's left of his stash, half-preoccupied with the thought that each drag brings me closer to the point where I have to get some more.

Just as I flick the second butt over the wall and turn to head indoors, I hear a rickshaw sputter up to the gate and honk. Murad Badshah's massive form is squished into the driver's area, and he waves a hello when he sees me, sending a stream of paan-red spit over his shoulder. I open the gate and he pulls inside like an adult riding a tricycle. "Greetings!" he exclaims, hauling himself out of the rickshaw with some difficulty.

"Hello, gangster," I say to him.

Murad Badshah's my dealer: occasionally amusing, desperately insecure, and annoyingly fond of claiming that he's a dangerous outlaw. He speaks what he thinks is well-bred English in an effort to deny the lower-class origins that color the accent of his Urdu and Punjabi. But like an overambitious toupee, his artificial diction draws attention to what it's meant to hide.

His hand engulfs mine, and I find myself pulled into a damp and smelly embrace, the side of my face pressed against his shoulder. "A very good evening to you, old boy," he says.

"Do you have any cigarettes?"

"But of course."

"My savior."

"More than you know." He flashes a grin down at me. "I also have some first-class, A-one quality charas."

We climb a rickety ladder to the roof of my house and sit down on the bench I keep up there for pot smoking and kite fighting. I roll a joint, and as we smoke it, Murad Badshah asks me how my job search is going.

"Badly. They want foreign qualifications or an MBA."

"It's all about connections, old boy." He takes a hit. "How did you get your previous job?"

"Through a family friend," I admit. Ozi's father, as a matter of fact.

Murad Badshah grins. "Perhaps you should see the gentleman again. What he did once he can do twice."

"Maybe he can." But I don't want to ask for Khurram uncle's help.

I look up, squinting into the sun. A hawk circles in the sky over my neighbor's house, where a baby lies naked on a sheet on the lawn. His ayah keeps a careful eye on him: he's too big for a hawk to carry away, but not too big for one to try.

"Quite frankly, Darashikoh Shezad, you're better off this way. Pinstriped suits are cages for the soul."

"At least a caged soul is well fed by its handlers."

"Well fed, my left buttock, if you'll pardon the expression. A man who works for another man is a slave."

I take the joint back from him. "Yes, but you need capital to start a business. I'm broke. The other day I received a notice that my electricity is about to be disconnected."

"All you need is human capital: a strong mind and an obedient body."

I look at Murad Badshah's obedient body. Even in the loose folds of his shalwar kurta, I can see the love handles sagging away from his waist.

"I have a proposition for you," he says suddenly.

"What?"

"I don't want to shock you, old boy."

"Just don't ask me to drive one of your rickshaws."

He reaches under his kurta and pulls a silver revolver out of the waistband of his shalwar. It gleams like well-polished cutlery, big and shiny and more than a little ridiculous.

"Is it real?" I ask him.

He looks offended. "Of course," he says.

"Why are you carrying it around?"

"Darashikoh Shezad, do you listen to nothing that I say?"

"You don't need to impress me."

He snorts. "Here, take it."

I drop my joint and put it out with my shoe. The gun is heavier than it looks.

"You are holding a Python. Three-fifty-seven magnum."

I nod and hand it back to him. "I don't like guns."

"Why don't you fire off a few rounds?" he asks. "Just point it up in the air. But be careful: it jumps."

I think of my mother and look away. "No thanks," I say. Sometimes indulging Murad Badshah can take more effort than it's worth. "Can you get me some ex?" I ask, reminding him that he's my dealer first and my friend only a very distant second.

Murad Badshah looks at me as if he wants to say more about his proposal. Then he seems to decide against it and says, "What is ex?"

"Never mind. It's a drug."

"The best I can do is charas, old boy. And heroin. I can always get you heroin. But I wouldn't recommend it." He puts his arm around me. "Come. Let's roll another joint."

I'm thirsty, and the smell from Murad Badshah's armpit is overpowering. I want to get rid of him. "Can I offer you a beer?" I ask, standing up.

He shakes his head, still seated. "You know me better than that, old boy. I want the pleasures of the afterlife. Charas is a gray area, but alcohol is explicitly forbidden."

"Some men drink the blood of other men, all I drink is wine," I quote.

"Saqia aur pila. Wonderful qawali. But I think the verse refers to the wine of faith, my friend."

Once I've paid Murad Badshah for the pot and I'm alone again, I open a bottle of Murree beer. I don't like it when low-class types forget their place and try to become too frank with you. But it's my fault, I suppose: the price of being a nice guy.

Settling in front of the television, I watch videos on Channel V, and remind myself that when I have some cash coming in I need to call a technician to adjust my satellite dish. The sound quality just isn't what it should be. I eat my dinner on a TV tray and open a beer. Manucci has fallen asleep at my feet. He loves to sleep in the living room when the air conditioner is on, and I don't blame him, because the servant quarters are too hot in the summertime.

The phone rings and wakes me up. I've dozed off in front of the television. Manucci's still asleep.

It's a woman's voice, husky, like she's just gotten out of bed. "Daru?" she says.

"Nadira?"

There's laughter on the other end. "It's Mumtaz. Who's Nadira?"

My mouth tastes awful. "No one," I say. "Just a friend."

"Listen, Daru, can you do me a favor?"

"Is everything all right? Where's Ozi?"

"Everything's fine. Ozi's in Switzerland on business. I need to go to the old city, but I don't know the roads in that part of Lahore and I don't want to take a driver. Do you think you could come with me?"

This is very strange. Why is Ozi's wife calling me up in the middle of the night to go for a drive? "Are you serious?"

"Yes. You don't have to if you don't want to, but it's important to me and I'd appreciate your help."

"Where are you?" I ask her.

"Outside your gate."

"What?"

"I'm calling you on my mobile."

Her mobile. How classy. I think quickly: What can be wrong in going with her? Ozi would want me to help her out. On the other hand, the last thing Ozi probably wants is for his wife to be cruising around Lahore with single men while he's out of town. But my curiosity gets the better of me. "I'm coming," I say.

It's dark outside. None of the streetlamps work and the sharp crescent moon does little to light the night. Mumtaz's car is parked with the engine running.

I get in, and she turns the music down. It's Nusrat, remixed and clubby, but damn good as always.

"Hi," she says with a grin.

"What's up?"

"I'll tell you as we go. Cigarette?"

I take one and she reverses onto the street, slips the car into first while it's still moving backwards, and accelerates away from my house.

"What have you been up to lately?" she asks.

"Looking for a job."

"Any luck?" She takes a turn fast and I tense my legs.

"No."

"What sort of job are you looking for?"

"The standard: banks, multinationals." We're on the canal now, zipping past weeping willows.

"Do you really want to work for a bank or a multinational?"

She seems distracted, intent on her driving, and I'm irritated that she's being flippant about what for me is a serious problem. "What do you mean?"

She flashes her beams at a truck and it pulls to the left to let us pass. "You don't seem like the sort of person who'd enjoy being a slave to a faceless business."

This is the very sort of attitude that pisses me off with most of the party crowd. They're rich enough not to work unless they feel like it, so they think the rest of us are idiots for settling for jobs we don't love. "I need the money," I explain to her, as I would to a child. "I don't have a choice."

"I know the feeling," she says as we descend into the Ferozepur Road underpass.

"Do you?"

She turns and gives me a surprised look. "No need to sound so condescending."

I realize that I've offended her, and suddenly I'm upset with myself. "I'm sorry."

She looks ahead again. "I wasn't talking about needing money. I was saying that I know what it is not to have a choice about working. I have to work, too."

I thought Mumtaz was happily unemployed. "What sort of work do you do?"

"It's a secret."

"What do you mean?"

"I'm going to tell you. I have to, I suppose, since I've dragged you out here with no explanation. It's very sweet of you to do this, by the way." Her hand touches my knee, briefly, before returning to the gearshift. "I have this thing about friends and secrets. Sometimes when I meet a person I like, I tell them a secret they don't know me well enough to be told. It lets me judge their potential as a friend."

"But what happens when they don't keep your secret?" I ask.

She opens a power window and flicks her cigarette out. "I don't know. They always have so far. But I don't meet many people I like."

I light another cigarette and pass it to her. "I'm flattered."

She accepts the cigarette with a nod. "You should be." We speed through the Jail Road underpass. "But let me tell you what I think about secrets before you decide if you want me to tell you one. Secrets make life more interesting. You can be in a crowded room with someone and touch them without touching, just with a look, because they know a part of you no one else knows. And whenever you're with them, the two of you are alone, because the you they see no one else can see."

I think of the look Nadira gave me at the party.

Mumtaz turns to me and smiles. "Do you still want me to tell you?" she asks.

"How could I not?"

"But if I don't feel good about it once I've told you, we'll probably never be friends. Doesn't that possibility frighten you?"

"It is pretty drastic," I admit. "But tell me and let's see what happens."

She looks at me and I see that she's smiling at herself. "Here it is. I know the identity of Zulfikar Manto." She takes a left on Mall Road.

"The journalist?"

"Precisely."

"The one who wrote that article about the missing girl in Defense?"

"Among other things, yes."

"But I didn't know his identity was a secret."

"It is. He submits his work by mail and collects his checks from a post office box. No one knows who he is except the editor of the paper that publishes his pieces."

She downshifts to second in front of Bagh-i-Jinnah and overtakes a group of teenagers in a car with big alloy wheels and a spoiler.

"So who is Zulfikar Manto?" I ask.

She laughs. "Me."

"You?"

"Me. I am Zulfikar Manto."

I start to laugh, too. "But why? Why don't you just write the articles under your own name?"

"That's a little complicated. Anyway, life is much easier if I'm not working as a journalist and Zulfikar Manto is."

Mumtaz assumes a mock-serious expression as we pass a mobile police unit near Charing Cross, and I feel like a character in an espionage film.

"That's incredible," I say.

She nods.

"Are you glad you've told me this?" I ask.

She's silent for a moment. "I don't know," she says finally. "It felt good to tell you, but I'm a little uncertain about how I feel just now."

I'm concerned. "What does that mean?"

"It means we'll have to see what happens." She shrugs. "But no more questions. This is where I need your help. We're getting close to the old city, and I don't know my way from here."

We pass the High Court. "Where are we going?"

"Heera Mandi."

I start to laugh. "You've got to be kidding."

"I'm dead serious. I have to interview the madam of a brothel, and I can't be late."

This is turning into a very strange night, but I'm enjoying myself. I like the way Mumtaz drives, with a sort of controlled aggression. Actually, she drives the way I like to think I drive. I direct her, glad she never asks how I know where Heera Mandi is, and point out the sights along our way like a tour guide: "That's Town Hall. Take a right here, on Lower Mall Road. That's Government College to your right. Take a left. That's Data Darbar. You should check it out sometime. This is Circular Road. See Badshahi Mosque? Minar-i-Pakistan's behind it. Okay, slow down. Take a right. This used to be a gate. Now we're in the old city."

"Who are all those people on the left?"

"Heroin junkies. We're almost there. You do realize that there won't be many young women dressed the way you are?"

"I hope not. It's been a long time since anyone accused me of dressing like a prostitute."

"What I mean is, we might attract the attention of the cops."

"I can handle cops. Besides, I've brought a lot of cash."

Soon enough we're there, and even though it's a little late for Heera Mandi, the place is still crowded. Mumtaz says we'll wait in the car, for what I'm not sure. People stare at us, making me nervous. Then a man almost as big as Murad Badshah knocks on our window, his eyes bloodshot and the ends of his mustache curled into points.

"Let's go," I say.

"Wait," she says. "Open it."

He leans in, ignoring me. "Are you here to see Dilaram?" he asks Mumtaz.

"Yes," she answers.

"Come quickly."

We open our doors and get out, but he stops me with one hand. "Not you," he says.

I lock eyes with him and remove his hand from my chest.

"It's okay, Daru," Mumtaz says. "Wait here. I'll be back soon."

I continue to glare at the pimp, my heart pounding. I wonder if Mumtaz would be impressed if I beat the hell out of him.

"Please, Daru," she says. "You don't know how hard it was to arrange this interview."

"It isn't safe for you to be here alone," I tell her.

"I'll be fine," she says, tossing me the car keys.

"Why can't I come?"

She tilts her head to one side, smiling like she wants to rumple my hair. "You look so disappointed. Let me ask her. If she agrees, I'll come back for you."

Before I know it, Mumtaz is running off with a giant pimp into some back alley in Heera Mandi and I'm sitting alone in her car. I am such an idiot for doing this. What will I tell Ozi if anything happens to her?

She isn't gone for long, but I'm already imagining an elaborate rescue scenario when she reappears. "You can come," she says. "But only if you promise not to do anything macho."

"I promise."

I have to walk quickly to keep pace with Mumtaz and the pimp. We pass a few men in the alley: satisfied customers, judging by their vacant smiles. Definitely stoned. Maybe even a little heroin. One is fastening his nala with both hands.

Then we enter a building, climb two flights of steps, pass through a door that opens only when the pimp knocks out a little code, part a curtain of beads, and find ourselves in a room with a shuttered window, dimly lit by a clay oil lamp which sits on a low table.

Reclining against a long, round cushion is a middle-aged woman with finely plucked eyebrows, her fleshy body well proportioned and voluptuous. She takes a gurgling puff from the hookah beside her and with the tiniest dip of her chin indicates that we should sit.

"It's a man's habit, but I love it," she says, taking another puff. Her voice is throaty, like Mumtaz's, but much deeper.

Then she points one henna-decorated finger at me. "Have I seen you before?"

"No," I say.

The woman chuckles. "Of course not. Your father, perhaps, but not you."

A disturbingly young girl with long eyelashes brings in tea. She wears bells on her ankles that chime as she walks, and I find myself hoping this is the only service she's made to provide, although I doubt it very much.

"You're not bad-looking," the woman says to Mumtaz, who smiles and lowers her gaze politely. "A nice face. And good hips. But your breasts aren't generous. You should eat more."

Mumtaz starts to laugh. "They're bigger than they were. I've fed a boy."

"With those?" The woman considers. "Perhaps it's because you have broad shoulders that they seem small." She smiles. "Are you looking for work?"

Mumtaz flashes a sly grin. "Your tea is delicious, Dilaram."

"Thank you. Like all things in my profession, it is a learned art."

"How did you come to begin learning?" Mumtaz asks, slowly taking out a minicassette recorder.

Dilaram laughs solidly, her body rippling. "It's quite a funny story really. I was a pretty girl, like this one here." She smiles at our adolescent tea server. "Only younger. The landlord of our area asked me to come to his house. I refused, so he threatened to kill my family. When I went, he raped me."

Mumtaz shuts her eyes.

Dilaram chuckles. "I was so skinny. Not like a woman at all."

"He paid you?" Mumtaz's voice is so soft I can barely hear her.

"No."

"Then what happened?"

"He kept making me come. He let his sons rape me. And sometimes his friends. One of them was from the city. He gave me a silver bracelet."

"Why?"

"He said it was a gift. Then I became pregnant." She laughs. "Imagine, my mother was also pregnant at the time."

"So what did you do?"

"The landlord told me the man from the city wanted to take me to Lahore to marry me. I didn't believe him. But the villagers told me it was the only way to recover my honor, so I went."

"Did he marry you?"

"No. He took me to a hakim who ended my pregnancy. Then he told me he had bought me from the landlord for fifty rupees. He said I would have to give him fifty rupees if I wanted to go back to my village."

"But you didn't have the money."

Dilaram chuckles. "He brought me to Heera Mandi and made me have sex with men until he had his fifty rupees."

I look at Mumtaz, but she doesn't notice me. The women are completely focused on each other.

"Then did he let you go?"

"No. He told me the villagers would not accept me back because I had lost my honor. I believed him. The others knew stories of girls who had returned to their families and were killed by their fathers or their brothers. So I stayed on. I worked for many years, until I was no longer young and had few clients. By then the man had grown old. He needed my help to run this place. Once it was clear to the girls and the clients that I was in charge, he died. Some people said I poisoned him." She laughs silently, shuddering.

I light a cigarette as the interview continues, and not seeing an ashtray, I tip the ash into the palm of my hand. Dilaram seems a little too well-spoken for an uneducated village girl, sounding more like a wayward Kinnaird alumna to me, actually, and I begin to wonder whether she's making up her story as she goes along.

Occasionally I turn to look through the curtain of beads behind us. The giant pimp observes us closely, his arms crossed in front of him. I don't see any of Dilaram's prostitutes or their clients, but through the walls I hear sounds which convince me that business is continuing despite our presence.

When the interview is over, Dilaram watches us go, laughing to herself. Our eyes meet for a moment, and I'm startled by the anger in her glance.

Neither Mumtaz nor I say anything until we're on the canal. She's driving fast, shifting up through the gears, and I want to ask whether she believes Dilaram's story, but something in her expression makes me think better of it.

I light a cigarette, the last from her pack, and pass it to her.

"Thanks for coming," she says.

She passes the cigarette and we share it, each taking a few

drags before passing it back. Soon we're back in New Muslim Town, near my house. I want to touch her, to make some connection before she drops me off and I'm alone again. But she does it for me.

She pulls up to my gate and stops. Then she turns and kisses me on the cheek, her hand curling around the back of my head, touching my neck and my hair. We stay like that for a moment, and I don't move, my arms at my sides, afraid of doing anything to make her leave. But she leans away from me and smiles, and I have to get out. We don't say goodbye.

I watch the taillights of her car flash red, and then she's gone around a turn. I know I'm standing still, but I feel like I've stumbled and I'm starting to fall.

The day after I become privy to the secret of Zulfikar Manto, I find myself in a suit and tie, my shoes shining more brightly than new coins in a beggar's bowl.

Butt saab is a master of the French inhale. He sits behind his desk, smoke slipping out of his mouth and up his nostrils, and watches me with the half-lidded, red-eyed superiority of a junior civil servant, which I'm told he once was. A flick of his tongue sends a tight gray ring drifting over my curriculum vitae. Mercifully, it disperses before reaching me.

"Normally, I wouldn't have agreed to see you," he says. "We have a hiring freeze in place at the moment. But your uncle is a friend, so I'm making an exception."

Eight banks, eight c.v.'s, seven flat-out rejections. This is my first actual interview. "Thank you, Butt saab."

"Where else are you looking?"

I tell him.

"And what have they told you?"

"They say I don't have a foreign degree or an MBA."

"And?"

"They haven't given me an interview."

Butt saab drops his cigarette into his almost-empty teacup. It hisses and he lights another. "Listen. I don't have a foreign degree. And I don't have an MBA. And we've hired three people this year, despite our hiring freeze, and they don't have foreign degrees or MBAs either. Well, two do have MBAs, actually. And, come to think of it, one has a foreign degree as well. But you have a master's and a fair amount of experience. You'd be as good as any of them, if I had to guess."

Sounds promising enough, but there's no encouragement in Butt saab's expression. "I know banking," I say. "And I'm hungry for a chance. I'll work hard."

"That's the problem. Work hard at what? There just isn't that much work these days." Another French inhale. "We have more people than we need right now. And the boys we're hiring have connections worth more than their salaries. We're just giving them the respectability of a job here in exchange for their families' business."

I nod. There doesn't seem to be much for me to say.

"I'm meeting with you, to tell you the honest truth, as a favor to your uncle," Butt saab continues. "Unless you know some really big fish, and I mean someone whose name matters to a country head, no one is going to hire you. Not with the banking sector in the shape it's in."

I try to smile. "I take it your country head doesn't know my uncle."

Butt saab laughs. "Mr. Shezad, I know your uncle. He's a good friend of mine. But if I were country head right now, I still wouldn't be able to hire you. Things are tight these days and favors are expensive."

A boy brings in another round of tea, our second in ten minutes, and sets the tray on top of my c.v. Butt saab offers me a cigarette that I accept, but my attempt to match his French inhale gets caught somewhere up my nose and makes my eyes water. I content myself with a smoke ring instead.

Outside the bank I sit in my car and watch them go in, guys my age in blue shirts and light suits. Sunglasses, longish hair slicked back. Bored, a little sluggish after lunch, but comfortably certain of an afternoon that won't stretch out too long and a paycheck at the end of the month. I never particularly liked my job, and wanting now what I didn't like but once had is enough to make me look down when former colleagues glance in my direction. It's too hot to sit in my car, so I turn the key in the ignition and head home, my perspiration smelling of an old iron and too much starch.

On Sunday I go to the weekly family luncheon. I tend to avoid these things because they depress me. But I make an exception today, because I'm bored and a little lonely, and I don't feel like sitting around the house by myself with nothing to do. Besides, my cash is running low and I could use a free meal.

The family luncheons are invariably at Fatty Chacha's place. My house is small, but my uncle's is smaller. He has no satellite dish, one car, and three kids, and his wife is so quiet that Dadi, who lives with them, calls her daughter-in-law "the philosopher." Dadi is the real spirit behind these get-togethers. She hates being separated from family, hates rifts and divisions, maybe because she's lost so much to partitions: her husband on a train from Amritsar to Lahore, and her eldest son, my father, in Bangladesh.

When I walk into the house through the open front door, Dadi, Fatty Chacha, my aunts—Tinky Phoppo and Munni

Phoppo—and their spouses and children are already eating. They look at me in surprise and then surge in a collective welcome that leaves my cheeks damp and marked with lipstick and my right hand a tad sticky from the food they were consuming.

It's all a little too eager. I sense something somber sitting behind their enthusiasm, something not-so-normal behind their normality. A little paranoia crawls into my lap, purring loudly, making me think maybe I'm the cause, reminding me how obvious it must be that my life is going nowhere.

My cousin Jamal gets up so I can sit, but I wave him back down.

"Come here," Dadi says, patting the arm of her sofa.

"Yes, Dadi?" I say, sitting there, my head several feet above hers.

"Where are you these days?" she asks.

"Where am I these days?"

"Have you found a job?"

"Not yet."

"When are you getting married?"

"As soon as you find me someone, Dadi."

"Two such lovely girls are sitting right here."

Tinky Phoppo smiles. Her daughters blush and look down.

"Let him eat," Fatty Chacha says, handing me a plate piled high with food.

"Do you need any money?" Tinky Phoppo's husband asks, his wife's elbow pressed firmly into his side. He isn't corrupt, so they survive on his pitiful salary and a small inheritance, including the Swiss watch that he likes to drop into a glass of water from time to time to demonstrate that it's waterproof and therefore authentic.

I start eating. "I'm okay for now," I lie, because they have no cash to spare.

Muhammad Ali, Fatty Chacha's son, tugs on my sleeve. "Daru bhai, do boxing with me."

"Show me what you know," I say.

He puts on a few moves. Not bad for a six-year-old. "Amazing," I say. "You'll be better than Muhammad Ali."

"I am Muhammad Ali," he points out.

"The greatest boxer ever was also named Muhammad Ali," Fatty Chacha explains.

Muhammad Ali laughs. "Noooo," he says.

"Yeeees," says his dad.

Fatty Chacha was a boxer when he was younger, although to look at him now, you wouldn't guess it. I think he was a bantamweight, but he's since put on a generous paunch, so he's basically a big belly with skinny legs and arms. He learned from my father, who learned from Dada. And Fatty Chacha taught me.

Jamal extends a plate to me and says, "Mango?"

I cut one open and eat it with a roti.

Dadi nods in satisfaction. "This one is really my grandchild," she says.

"I'm also really your grandchild, Dadi," Muhammad Ali says, grabbing her from behind.

"Of course, of course," she says, laughing. "You are all my grandchildren."

Munni Phoppo looks at Jamal anxiously, but he gives me a brave wink. Jamal knows he's adopted, and he makes no bones about being happier with his fingers on a computer keyboard than in boxing gloves. Maybe he'll be the first Shezad male to make a success of his life.

I wink back at him.

When we're done eating, Dadi tells me that her shoulder is hurting again, which is her way of telling me to massage it. She likes my massages. She says I do it like my father did. I bend to my task behind her, pressing away, my eyes on the few wisps of white hair which grow on her bald head. Dadi feels as ancient as she looks, and when she tells me to do something I do it instinctively, as though the command passes to me through my genes rather than my ears.

Except, of course, that I won't marry one of my cousins.

After the meal is done and the family has finished chatting and digesting, a process which takes a couple of hours, there's a break in the cricket match we've been watching on TV and the clan begins to disperse. Jamal, who's been learning to drive, demonstrates his reversing technique to me on his way out. Then he pulls away from the house with a little screech, probably for my benefit, and I can see his parents screaming at him as their old VW Beetle zips down the road.

Once my aunts' families have gone, Fatty Chacha and I go to the children's bedroom with some tea. The room is small and plastered with fading stickers. The fan above gives a metallic groan on each slow revolution.

"So, champ," Fatty Chacha says, "how are things?"

"Fatty Chacha, I'm not having any luck."

He shoves his hand inside a box of Marie biscuits. "How about my friend?"

"Butt saab," I say, stressing the *saab*, "told me other people were better connected."

He bites into a biscuit and it breaks, parts of it falling into his lap. "That's ridiculous."

I shrug.

He brushes some crumbs onto the carpet. "I'll have another talk with him."

"It won't help. He said there was nothing he could do." I put down my cup. "Fatty Chacha, this tea is awful."

"I know. I don't understand how you can make bad tea, but this new boy manages to do it every day. You don't know how lucky you are to have Manucci. Here, have a biscuit." He offers the box to me.

"Thanks," I say, taking one.

"Your father was the well-connected one, champ. I don't know anyone else who owes me a favor and might be of some use to you. But let me make some calls."

"Thanks, Fatty Chacha." The biscuit is stale, but I eat it anyway.

"Do you need some money for the time being?" He offers the box of biscuits again.

"Could I borrow two thousand?"

Fatty Chacha looks uncomfortable. "Of course," he says. "Let me give you five hundred now, and I'll take out some money from the bank tomorrow."

Maybe I should have asked for less, but I don't want to embarrass him by withdrawing my request and I really need the money. I sit with Dadi for a while, but she's fast asleep, and as much as I'm enjoying the air-conditioning in the living room, eventually I have to go.

Fatty Chacha insists I take the leftovers with me: three glass bowls capped with tin foil. They make my car smell, and the smell makes me hungry even though I've just filled my stomach with as much as I thought it could hold. Lately I've been eating more than usual, and I wonder why my body has chosen this moment to give me such an appetite, when I can least afford it. Then again, animals tend to fatten up in anticipation of lean times ahead. I belch loudly as I drive, quite a roar, freeing up some space inside.

CHAPTER 6

the big man

Murad Badshah, MA, rickshaw fleet captain and land pirate, at your service. Allow me to begin at the outside and move in.

Huge (and also massive, enormous, and gigantic) describes me well. I am very, very rarely called fat. Perhaps you smile thinking this is because I inspire a certain sense of caution in more modestly proportioned persons? I must most respectfully take issue with you on this matter, and I beg your indulgence as I present a simple proof.

What is fat?

"Fat" is a small word which belies its size in the girth of its connotations. Fat implies a certain ungainliness, an inefficiency, a sense of immobility, a lack of industry, an unpleasant, unaesthetic quality; unmotivated, unloved, unnatural, unusual, uninspired, unhappy, unlikely to go places or to fit, under the ground with a heart attack at fifty-five. In short, fat somewhat paradoxically involves the lack of many attributes which, you must concede, are generally held to be good.

When the word "fat" is mentioned, people do not tend to

think of the awesomely powerful rhinoceros, the supremely efficient and magnificent sperm whale, the deadly grizzly of North America. They do not say, "fat as a well-fed tiger." No, they say, "fat as a pig," a creature which eats its own feces and has never in our literature been a symbol of dignity.

Very well, then. The collective consciousness has assigned to fat a meaning, and as I speak this language I must accept fat on these terms. Fat is bad.

And so I am certain you will not disagree when I say the word can hardly be considered to apply to me. I am weighty, yes, but I carry my mass wonderfully. I am quick, light on my feet, and graceful. I have poise; delicacy and elegance characterize my every movement. My fingers are nimble, my hands deft. It is no secret that I dance well and most willingly. Furthermore, I possess those very qualities the lack of which is assumed by the word "fat": industry, drive, dexterity, cunning. I am the living embodiment of so many unfat qualities that their enumeration would be a project of enormous scope.

If A has fundamental characteristics the very absence of which characterize B, it cannot be said with any degree of accuracy (or, may I add, sophistication) that A is B.

Thus, I am not fat. *Quod erat demonstrandum.*

But I do stutter, it is true.

You pretend not to understand the logic which links this last statement to that which preceded it? Come, come, now. There is no need for such modesty on your part. A stutter, like fatness, is considered a bad thing, a flaw. I simply wish you to understand that I am not perfect and I am aware of my imperfection. I stutter. I stut-tut-tut-tut-tut-tutter. You perhaps have noticed that my mind works at quite an exceptional speed? (I hope you share my feelings about modesty.) As a child, my mouth struggled to keep pace with my thoughts, but the race was so unequal that my tongue would inevitably stumble like a blind camel with vertigo. It took me many years to realize that the secret to speech lay in speaking slowly, training my trotting tongue not to chase my galloping mind.

So I do not stutter obviously or often, but I do stutter. And strange though it may seem, I am proud of my stutter, much as a comely woman is proud of the black lump which on her face is called a beauty mark.

But enough small talk. Let me tell you how I met Darashikoh Shezad.

My father was a gold jeweler, the son of sons of gold jewelers from time immemorial. He died before I was born, in a freakish accident involving a cigarette and the open valve of a balloon vendor's gas cylinder. My mother was of a more modest background and unloved by the members of her husband's family, who at the time of my father's immolation had no knowledge of my imminent arrival. We were soon living with her brother, my uncle, who worked for the British Council library.

So it was that I had access to all the books I could want and the opportunity to learn the nuances of English speech from a people who, if nothing else, do one thing excellently: speak English.

I received my MA in English twenty-some years later and was of course unable to find a job. To sum up what followed: I went to see my father's eldest brother, whom I had never met, and in a five-minute interview was given a sum of money (in exchange for a promise never to show my face in his shop again) that I used to purchase a rickshaw. In the short years since then, I acquired four more, and am now captain of a squadron of five little beauties.

My rickshaw fleet specialized (as much as it is possible to do so in my line of business) in servicing the students and faculty of my alma mater. It so happened that on one rainy day an occasional client of mine, the inimitable Professor Julius Superb, brought one of his favorite students into my rickshaw with him. I had made Dr. Superb's acquaintance in my days as a master's candidate at the university, and he always sought me out when he had rickshaw requirements to be met. He introduced me to his student, we shook hands, I felt a strong grip, and the seeds of a partnership in crime were sown. When next Darashikoh needed conveyance, he sought me out.

Darashikoh was an intriguing fellow. Excuse me for speaking of him in the past tense, but that is how I think of him. He was ruggedly handsome (like knows like, as they say) but cold, with a steady gaze and a cruel mouth. A solid boxer with a quick mind. We talked, and I took a liking to him, and he to me, and we became friends.

Socially we moved in somewhat different circles, although I must say his friends were always very respectful. We met for tea and talk on Tuesdays, after which I gave him a ride (gratis) to wherever he was going. Our conversations ran from economics to automotive maintenance, broken noses, and Aretha Franklin. (A word about this last: a foreign tourist once left a cassette in the back of my rickshaw, and when I took it home and played it, I discovered the Queen of Soul. Life was never the same. In the past, when people said America has never given us anything, I used to agree. Now I say, "Yes, but America has given us Aretha Franklin, the Queen of Soul," and they look at me strangely. I never explain any further: one cannot explain Aretha Franklin; either you are enlightened or you are not. That is how I view the matter.)

With the arrival of yellow cabs in Lahore, the rickshaw business took a bad turn. Profits became increasingly slim, and to say competition was fierce is an understatement of unusual proportions. Business is a tough business, as they say, and I am fairly handy when it comes to mixing it up. In my post-MA years I have been shot at three times, hit twice (stomach and thigh), and was unfortunately once obliged to kill a man with a wrench. I took to carrying a gun quite some time ago, and it was but a short step from protecting my own on the high seas of Lahore's streets to realizing that piracy was the wave of the future. The marauding yellow cabs had devastated the rickshaw industry, so I conducted a little redistribution of wealth on my own. Robbing yellow-cab drivers as they slept put my finances back in the black.

But this didn't last. Imitation is the sincerest form of flattery, as they say, and I was flattered to the point where yellow-cab drivers were forced to take precautions, parking to sleep in places that were extremely inconvenient from my point of view, carrying less money, and so on. Pickings became slim and profits dropped off.

Around this time Darashikoh was in rather difficult straits himself: he was in debt, had no job, and was saddled with the heaviest weight of pride and self-delusion I have ever seen one person attempt to carry. I trusted him, knew he was bright, ruthless, capable, and that he could tolerate my sense of humor. And so it was that I enlisted him in my plan to rob boutiques, and together we formed a duo that would strike fear into the hearts of purveyors of fashionable clothing everywhere.

It was a summer of great rumblings in the belly of the earth, of atomic flatulence and geopolitical indigestion, consequences of the consumption of sectarian chickpeas by our famished and increasingly incontinent subcontinent. Clenched beneath the tightened sphincters of test sites and silos, the pressure of superheated gases was registering in spasms on the Richter scale.

Lahore was uneasy, and Immodium in short supply.

The perfect time, I thought, for my plan.

Allow me at this point the luxury of a minor digression. Although I proudly admit to being a robber (attaching as I do a certain prestige to my calling), I must make it quite clear, so clear that there is no room for doubt, that I am not a murderer. And while it is true that outlaws of both departments are schooled by the faculty of lawlessness, it is equally true that they are separated by a moral chasm as vast as the difference in syllabi which divides BA candidates from those pursuing a BSc.

You see, it is my passionately held belief that the right to possess property is at best a contingent one. When disparities become too great, a superior right, that to life, outweighs the right to property. Ergo, the very poor have the right to steal from the very rich. Indeed, I would go so far as to say that the poor have a duty to do so, for history has shown that the inaction of the working classes perpetuates their subjugation.

However, because I believe in the primacy of the right to life, I also believe that killing is wrong unless done in self-defense. Although many of my more frivolous friends and acquaintances accuse me of dieting to reduce my weight, the truth of the matter is that I do not eat meat because I am so strongly opposed to killing, and because my sense of compassion is so fat (here defined as grand, expansive, and all-encompassing) that it extends to species beyond our own.

The professional murderers I have known tend to disagree. Their arguments run as follows.

"Murad, old chum," they say. "Your moral structures are but feeble attempts to come to terms with the reality of killing, and excuse us for saying so, but you really do miss your mark. When a bird takes wing and you bring your gun to your shoulder and track it and pull and send bits of metal hurtling through the air, ripping through its little feathered body, thereby causing it sufficient physical trauma to begin a process of cessation of vital bodily functions, what do you have? A moral issue? Sport? An illustration of the essential brutality of the universe and the simultaneous meaning and meaninglessness of existence? Of course not. You have a tasty morsel waiting to be seasoned and served with carrots.

"What once was a free creature which happily flitted about, cheating on his mate and slurping worms out of the soft ground with a flick of his head as if to say, 'Ah, this is the life,' is now something stuck between your teeth in such a manner that the toothpick you use to pry it loose leaves your gums feeling just a little bit raw in that deliciously painful but pleasurable way which reminds you of days long since gone when you spent hours twisting at your loosening milk teeth.

"But you can always justify killing animals on the grounds that you want to eat them, or wear them, or that they smell bad, look funny, bother you, threaten you, and have the bad luck of being in your way. What about killing humans? Well, aside from a few die-hard individualists on the fringe, the general consensus among people these days seems to be that eating and wearing other people is just not on. Wearing a suit which costs as much as a farmer will make in his lifetime is acceptable, but actually putting his eyeballs on a string and letting them dangle above tastefully exposed cleavage is bad form.

"That said, killing someone because of the other reasons we mentioned above (smell, looks, bother, threat, or bad luck) is quite acceptable. You want deodorants, you know that one in 6.87 million will die from a violent allergic reaction, you shrug and churn the stuff out, and some poor fellow suffers a pain in the armpit beyond imagining and dies, and that's that: acceptable. You drive cars, knowing eventually you will probably kill somebody or be killed, but 'Hurry up, I don't want to be late for my threading,' and you're off. No regrets. Or someone who has never been to your farm and seen the cute dimples your youngest daughter is already showing when she smiles decides a line on a piece of paper should be a little to the left, and in the name of God and all that is right, to war boys: kill, kill, kill! Yours not to reason why, but damn it hurts when a land mine blows off your leg.

"So, Murad, old chum, people kill people all the time, and usually with the barest minimum of fuss. You really must keep a sense of humor about it all. There is no moral issue here. Better to laugh at what you do not understand than to take it seriously and end up giggling hysterically in a padded cell off Jail Road."

Now, I concede that the murderers do have a point. But I was brought up by my mother to have a strong sense of wrong and right, and in the end I can only say, quite feebly I admit: Placing so little value on human life is wrong.

As for myself, I had no choice. The first and only time I killed a man, it was either him or me, and even so the memory of it saddens me immensely.

Let me elaborate.

I was (why deny it?) something of a celebrity in the transportation industry in those days. The wave of yellow-cab robberies by rickshaw drivers had crested, and the sense of empowerment which coursed through my fellow drivers of three-wheeled vehicles was electric. It was widely and correctly believed that I was the originator of the idea that the rickshaw's salvation lay in erecting a little barrier to the entry of the yellow cab in our market. Entry barriers are common to all industries, and the spree of robberies of drivers of four-wheeled entrants by drivers of the established three-wheeled holders of market share was simply an example of laissez-faire market economics, as I am sure the good Dr. Superb would tell you.

Naturally, the yellow-cab drivers had a different point of view. I was an infamous figure of almost mythical proportions to them, a Redbeard or Red Baron (indeed, my rickshaw sported a little red pennant from her rear mast, a radio antenna), and every second robbery was linked to me in some way. A bounty of ten thousand rupees was placed on my head, soon upped to fifty thousand, and from there to two lakhs. At least three men were killed by bounty hunters and irate yellow-cab drivers in cases of mistaken identity. And I wasn't always so lucky: two bullets found me out in my hiding places, as I mentioned earlier, and I submit that I shed more than my share of blood.

Eventually, after heavy casualties on both sides, a truce was agreed to, and rickshaw drivers and yellow-cab drivers joined one another in putting an end to the cycle of robbery and reprisal. By this point, most of the robbing was being done by professional thugs who had nothing to do with either side but simply saw a good opportunity and did not discriminate between the types of vehicles they robbed. So both three- and four-wheeled transporters banded together against this common threat.

The bounty on my head was withdrawn, and I came out of hiding a hero to rickshaw drivers and a feared but respected former adversary to yellow-cab men. All sorts of rumors were circulating: that I had killed six men with my bare hands and eaten their livers, that I could shoot the cap off a bottle of Pakola at twenty paces, that I had once caught a bullet in my teeth and spat it away unharmed. Truth be told, I had never killed anyone, was a fair shot at best, and had teeth so weak I avoided eating sugarcane, but I encouraged the rumors, because they deterred would-be aggressors and, to be frank, flattered my ego.

Now, I was strutting about proudly in those days, and it goes without saying I should have been more careful. Some lad got it into his head that I had killed his father, a yellow-cab driver, and he swore to himself that truce or no truce, he would get revenge. The day before it happened, my sources later told me, he was heard boasting that he would not only kill the great Murad Badshah but would humiliate me besides. And he came after me with his father's gun.

There are three lessons to be learned from what followed, aside from my general point about death and killing. The first is that the gun of the father is always the undoing of the son. The second is that it is never wise to call someone something which he is not. And the third is that a man's weakness can at times be his greatest strength.

Gun in hand, the boy arrived at the little depot where I maintain my rickshaws. I was in the small, dimly lit back workroom, tinkering about with a broken-down engine and holding a fancy Japanese wrench given me by a friend who retired from the rickshaw business when things first began to get rough, not because he was afraid, but because his wife said he was losing his hearing driving a noisy rickshaw all day and ought to be working a register in her brother's store instead. A few children were playing in the street outside, and our would-be murderer, seeing this audience and rising to the role he fully expected to play, cried out theatrically as he entered my depot, "Your time is up, fat man!"

If he had been silent I might well have breathed my last that day.

Instead, I surged to my feet and would have roared, "What [obscenities] said that?" but as so often happens in moments of intense excitement, my stutter locked onto my voice like a fearful lover and prevented me from uttering a sound. I was growing red, my mouth working desperately, when the boy strode purposefully into the workroom with a glint in his eye and the tip of his tongue between his lips. In the dimness, he did not see me beside the door. But I saw his gun, and without thinking, I swung my wrench in a mighty blow that caught him at the back of the head, where the spine meets the skull, and with a sound like stepping on a soft-shell turtle his life was over.

I have many regrets about that day. Perhaps I could have disarmed him. Perhaps I could have struck him with less force. But life seeks to preserve itself, and I acted as any man who wants to live would have acted. I derived no pleasure from it, and of all the stories you may hear of the men who have died at my hands, only this one is true, and my career as a robber would have been more illustrious were it not.

Perhaps you will now better understand why I, an infamous criminal, was so horrified by the events of that ill-fated robbery, when my friend and colleague Darashikoh revealed his capacity for cold-blooded murder.

It was a dark and stormy night.

Do you smile at this introduction? Allow me to submit for your consideration the saying that tales with unoriginal beginnings are those most likely later to surprise.

So, the night was dark and stormy.

Lightning flickered above the city, a crescent moon sneered through a gap in the clouds. The boutique huddled against the storm, a tiny island of light on an unlit street.

I wore red, the darkest crimson, a color that blends into black in the dark and flatters my figure by day. My kurta fluttered behind me in the breeze, and a concealed revolver itched where it pressed against my hairy belly. Darashikoh was inside, for all the world a tastefully dressed patron of the shop, but he carried death in his undershorts and hunger in his heart. I had done all this before, but the thrill, the excitement, the electricity of anticipation never goes. Yes, armed robbery is like public speaking. Both offer a brief period in the limelight, the risk of public humiliation, the opportunity for crowd control. And in both, what you wear is an often ignored but vitally important factor.

The signal I awaited was simple: when Darashikoh placed his

pistol against the head of the guard standing just inside the entrance of the shop, clearly visible through the window display, I was to come in and fleece the place.

The signal was given and I walked in. If you learn nothing else about violent conflict, learn this: never rush. Take your time, evaluate the situation, then act. When you have multiple tasks to perform, proceed sequentially, or you will make a mess of them all. Think of it as being assigned to read a long, convoluted poem, if that helps you. My tasks at this stage were to enter, control the crowd, rob them, and leave.

The shop guard, a rather sweet fellow with a shotgun and a leather bandolier of cartridges, seemed almost ready to cry by the time I entered, walking purposefully but without undue haste. From my long years in the service profession I have learned both that the customer is always right and that if he steps far enough out of line, threatening him with execution-style murder is a valid although rarely exercisable option. I am told my smile and manner succeed in conveying this duality of knowledge and so it is easy for me to maintain the utmost respect while inspiring terror of bowel-moving proportions.

With a cheery "If you please," I proceeded to lighten the burden of wealth that bore down so heavily upon this establishment's clientele. My revolver gleamed with the sweat it had accumulated while pressed against my skin, and it was slippery in my hand. I looked about me as I proceeded, and so I saw the vacant look in Darashikoh's eyes as he stood with one foot on the guard, who was by now lying flat on the floor.

It happened when I turned my back on him.

I was encouraging an elderly lady to help her husband remove a lovely watch with a complicated clasp when I heard a sound behind me, the sound of feet moving quickly, and I whirled just in time to see Darashikoh raise his gun.

The moment is frozen in my memory: the blank faces above their expensive outfits, the colorful clothing on shiny metal racks, the motionless, impossibly slender mannequins, the gasping inhalation that preceded the woman's scream, the change in pressure as the door of an air-conditioned space is opened, Darashikoh's left hand flashing up to steady his aim. And then the scream—shrill—a sound that raises hackles.

And finally, so long awaited that its coming was a shock, the explosion of the gunshot.

And Darashikoh changed before my eyes.

It was unsettling, even for me, a man not easily unsettled.

I had forgotten how much it affected me. I hope you will not mind if I now take my leave.

CHAPTER 7

four

I wake up sweating, staring at a motionless ceiling fan. Damn. They've cut my electricity. I call the power company, hoping that it's just load-shedding or a breakdown, but a smug voice at the other end tells me that my account is in arrears and my service has been discontinued.

I yell for Manucci, and he sticks his head into my room with a smile. "What are you smiling at, idiot? Our electricity is gone."

"It will come back, saab," he says, still smiling. The boy has no fear of me.

"No, it will not come back. They've cut us off. We're back in the seventeenth century."

He nods solemnly.

"Make my breakfast. I'll have eggs. No, it's too hot. I'll have a glass of milk and a sliced mango. Then run to the bazaar and get some candles. And some hand fans."

He starts to shut the door to my room and then stops. "Saab, money?"

"What happened to the money I gave you?"

"It's finished."

"What do you mean, finished? Stop smiling, you crook, this is serious." I take two hundred rupees out of my wallet and give them to him. "I want a full accounting when you get back."

I take a shower and plop down on my bed, still wet, with a towel wrapped around my waist. At least I'm not hot this way. Having the power cut is serious. I was a month behind on my payments even before I lost my job, unprepared as usual for the summer spike in my bill that sucks a quarter of my paycheck into the air conditioner, and now I owe them half a month's salary. Power prices have been rising faster than a banker's wages the last couple of years, thanks to privatization and the boom of guaranteed-profit, project-financed, imported oil–fired electricity projects. I was happier when we had load-shedding five hours a day: at least then a man didn't have to be a millionaire to run his AC.

I'm eating the mango when the phone rings. A voice jumps out of the receiver like a snappy salute, and even though I haven't spoken to Khurram uncle in quite some time, I know at once it's his. He has an unmistakable tone of command I associate with Sandhurst and the experience of sitting comfortably in an office while ordering men to die.

"Darashikoh," he says, "Aurangzeb tells me you've encountered a spot of difficulty finding a position."

So he knows I've been fired. "Yes, sir," I answer.

"Well, son, I think it's about time you called in the heavy guns. I know Aurangzeb has requested your presence at the house this evening. Come by my quarters at twenty-two hundred and we shall see if I can't straighten things out."

"Yes, sir."

"Very good."

Khurram uncle was my father's best friend at the military academy. He occupied a cushy staff position as an ADC in Rawalpindi in '71, while my father died of gangrene in a prisoner-of-war camp near Chittagong. Then he slipped into the civil service, specializing, it's said, in overpaying foreign companies for equipment and pocketing their kickbacks.

I have no real memories of my father. I turned two the summer his regiment was sent east. His photos and the stories I've heard have built in my mind the image of a quiet, courageous man, a soldier's soldier. He was the best boxer at the military academy, and he drove a motorcycle. I have his ears, people say. Strange things to inherit, ears. Small and lobeless, like a pair of half-hearts. Otherwise we look nothing alike.

Khurram uncle was the first person to notice the similarity. I must have been seven or eight. Ozi and I had come back to my place from a football match and my knees were bloody. Khurram uncle was paying a visit to my mother. As she cleaned my cuts with Dettol, and I cried because of the stinging, I remember Khurram uncle taking one of my ears between his thumb and forefinger and saying, "Strange ears. Connected to the jaw. Just like his father."

Khurram uncle visited our house fairly regularly. He always asked if we needed anything, and he often brought me presents. Sometimes he gave me clothes from abroad. I remember my first pair of high-top sneakers. Ozi told the boys in school that they were meant for him but were too small, so his father gave them to me.

I saw less and less of Khurram uncle as I grew older, especially after Ozi left for America. The summer my mother died, I went to a restaurant with some friends and found her having lunch with Khurram uncle. She told me he had found me a job at a bank. I don't remember being happy at that moment. Maybe no one wants to stop being a student.

The last time I saw him was at her funeral. He was crying. Ozi's mother was sick and couldn't come. Khurram uncle told me to contact him if there was ever anything I needed. I never did. But even though we weren't in touch, I kept hearing about him, that he'd built a mansion in Gulberg, that he was being investigated by the Accountability Commission.

I never said anything when people spoke of him. I'd been doing well enough for myself. I was getting by without any more of his handouts. And I was quite content not to see him.

But tonight I swallow my pride, hold my nose, and arrive at his place promptly at ten.

"Darashikoh, my boy," Khurram uncle says when I'm taken to him. "Why haven't you come to see me before this? There's no need for formality between you and me. You're a bright lad; all you need is a few doors opened for you and your merits will carry you far."

I thank him and sit down.

"So, what kind of work is it you're looking for?" he asks me.

I lean forward in my seat. "A bank or a large multinational."

"Have you thought about car dealerships?"

He doesn't seem to be joking. "Not really."

He takes a sip from a glass of whiskey and taps his shoe with a walking stick. "There's good money to be made, and someone with your brains could be quite an asset to a car dealer."

I feel the blood rush into my face, burn hotly in my ears. "I'm not—"

"Now listen to me, Darashikoh. This is no cheap little used-car dealing operation on some side street. I'd never ask you to consider something like that. No, I'm talking about a modern business, a professional showroom on Queen's Road, with well-dressed salespeople and well-heeled clients. A place where you will have twenty-five thousand rupees in your pocket at the end of every month."

"I'd really like something with a bank or a multinational."

"Ah, boys these days. They don't know a good thing when they see it. Still, nothing is too much for the son of my dearest comrade-in-arms. Let me see what I can do." Khurram uncle takes another sip from his whiskey. He hasn't offered me any, which is no surprise, since he doesn't permit Ozi to drink in his presence, even though he knows Ozi drinks. Maybe it's a little like Khurram uncle's attitude toward corruption.

A young Filipina leads a child in by the finger. "This is Muazzam," Khurram uncle says proudly. "Aurangzeb's son. Would you like to give him a hug?"

"I know Muazzam," I say, taking the child into my arms. He struggles to pull free, like he's afraid of me, and his nanny quickly retrieves him.

"Children are excellent judges of character, you know," Khurram uncle says with a loud guffaw. "Well, off with you now, my boy. I'll keep you posted."

I head upstairs, feeling a little disgusted with myself.

When Ozi opens the door to his suite, though, surprise drives all thoughts of my meeting with Khurram uncle out of my head. Ozi embraces me hard, like a friend preventing a fight, or a boxer tying up an opponent with shorter reach. The smell of his after-shave envelops us both, and his voice tickles my ear as he whispers, "I'm so sorry, yaar. I know it was just supposed to be the three of us tonight, but there's been a change of plans. I hope you don't mind."

"Of course not, yaar," I say, confused.

"And I tried to call you about dinner, but I couldn't get through. Besides, we had sushi flown in from Karachi and I know you don't like fish."

And with that he steps aside and lets me pass, and I begin to understand what he's talking about. I have arrived at a full-fledged invitational dinner only semi-invited. That is, I was told to come late for drinks, while the other guests came early and polished off an exotic air-transported meal. I know a snub when I see one, and this is a serious snub, especially since I love fish and know damn well that I've never told Ozi otherwise.

But why wouldn't Ozi want me around?

It takes me only a cursory examination of the room to answer that question: Ozi's made new friends.

Dressed in elegant evening wear, chins held aloft, are key components of Lahore's ultra-rich young jet set, only five couples in all, but enough of a presence to indicate that Ozi has been granted a trial membership in their crowd.

The introductions begin. I know their names. Some venture an "I think I've seen you around," but most don't bother. They've sized me up, figured out I'm a small fish, and decided to let me swim by myself for the evening. I spot Pickles, sporting flat-fronted black trousers and a bicep-revealing V-neck T.

"Darashikoh, right?"

Yes, you pretentious bastard. Darashikoh, the same boy who thrashed you after PT behind the middle school building. "Right. How are you, Pickles?"

He seems less than ecstatic at my use of his pet name. "Very well. Yourself?"

"Couldn't be better," I find myself saying.

"Really? What are you doing these days?"

I raise my chin. "Family business, you know. Import-export."

"Clothing?"

"Of course."

"Great," he says. "What do you think of that Australian buyer everyone's been talking about?"

I feel the illusion I've twirled around me like a sari start to come undone and fall to my feet. "You know, Pickles, there's no quick answer to that one. Let me give you a call to discuss it further."

He winks. "I already know the details. I just wanted to know whether it's true."

I can't tell whether he's referring to a sex scandal or a business blunder. "It's true," I say.

He laughs. "Here's my card," he says, whipping out a pen to write something on the back. "And that's my mobile. We should do lunch."

"Thanks," I say, taking it from him. He looks at me expectantly, but I see Mumtaz coming into the room and excuse myself with a smile. Pickles probably thought I was dying to give him my card, and I suspect I've risen several levels in his estimation by not doing so.

Mumtaz gives me a quick kiss on the cheek. She looks harried, and nothing about her suggests that our midnight run to Heera Mandi ever took place.

"Is everything all right?" I ask her.

"Yes. Sorry. Muazzam's making a nuisance of himself downstairs. He won't go to bed, and Ozi's father gives him candies whenever I scold him. He probably has nothing but liquid sugar in his bloodstream at this point. He may never sleep again." She smiles at me. "How are you?"

"Good. What is this?"

"Lahore's rich and famous."

"Are they your friends?"

"I've met most of them before."

"So they're Ozi's friends?"

"Some are. The rest will be. He's good at this sort of thing, my husband. Can I get you some wine?"

"I'm not a wine drinker."

She looks at me thoughtfully. "You sound upset. Is it because Ozi didn't invite you for dinner?"

"No."

"Don't feel bad. He wasn't sure you would like this crowd."

"Why didn't he just tell me not to come at all?"

"He wanted to see you. So did I. Listen, I'm not a wine drinker either. Let me get us both a Scotch."

I nod, feeling a little better. When she returns, we toast each other silently, and then she says, "Look, you have to try to enjoy yourself. Pretend that you're an anthropologist observing the rituals of some isolated tribe."

It isn't hard to do.

A woman whose tied-on top reveals armor-plated abs starts clapping her hands above her head. "Quiet, everyone," she says. "Who wants to go swimming?"

Another woman, very drunk and visibly undernourished, starts chanting, "Swim-*ming!* Swim-*ming!* Swim-*ming!*"

"In Ozi's pool!" yells the first.

"O-*zi!* O-*zi!* O-*zi!*" chants the second.

(I record the first entry in my ethnography: *It appears that intermarriage has severely retarded the mental development of some members of the tribe*.)

"Forget that you're Over Here! Pretend that you're Over There."

(*The utopian vision of Over There or Amreeka promises escape from the almost unbearable drudgery of the tribe's struggle to subsist*.)

There's some scattered clapping but no real enthusiasm for the idea. More drinks are tossed back. I see the rare sight of an iced martini glass being filled with gin and a splash of vermouth, then stirred gently and served with an olive. Ozi is really going all out. I wonder how much he's spent tonight. Fifty thousand rupees? More?

After a while I tire of pretending I'm an anthropologist and focus on my Scotch, killing time by swirling ice cubes. Luckily, the end isn't long in coming.

The Amazon and her famished friend start making a racket again. "Par-*ty!* Par-*ty!* Par-*ty!*"

As if on cue, people start downing their drinks and rounding up their mobile phones. I follow the pack downstairs. In the driveway I don't stand next to my car. It's silly, I know, but I lean against Ozi's Pajero instead. Eventually my friend's guests have gone and it's just Ozi, Mumtaz, and I.

"So what's the plan?" I ask.

"Pickles's cousin is having a party at his farmhouse," Ozi says. "You have to come."

"I'm not invited," I say. And I don't have a date.

"We'll get you in," Ozi says, clapping my shoulder. "Never fear, yaar: I'm back in town."

We're getting into our cars when Ozi stops and asks, "Is Muazzam in bed?"

"I've handled him all night," Mumtaz tells him. "You check."

Ozi shakes his head and goes back in. Mumtaz stares after him, as though she's tracking his progress inside. She looks exhausted.

"How's my friend Zulfikar Manto?" I ask her.

Life seems to rush into her face. She raises an eyebrow and sends a slow glance to either side, pretending she's making sure we aren't overheard. Then she grins. "The prostitution article came out today."

"And? I haven't been reading the papers."

"Big response. I spoke with the editor, and he said he's been swamped with calls."

"Good?"

"Mostly furious. Which is good. It means people read it. One even threw a rock through the paper's window."

"Was the editor upset?"

"He said they're used to it. They buy cheap glass."

The door opens, spilling light, and Ozi comes back out. "He's asleep," he says.

I follow Ozi's Pajero in my Suzuki, struggling to keep pace. We head down the canal toward Thokar Niaz Beg, take a left, cruise by what everyone calls the Arab prince's vacation palace, wind from a side street to an unpaved road to a dirt path, and finally end up at a gate in a wall that literally stretches as far as I can see into the night. Even out here we find the obligatory group of uninvited, dateless guys trying to get in, their way barred by a mobile police unit responsible for protecting tonight's illegal revelry.

Ozi and Mumtaz show their invitation to a private security guard, and he lets them drive through. He stops me. "Invitation?"

"I'm with them," I say.

"Sorry, sir." He isn't apologizing. He's telling me I can't go in. Luckily, I see the white reverse lights of Ozi's Pajero come on ahead.

All three of us get out. "We told you he's with us," Ozi says.

"Sorry, sir. Orders."

"No sorry. Let him in."

"It's okay," I say to them. "I'm tired anyway. I'll just go."

"Don't be silly," Mumtaz tells me. "You're coming in."

A Land Cruiser pulls up behind us, blocking my exit. Pickles gets out and the guard touches his cap to him. "What's the problem?" Pickles asks.

"They're not letting Daru in," Mumtaz tells him.

Pickles nods to the guard.

And that's that.

The driveway, made of brick and in better condition than most roads in the city, purrs under my tires. We park near the farmhouse, big and low, with wide verandas, and I notice the difference in the sounds of slamming car doors: the deep thuds of the Pajero and Land Cruiser, the nervous cough of my Suzuki.

It's early summer, which means I'm not likely to go to another big bash for a while, so I put on my best party-predator smile, run my fingers through my hair, and light a cigarette, trying to get in the mood.

The party turns out to be a real insider's affair. Just a hundred people, the who's who of the Lahore party crowd, all hip and loaded and thrilled about Santorini in June. Even the music isn't the standard club collage but rather some remixed desi stuff that I've never heard before (because, I'm soon told, the DJ mixed it specially for this party and sent it in from London).

I wander around, checking out the scene. Our host, Pickles's cousin, is wearing a white linen shirt, thin enough to suggest an underlying mat of chest hair even though he has only the top button open. His sleeves are rolled up over thick, veiny forearms, and one of his fists clenches a bottle of rare Belgian beer. Long hair is moussed back along his scalp, giving his forehead a greasy gleam, and his nose sits like a broken gladiator above the huge grin he's flashing at everyone and everything around him.

I'd smile, too, if I were him. His party is a smashing success. The dance floor is packed, and the dancing sweaty and conversation-free. Businessmen and bankers crowd the bar, fetching drinks for models with long, lean, nineties bodies. A lot of skin is on display, like something out of a fundo's nightmare or, more likely, vision of paradise. Tattoos, ponytails, sideburns, navel rings abound: this is it, this is cool, this is the Very Best Party of the Off-Season.

And I'm single, with no job and no money, and no real hope of picking up anyone.

Nadira's here, some hotshot in tow, and I try to avoid her even though I know the party's too small for me to hide successfully. I wish I'd brought some hash.

I look around for Raider. I don't know how he does it, because he isn't rich or anything, but the better the party, the more likely he is to be there. I find him kissing Alia under a mango tree.

"Daru," he says, clearly delighted. "Where have you been, partner?"

"Do you have a joint?" Alia asks.

"I was just about to ask you guys the same thing," I say.

They exchange grins. "No joint, yaar," Raider says. "But I have you-know-what."

"Raider, if I didn't know better, I'd suspect you were Lahore's number-one ecstasy supplier."

"Who's that?" Alia asks, looking in the direction of the house.

I see Mumtaz and wave. She walks over.

"Does anyone have a joint?" she asks.

Raider and Alia laugh and introduce themselves. "I like you already," Alia says to Mumtaz.

"I was just telling Daru that we have some ex," Raider says.

I wish he would learn to be more discreet.

"Really?" Mumtaz says, with unexpected enthusiasm.

"Only one," Raider says.

Mumtaz looks at me. "Do you want to?"

"Do you think it's a good idea?" I ask her.

She takes my answer as a yes. "How much does ex cost here?"

"Nothing," says Raider, handing her a little white pill.

"Two thousand," I tell Mumtaz, hoping the price will discourage her. What would Ozi say?

She takes out some cash, peels off two notes, and hands them to Raider. Then she places the pill in her palm and breaks it with her thumbnail.

"Cheers," she says, downing her half.

I look at the broken pill in my hand: smooth curve, rough edge. Might as well. "Cheers," I say, placing it on my tongue and swallowing.

"It won't kick in for a while," she tells me. "I'll see you guys in a bit."

I nod and she heads back inside.

"Wow, I think I'm in love, yaar," Raider says admiringly.

"So am I," says Alia. "Who is she? I've never seen her before."

It somehow sounds inappropriate to say, "Ozi's wife," so I say, "Just a friend."

They both laugh. Then Raider starts stroking Alia's arm, and I can see that I should leave. "Check on us from time to time," Raider says. "We'll be right here till dawn."

I wander around, making small talk and avoiding Ozi, because I'm still upset at not being invited for dinner and also because I'm feeling guilty about having ex with his wife. But eventually he catches my eye and weaves his way over, half-dancing to the music, flashing his famously irresistible grin.

"What's the matter?" he asks.

"Nothing."

He puts me in a headlock and messes up my hair with his free hand, laughing. I push him away.

He looks surprised and hurt, and I feel bad, because I pushed him with more force than I'd intended. "Sorry, yaar," I say, trying to sound playful but failing miserably.

"You're mad at me, aren't you?"

I shrug.

"You think I'm doing a little social climbing," he goes on. He's slurring slightly.

I don't answer.

"Lahore's boring, yaar. Deadly dull. They provide some entertainment."

"They seem like good friends," I say, acid in my voice.

He embraces me, and I know the ex must be kicking in,

because I'm very aware of the contact between us, his shirt, slightly sweaty, the muscles of his back, our breathing.

"That's why I love you, yaar," Ozi's saying. "You always look out for me. But I don't want to be friends with those people. We'll be friendlies at best. People who party together. But that's good enough. That's all I want from them. They're the best party in town."

I feel my attention drifting with the ex, flowing in and around his words, and my gaze slips around the room, looking for Mumtaz.

"It's not my crowd," I say, trying to hold up my end of the conversation.

"That's because you can't afford it. But you're lucky in a sense. Being broke keeps you honest."

I stare at Ozi's mouth. I'm not sure if I thought those words or if he said them. But I want to get away from him. I need to breathe.

"Let me get us some more drinks," he says.

I nod, but I'm starting to ex with unexpected intensity, and once he's gone I head outside to be alone as I adjust, as I shed my sobriety for a newer, livelier skin. The stars look big tonight, and I float over the lawn in the direction of the mango tree.

"Partner," someone calls out.

I look. "Hi, guys," I say.

Raider and Alia are giggling. "She went that way," Alia says.

"Who?" I ask.

"Mum-taaaz," she says, stretching the word lovingly.

I walk in the direction she tells me. I feel my pores opening, sweat and heat radiating out of my body. A firefly dances in the distance, leaving tracers, and if I turn my head from side to side, I see long yellow-green streaks that cut through my vision and burn in front of my retinas even after the light that sparked them has gone.

I emerge from the mango grove into a field. In the distance

unseen trucks pass with a sound like the ocean licking the sand. A tracery of darkness curls into the starry sky, a solitary pipal tree making itself known by an absence of light, like a flame caught in a photographer's negative, frozen, calling me.

A breeze tastes my sweat and I shiver, shutting my eyes and raising my arms with it, wanting to fly. I walk in circles, tracing the ripples that would radiate if the stars fell from the sky through the lake of this lawn, one by one, like a rainstorm moving slowly into the breeze, toward the tree, each splash, each circle, closer.

And with a last stardrop, a last circle, I arrive, and she's there, chemical wonder in her eyes.

"Hi," she whispers.

"Hi," I say. It's as if she's not Ozi's wife but someone new, someone I haven't met before. "What's your name?" I ask.

She smiles. "My name?"

"Your full name," I say, the words coming slowly. "Before you were married."

"Mumtaz Kashmiri. It still is. I didn't change it."

"Kashmiri." I let the word flow over my tongue, my lips kissing the air in the middle of it.

I shut my eyes and lean against the pipal tree, my world tactile, a dandelion of feeling. Cotton flows over my body, dancing with my breathing, and through it the slender tree trunk at my back, its grooves, its notches, its waves on my skin, tendrils of nerves smiling. It trembles. Kashmiri is leaning against the tree and I feel a hint of her weight pushing through the trunk. My shoulders sense the nearness of hers, but nothing more, no touch, the tree between my neck and hers, my spine and hers.

I want to touch her, to kiss her, to feel her skin. My hands explore my own arms, the arms they come from, my skin pure pleasure, exciting me.

And terrifying me. With a shock of knowledge, of waking

while dreaming, I know what I'm thinking is wrong, that the woman behind me isn't Kashmiri but Mumtaz, Ozi's wife, and I can't betray him, betray her, betray them by touching her.

I push against the tree and run away, stumbling, the unreal night playing with me, gravity pulling from below, behind, above, making me fall. And I run through a world that is rotating, conscious of the earth's spin, of our planet twirling as it careens through nothingness, of the stars spiraling above, of the uncertainty of everything, even ground, even sky.

Mumtaz never calls out, although a thousand and one voices scream in my mind, sing, whisper, taunt me with madness.

Then I'm in my car, driving home. I lose my way, but this is Lahore, and by dawn I'm in my bed, the growing heat welcome as pure, reliable sensation.

My back begins to ache as I sleep, waking me, and by midday spasms of pain rip down my vertebrae, arching my body like a poisoned rat's, forcing me to grit my teeth and hug my ribs against this, my ecstasy's aftermath.

I'm lying in bed with the taste of Panadol in my mouth, trying desperately not to move, when Ozi comes in and, before I've recovered from the surprise of his unexpected appearance, tells me the neighbors have gone nuclear.

"Shit," I say.

"Why are you still in bed?"

"I sprained my back."

"Bad?"

I nod.

"Sorry," he says, sitting down. The foam mattress stretches with his weight, tugging at my back like a torturer tightening the rack.

"How do you know?"

"Everyone knows. It's mayhem outside. I had to drive through a demonstration just to get here."

"So what happened?"

"They tested three. A hundred kilometers from the border."

"How symbolic."

Ozi shakes his head. But he's grinning. And in spite of the spasms ripping quietly through my back, I notice I am, too.

"Why are we smiling?" I ask him.

"I don't know. It's terrifying."

"You know the first place they'd nuke is Lahore."

"Islamabad."

"No, Lahore. If they nuked Islamabad, no one would be able to stop it."

"Stop what?"

"Us. From nuking them."

"We'll nuke them if they nuke Lahore."

"No, we'll nuke them before they nuke Lahore."

"What do you mean?"

I try to stop grinning, but I can't. "We'll nuke them first. They're bigger. They don't need to nuke us. Some skirmish will get out of hand, they'll come marching our way, and then we'll nuke them. One bomb. For defensive purposes."

"And then they'll nuke Lahore?"

"Where else?"

"What about Karachi?"

"Too important. If they nuke Karachi, we'll nuke a few of their cities."

"Peshawar?"

"Be serious."

"Maybe Faisalabad."

"That's true. They might nuke Faisalabad."

He looks at me and starts to laugh. "Poor Faisalabad."

I try to fight it, but I'm laughing, too, holding my ribs against the pain, strangling each chuckle into a cough that bounces down my back like a flat stone cutting the surface of a lake.

I laugh until tears run down my face. "They're screwed."

"Faisalabad." Ozi can hardly breathe, he's gasping so hard.

"One more reason not to live there," I say when I can speak again.

Ozi sighs, shutting his eyes, his face exhausted, spent. "That hurt," he says.

"Imagine how I feel."

He leans forward. "Do you want a cigarette?"

I tilt my head. "What do you mean?"

He pulls a pack out of his shirt pocket. "Reds?"

"Reds."

He lights one for me, taking a long drag without coughing. "Here you go."

I take it from him. "I thought you'd quit."

"I have. That was my first puff in years."

Suddenly I'm aware of a connection I haven't felt in a long time, a bond of boyhood trust and affection. I look at Ozi and see my old friend's image, a younger face projected onto this fatter, balder screen. A hundred of my teenage adventures must have begun with Ozi inhaling a cigarette and blowing the smoke out the side of his mouth, the same side that smiles when he flashes his usual half-grin. That grin used to make me wonder what it would take to pull a full smile out of him. And his crazy ideas were like answers to that question. I remember the time we jumped the wall of Ayesha's house and her father set his Dobermans on us, whether because he thought we were robbers or because he was overprotective of his daughter, we never discovered. We had to climb a mango tree to get out: the top of the wall was too high to reach by jumping. And Ozi let me climb first.

I take a hit, jointlike, from the cigarette he's given me, filling my lungs and holding it in. "Thanks, yaar."

He looks away.

I shut my eyes and savor the smoke.

When I open them again, he's watching me.

"I've been having some problems with Mumtaz," he says unexpectedly.

"What do you mean?"

"I think she's unhappy."

I feel guilt pinch me on the ass and grab a quick feel. "Why?"

"I don't know, yaar."

"What makes you think she's unhappy?"

"Little things. She never wants to talk. She's always tired. She's snappish with Muazzam."

"Lahore isn't New York. Maybe she doesn't like the city."

"That isn't it. She was like this in New York. Besides, she wanted to come back."

"Then what do you think it is?"

"I don't know."

"Maybe you should ask her."

"I have. I do. I ask her all the time."

"What does she say?"

"She says she's unhappy."

"Then she probably is."

He smiles. "I know."

"How long has she been like this?"

"Months. Maybe a year."

"It could have nothing to do with you. People go through difficult times."

"But I don't like to see her this way. I miss her."

I nod, finishing off the cigarette and stubbing it out on the table. One more burn mark in a constellation of burn marks.

Ozi is pinching the point of his chin as though he's discovered he missed a spot shaving this morning.

"You know," I say, trying to cheer him up, "they really might nuke Lahore."

He stops playing with his chin. "We're going to test, too."

"When?"

"Who knows. I hope we do it soon."

"Why? We know we have the bomb."

"We want them to know."

"They know." I say it casually. As casually as I can. Because unsaid between Ozi and me, unsayable, is a possibility, a doubt: What if our bomb doesn't work?

Ozi's sweating. His face shines and he wipes it with the tips of four curved fingers held together. "It's damn hot. How long has the power been gone?"

"Just a couple of hours," I lie.

"Load-shedding or a breakdown?"

I shrug.

"You need a generator," he tells me.

Ah, Ozi. You just can't resist, can you? You know I can't afford a generator. "Do I?"

"Of course. How can you survive without one?"

"Most people do manage to, you know."

"I wonder if we still have the small one from the old house. If we do, you might as well take it."

"I'm fine." I don't need your secondhand generator, thanks very much. And I don't have the money to buy fuel for it in any case.

"I'm surprised I didn't notice the heat until now."

"Nothing like nuclear escalation to make people forget their problems."

He winks. "And on that note, I'd better push off. Some of us have to work, you know."

He says it as though he'd like to be unemployed.

I feel myself getting angry, and the connection between us snaps in silence. "Not if they nuke Lahore," I say under my breath.

He leans over and puts the pack of reds on my bedside table. I don't want it now. But, as with all his gifts, I take it anyway.

My back is better by the time Ozi kills the boy.

It's a Sunday, the neighborhood nuclear test count is up to five, and I'm on my way to Jamal's office. Strange that my sixteen-year-old cousin should have an office, but he's been working for a week now, on weekends and in the evenings, after school.

The address he's given me turns out to be a house in Shadman with two nameplates: a white one above with *Alam* in faded black lettering and a sleek silver rectangle below which reads CHIPKALI INTERNET SERVICES. I enter through a side door marked *Headquarters* and shut it silently behind me, feeling the chill of air-conditioning at full blast.

Jamal and his partner, a short boy with bad posture and a white boil on his neck, just under the straight line of his clipped hair, sit with their backs to me, staring at a computer screen the size of a television. Various pieces of high-tech equipment are scattered about the room, connected by wires and plugged into an enormous surge protector. I sneak up on them and tap Jamal on his shoulder.

He turns, startled, then smiles and gets up. His partner looks embarrassed.

"What are you two doing?" I ask. "Looking at naughty pictures?"

They blush together and begin to explain.

"No, Daru bhai—"

"We were just—"

I move them apart with my hands and glance between their shoulders at the monitor. But instead of naked women I see a jerkily expanding mushroom cloud, a burst of digital pastels. "What's this?" I ask.

"We downloaded it from one of the sites covering the nuclear tests," Jamal tells me.

We watch the clip run through in somber silence. People have begun to say we might be attacked before we can get our own bombs ready.

"But I thought their tests were underground," I say.

"This isn't one of theirs. It's an American test. An H-bomb."

"We're going to use it for a client's site," his friend adds, his voice a nasal whine.

I pull my eyes away from the screen. "A client? You have clients?"

"Three," he says proudly.

"And what do you do for them?"

"We design and host Web sites," Jamal explains. "Completely customized, maintained on our server."

I smile. "And how much do they pay you?"

"It depends on the work. They can pay us once, up front, a lifetime fee that covers design, maintenance, everything. Or they can pay us monthly."

"And how much do you expect to make on average, from one client?"

Jamal tells me. And I'm shocked.

"But why would they have you guys do the work? Why wouldn't they go to professionals?"

Jamal's friend turns his face away haughtily. "We are professionals."

I've decided I don't like him.

"We're cheap," Jamal says. "And we're really good, Daru bhai.

Besides, we're learning fast. And our first three clients aren't paying that much. We're giving them a discount, as an introductory offer, you know, as we get started."

"How much of a discount?"

"Ninety percent."

"That still isn't bad. And have they paid you?"

"Not yet."

"I'm expecting a dinner from you when they do." It's a joke, but immediately after I've said it, I feel ashamed, because I could actually use a free meal.

"Of course, Daru bhai."

They offer me a chair and take me on a tour of their handiwork, showing me sites they admire and want to copy, as well as the Chipkali Internet Services home page, which they designed themselves. I'm happy to see Jamal so excited, but the more he tells me, the more worried I become. The equipment all belongs to his friend. The office is in his friend's house. The clients have come to them because of his friend's family. The entire venture is being bankrolled by his friend's father, who works in Bahrain and happily buys his son any computer-related gadgetry he wants. And unlike wide-eyed Jamal, with his delicate fingers and soft, protruding lower lip, his friend looks very business-savvy. I feel uneasy. I hate to see Jamal depending on this guy and being hurt. But there's nothing I can do. And maybe there's nothing to worry about, maybe I'm just unsettled by the fact that my little cousin, who's still in school and twelve years younger than I, is working and I'm not.

I don't stay long.

Stepping out into the hot day, I shiver at the sudden change in temperature. The sun beats down on the roads, searing the last blades of green from otherwise completely brown dividers of parched grass. I stop at Liberty Market for a long glass of fresh pomegranate juice.

The shopkeeper looks edgy, and the boy who brings me my drink doesn't smile. Probably tense about this nuclear thing.

Or maybe it's just the heat.

I sip slowly through a waxed-paper straw while I watch two dogs in the shade not far from my car. An emaciated bitch lies on her side, so thin it seems the skin covering her ribs will soon dissolve in the heat, exposing the white bones of her skeleton. She looks dead except for the slow rise and fall of her flank as she breathes, too tired to be bothered by the flies or the big, healthy pup who nuzzles at her dry tits, his tail moving rapidly from side to side as he sucks the last drops of life out of her.

Paying up, I drive off.

I'm on Jail Road, stopped at Samugarh Chowk, when I notice a Pajero in my rearview, the polished red of its exterior striking on a road where everything else is dulled by a layer of dust. A squint and I recognize Ozi, so I roll down my window to give him a wave. On my left a boy pushes off unsteadily to cross the road on a bicycle that's too big for him.

Ozi hasn't noticed me. He's bearing down on the red light at full speed. Out of the corner of his eye, the boy sees the Pajero and he bends forward, pumping hard. I feel sorry for the kid, constantly afraid of being hit by maniacs like Ozi, and the arm I stick out my window starts flapping up and down instead of waving, telling my friend to stop even though I know he hasn't seen me and doesn't mind putting a little fear into people whose vehicles are smaller than his.

Ozi's Pajero roars by me, piercing the intersection. The boy is staring straight ahead, his eyes desperately focused on the opposite curb, now not far away, when his foot slips from the pedal and he wobbles, his pace broken, and I think, Shit, Ozi's cutting it too close. Then the quick flash of brake lights, a sudden scream of rubber sliding like skin on cement, too little too late, the front of the Pajero dipping like a bull ready to gore, a collision unheard because of the squeal of locked tires. A brief silence. The sound of an engine gathering itself as the Pajero charges away.

The boy's body rolls to a stop by a traffic signal that winks green, unnoticed by the receding Pajero.

I drive to where the boy lies on the asphalt. His head has been partly crushed, flattened on one side, but the rest of him seems almost untouched except that one of his shoes is missing and a little brown foot sticks out of his shalwar. I think he's dead, but as I stand over him his arm twitches and someone says, "He's alive."

I look around. A crowd has gathered to stare, but no one does anything. I put my hands under the boy to lift him. The back of his head is soft and sticky, and I swallow against what rises in my stomach as I smell the smell. Another man helps me, and together we place him on the back seat of my car and drive quickly to Services Hospital.

I press down on my horn until two orderlies rush out to put the boy on a trolley and wheel him inside. Then I tell the man who came with me to stay and talk to the police until I return.

Ozi lives just off Main Gulberg Boulevard, so I'm at his place in a few minutes, punching my horn with the side of my hand again and again. The guards must know me by now, because they open the gate and let me in.

The red Pajero is parked in the driveway, Ozi watching a servant wipe the dent in its bumper with a wet cloth. My best friend is wearing sunglasses, a bright T-shirt, and knee-length shorts. He looks like an overgrown child. A child who gets everything. Gets away with everything.

I step out of my car and say very softly, "I saw you just now."

For a moment he watches me, silent, expressionless, as though he's trying to remember who I am. No, not remember: decide. Decide who I am.

Then he hangs his head. His shoulders fall. "There was nothing I could do. I didn't see him until the last moment." He looks into my eyes, begging to be believed.

"It was a red light."

"Do you think he's okay?"

I shake my head.

Ozi's lips stretch. Flatten. Not a smile: a twitch. "We'll take care of his family," he says. "I'll make sure they're compensated."

My throat constricts, choking me. I want to speak, but I can't work my voice.

Fingers curl, hands become blunt. Lungs half-fill, then lock, rib cage and chest now armor.

I focus on the underside of his jaw. His Adam's apple. The soft flesh there.

Ozi sees the violence in me. Recognizes it.

And, gently, he takes hold of my arm.

"Daru?"

Something claws its way out of me, tearing, ripping, forcing my eyes shut, as powerful and vicious as a sob.

And then it's gone, my anger, dispelled by his touch, by the tone of his voice. I feel weak and sick. Sunstroke. Dehydration. But I can speak again. "I'm going back to the hospital."

"Don't tell them about me."

I don't answer. I turn and get back into my car, rubbing my eyes with my fingers as I reverse out of the driveway. The back seat is covered with blood.

• • •

When I arrive at the hospital, a blue police jeep is already there and the cops are questioning the man who helped me bring in the boy. Their officer turns as I approach. "You brought the victim here in your car?"

"Yes," I reply.

"Then why did you leave?" he asks suspiciously. "Where did you go?"

"To look for the car that hit him," I answer. "But I couldn't find it."

I don't say anything about Ozi. The officer tells me that the boy is dead and I'm to come with them to the police station. A policeman rides beside me in my car, a rifle between his thighs. "In case you don't know the way."

I'm led past an interrogation room, I suppose to impress upon me the need to be forthcoming. Inside, an old man is screaming that an atomic bomb incinerated his wife. A brawny interrogator slaps him again and again, saying, "It was you, it was you," in a frightened voice that belies the bored expression on his fat face.

It takes the police a long time to record my statement, and I'm left uncertain whether they consider me a witness or a suspect.

When Manucci sees the blood on the back seat of the car, he just stands there with his lips pressed together like a kiss and questions ballooning behind his eyes. But I take one look at him and say, "Clean it," and he jerks to attention, running for a bucket of water and a cloth.

I have a hard time sleeping that night. But I decide one thing: I'm not going to take any of Ozi's father's help in looking for a job.

It isn't as hot as usual the next morning, so I'm still in bed when Manucci comes banging on my door.

"What is it?" I yell.

"Saab, an andhi is coming," he says.

I get up and pull open the curtains. It's dark, like late evening. "Shut all the windows," I say. "I'm going outside."

Lahore could use an andhi, especially if it brings rain. There's too much dust everywhere, and it's too damn hot too early this summer.

I walk out to the banyan tree in front of the house, stepping on my heels because sticks and rocks on the dead lawn stab my feet. A dusty smell hanging in the still air reminds me of the storms of my childhood, when the lawn had been green and lush and I hid behind the banyan tree because my mother would have made me come inside, hid even as the storm broke, because the banyan tree sheltered me from the wind and dust until the rain began to fall, and I ran dancing in it while it soaked me and washed away the heat, leaving everything cool and clean, it seemed, for days.

The lawn has died since then, but the banyan tree is still alive, wound about itself like iron cable. Its branches hang low, their canopy casting a shade over roots that grip and break the soil, grasping in every direction. The tree is old, much older than the house and the boundary wall that seems almost to have been built to hold it in and against which the tree is now beginning to push.

For some reason I find myself doing what I used to do as a child, even though now there's no one to hide from: going to stand in the lee of the banyan tree. I feel the pressure building around me, feel it between the hair of my forearms and the skin, along the back of my neck, the line of my shoulders.

The sun is completely blotted out by a dirty sky.

I shut my eyes as the wind picks up, whipping through the branches with a rising howl as dust sweeps over me, smoothly abrasive. The andhi builds, pushing me back a step, screaming in my ears, bending my outstretched arms as I stand my ground. It flings sand at me, sends leaves hurtling into me, but the tree breaks their force and I feel only brief touches on my skin.

Raindrops begin to shatter on my eyelids, on my ears, my throat, my stomach. The andhi roars now, violent and fully alive, and I keep my eyes closed as I wait for it to subside.

Suddenly something strikes my chest. My eyes snap open and I'm immediately blinded by the dust. I turn around and put my back to the wind, rubbing my fists into my stinging eyes. I fight to keep my balance, gasping, overwhelmed by the storm.

The andhi dies unexpectedly, without much rain.

My eyes are tearing and I open them, blinking to flush the dust out. I have a small cut on my chest, probably from a broken branch of the banyan tree. Around me everything is coated with dust, damp in patches from the spray. The sun is already burning a hole through the rusty clouds.

I'm filthy and it's begun to get hot again. The wind blowing through the branches of the banyan tree carries the smell of parched land that has waited too long for too small a drink. Rubbing the dirt in the corners of my eyes and fingering the cut on my chest, I go inside to take another shower.

They say the nuclear tests released no radioactivity into the atmosphere. Each a huge gasp, smothered unsatisfied.

CHAPTER 8

what lovely weather we're having (or the importance of air-conditioning)

Your robes are itching and you crook a finger at one of your clerks.

"Have we considered air-conditioning?" you ask him.

"One moment, Milord," he says, scurrying off.

He returns in a few minutes, hands you a sheaf of papers, and bows repeatedly. You are about to commence fanning yourself when the title page catches your eye: "Air-Conditioning," it says. Intrigued, you begin to read and encounter the following:

Anticipating your Lordship's request, an investigation was conducted into the role air-conditioning may or may not have played in the lives of the various witnesses expected to testify before your Lordship during the course of this trial. Clearly, the importance of air-conditioning to the events which constitute the substance of this case cannot be overestimated.

The pioneer of academic commentary in this field is Professor Julius Superb. Although his ideas received a cool reception when first aired, they are now widely influential and are discussed not only in doctoral dissertations but also in board rooms and living rooms throughout the land. Indeed, Lahore will not soon forget the Superb paper presented at the Provincial Seminar on Social Class in Pakistan.

Professor Superb walked to the auditorium with a determined smile on his face and a growing ink stain on his shirt pocket, the work of the unsheathed fountain pen he had used to add the final touches to his speech. Those of his students who saw him at the time recalled that he seemed distracted. This did not arouse their curiosity, as the professor was known for his absentmindedness.

Reaching the doors of the auditorium, he attempted to hurl them open, failed, and then struggled unsuccessfully until he realized that he was pushing, not pulling. His awesome mind broke the problem into discrete parts, solved each with the inhuman speed and precision of a supercomputer, and he was inside before fifteen seconds had passed.

Professor Superb then waited in the hushed gloom until it was his turn to speak. When the time came, he strode to the front of the auditorium, mounted the stage, cleared his throat, and delivered a few introductory remarks. Finally, he was ready.

"There are two social classes in Pakistan," Professor Superb said to his unsuspecting audience, gripping the podium with both hands as he spoke. "The first group, large and sweaty, contains those referred to as the masses. The second group is much smaller, but its members exercise vastly greater control over their immediate environment and are collectively termed the elite. The distinction between members of these two groups is made on the basis of control of an important resource: air-conditioning. You see, the elite have managed to re-create for themselves the living standards of say, Sweden, without leaving the dusty plains of the subcontinent. They're a mixed lot—

Punjabis and Pathans, Sindhis and Baluchis, smugglers, mullahs, soldiers, industrialists—united by their residence in an artificially cooled world. They wake up in air-conditioned houses, drive air-conditioned cars to air-conditioned offices, grab lunch in air-conditioned restaurants (rights of admission reserved), and at the end of the day go home to their air-conditioned lounges to relax in front of their wide-screen TVs. And if they should think about the rest of the people, the great uncooled, and become uneasy as they lie under their blankets in the middle of the summer, there is always prayer, five times a day, which they hope will gain them admittance to an air-conditioned heaven, or, at the very least, a long, cool drink during a fiery day in hell."

Smiling, the professor walked out of the hushed auditorium, his footsteps echoing in the silence.

Most of the students present were either asleep or too bored to pay attention. Others had not heard a word, because Professor Superb eschewed the use of a microphone, thinking himself a great orator when in actuality he had a faint and unsteady voice. However, some of those who were awake and listening in the first three rows later said they were transfixed by the speech. Among them was the professor's former pupil Murad Badshah, who regularly attended the Provincial Seminar Series.

Murad Badshah was never very fond of ACs. He was a man who liked to sweat, and he sweated well and profusely. In his own opinion, he had supremely athletic pores and a finely honed sweat distribution system which sent trickles of coolness wherever they were most needed.

He also enjoyed the natural aroma that clung to him like pollen to an errant bee.

But Murad Badshah was in the rickshaw business, and he had to accommodate passengers whose opinions (at least on this subject) often differed from his. Accordingly, he bathed three times a day in the summer: morning, midday, and evening. He found bathing almost as effective as sweating in its ability to cool his body, and thought of his combined bath-sweat cooling regimen as a way of augmenting rather than diminishing his body's natural cooling capacity.

ACs, on the other hand, he considered unnatural and dangerous. Your pores will get out of shape if you rely on ACs for your cooling, he would say. It's fine as long as you stay in your little air-conditioned space, but one day you might need to rely on your body again and your body won't be there for you. After all, fortunes change, power blackouts happen, compressors die, coolant leaks.

He loved load-shedding for this reason. It amused him to see the rich people on the grounds of their mansions as he drove past their open gates, fanning themselves in the darkness, muttering as they called the power company on their cellular phones. Indeed, nothing made Murad Badshah more happy than the distress of the rich.

Lazy pores, he would say to himself, and laugh joyously. And the rich people would stare at the retreating lights of his rickshaw on their darkened streets and wonder what anyone could possibly be so happy about when it was so damn hot.

Murad Badshah was a firm believer in the need for a large-scale redistribution of wealth. After Professor Superb's speech, he vowed to break the barriers that separated the cooled from the uncooled, like himself. Indeed, he used this principle to justify his piracy campaign against yellow cabs, since they were not only taking market share from rickshaws but were air-conditioned as well. He was fond of asking his victims, "Why should you be cooled?" A populist, he rebelled against the system of hereditary entitlements responsible for cooling only the laziest minority of Pakistan's population, and he embraced Darashikoh as a partner when the latter fell from cooling.

But in the Shah household, in the compound financed by the corrupt millions of Aurangzeb's father, the hum of the air conditioner was sucking the life out of a marriage. For air-conditioning can be divisive not only in the realm of the political but in the realm of the personal as well.

Aurangzeb loved ACs with a passion unrivaled by his love for any other species of inanimate object. He insisted that his father install central air-conditioning in their new house, that the system be supported by a dedicated back-up generator, and that he have a master remote control for the entire upstairs portion. He was never happier than when his bedroom was so cold that he needed a heavy blanket to avoid shivering in the middle of summer. Conversely, he liked it to be so warm in winter that he could comfortably sleep naked without so much as a sheet. Aurangzeb, more than most men, sought to master his environment.

Mumtaz hated ACs with the sort of hatred one normally reserves for members of other religions and ethnic groups. An AC had almost killed her when she was young. She came home from a school football match (she was a star midfielder with a vicious left foot), took off her clothes in front of the AC, caught pneumonia, and spent two weeks in a hospital with a tube draining her lungs, battling for her life. Although Mumtaz was only fourteen at the time, and although people told her she had brought her illness on herself, she swore never to forgive and never to forget. Having once been betrayed by an AC, she branded them all traitors, and avoided their use except under circumstances of egregious warmth.

And so it was that the marriage between Aurangzeb and Mumtaz was doomed from the start.

In New York, a city of hot, muggy summers, Aurangzeb insisted that only an insane person would sleep with the air-conditioning off. Mumtaz disagreed, but baby Muazzam settled the question: he would cry all night unless serenaded by the cool hum of the air conditioner. A triumphant Aurangzeb agreed to Mumtaz's terms of surrender: the AC would be left on at night, but at a thermostat setting of no more than three (with nine, of course, being the coolest).

When the couple returned to Lahore, where young Muazzam had his own room and a nanny, Mumtaz renewed her campaign. "We have to conserve electricity," she would say. "The entire country suffers because of the wastefulness of a privileged few."

"I couldn't care less about the country," Aurangzeb would reply. "Besides, you have a delusional and obsessive fear of pneumonia."

"I think you underestimate the risk pneumonia poses to all of us. Besides, I really do feel that we have a duty to use electricity responsibly."

"Then sleep outside. The AC is staying on."

The results of Mumtaz's renewed attempts to reduce the air-conditioning in the life she shared with Aurangzeb were minimal in terms of any change in the temperature. But her relations with her husband had grown chilly since their return from America, and his persistence on the AC issue did nothing to restore the warmth that had disappeared. In fact, now that they were back in Pakistan, Aurangzeb was far less conciliatory toward her than he had been before. For his part, he felt that she should be grateful for the style with which he (actually his father) supported them. He felt that the cars and clothes and dinner parties made him a good husband, and he resented her inability to demonstrate gratitude through obedience as his wife.

Mumtaz would later wonder whether Darashikoh's lack of air-conditioning played a role in attracting her to him. No one will ever know the answer to that question, but it must be said that if air-conditioning doomed her relationship with her husband, it doomed her relationship with his best friend as well. You see, Mumtaz was over-air-conditioned and longed to be uncooled, while Darashikoh was under-air-conditioned and longed to be cooled. Although they walked the same path for a while, Mumtaz and Darashikoh were headed in opposite directions.

Yes, and no matter how important air-conditioning was to Mumtaz, to Aurangzeb and Murad Badshah and Professor Superb, it was more important to Darashikoh Shezad, for it took his mother from him and propelled him inexorably toward a life of crime.

On a midsummer night that followed a day when the temperatures spiked into the hundred and teens, much of Lahore was plunged into darkness. The pull of innumerable air conditioners stressed connections and wires and the systems that regulated the eddying currents of electricity past their capacities, and one after another, they failed. The wind chose that night to rest, and neighborhoods baked in the still heat.

Perhaps it was not surprising that Darashikoh's mother decided to sleep on the roof on that tragic night. After all, she had often done so as a child growing up in Khanewal with no air-conditioning. She told her son and servants to carry two charpoys up to the roof, and such was her command over her household that they managed to do so.

Darashikoh would remember having a cup of hot tea with her before lying down on his charpoy, his arms crossed under his head, staring up at the stars. He fell into a deep sleep, so deep that he never heard the firing of the bullet that would claim his mother's life.

His mother may have been asleep as well, for when her son

found her dead the next morning, she was lying on her charpoy with her eyes shut. Or she may have been awake. She may have heard the repeated coughing of a Kalashnikov being fired into the sky. But even if she did, she probably thought nothing of it: there were two weddings in the neighborhood that night, so the celebratory sound of automatic gunfire was only to be expected. Of course, the bullets might not have come from those weddings. Someone might have fired a Kalashnikov in the air to announce a victory in a kite fight, a job promotion, or the birth of a child. A young man may have fired just to fire, or to let the neighborhood know that his was not a house to be robbed. Perhaps the weapon was fired at the moon, a metallic human howl.

Indeed, it is possible that only the one bullet was fired that night, for only one was found in the morning. It pierced Darashikoh's mother's throat from above, passed through the charpoy, and rolled, spent, to the edge of the roof. Her death was probably not instantaneous, since her spinal cord was not severed by the injury. The coroner was of the opinion that she bled to death in silence over the course of some minutes, unable to get up or to make a sound. The pool of her blood was already dry when the lightening sky roused Darashikoh from his sleep.

After that night, Darashikoh would have a recurrent vision which came to him not only when he was asleep but when he was awake as well. Once he was sitting with Mumtaz when the vision came, and he described it to her in this way: "I imagine Lahore as a city with bullets streaking into the air, tracers like fireworks, bright lines soaring into the night, slowing, falling back on themselves, a pavilion collapsing, the last dance of a fire before its fuel is consumed. And I lie on a field in the center of town, on grass fenced in by buildings, looking up at the stars with a sweet stem in my mouth, watching the brilliant arcs descending toward me."

Mumtaz could not understand why people fired into the air as though the bullets would never come down again. She said, "People don't believe in consequences anymore."

But Darashikoh believed in consequences. He knew that his mother would not have died if the AC had been cooling her room that night, and when he lost his job and had his power disconnected, he felt more than just the discomfort of the heat in his house. He felt an insecurity, a dis-ease that gnawed at him day and night. Perhaps he merely feared the loss of social status that the end of his air-conditioning represented. Or perhaps he feared something more profound and less easily explained. He needed money to have his power and air-conditioning and security restored, and he swore that nothing would stand in his way. He, a man who hated guns, came to accept that he would have to use one.

It is possible that Darashikoh could have learned something from his young servant, the mystically minded Manucci.

If one had asked Manucci during his days as a street urchin, as he sat, in defiance of municipal orders, astride the gun Zam-Zammah, Manucci would probably have said that ACs were hot. The first time he saw one jutting out into the street from the wall of a shop in the old city, he walked up to the noisy box and was amazed at the blast of hot air it sent straight into his face. Why do people turn on hot air in the middle of summer? he often wondered.

When he asked, people thought he was crazy. "What do you mean ACs make hot air?" they would say. "They make cold air. Everyone knows that. That's the way it is: ACs make cold air. That's what they're for."

"Do you have an AC?" he would ask. "No," they all had to admit. No one had an AC. The other beggars, the vendors, the runners at paan shops, the ne'er-do-wells: none of them had an AC. But they all knew ACs made cold air, everyone knew that. That's what ACs were for.

One day Manucci met an AC repairman. "You don't seem to be doing a very good job," Manucci told him. "All the ACs around here are making hot air."

"You're crazy, boy," the AC repairman said.

Manucci realized what all this had to mean. It meant people thought what he called hot air was cold air. So whenever he walked down the street past the back of a protruding AC, he would smile and say, "What cold air it makes. Wonderful."

And people would shake their heads.

But Manucci knew they would call him crazy if he said this air was hot, so he always said it was cold. And when they shook their heads at him he shook his head right back.

It was not until the day that Darashikoh's mother grabbed Manucci by the ear as he was trying to slip her wallet out of her purse and, deciding what Manucci needed was a home and some discipline, brought him back to her house, it was not until that day that Manucci finally went inside a building that had an AC. When it was turned on, he felt cold air blowing right into his face. And that is why he said, without blinking an eye, "This air is hot."

He was very pleased with this statement.

But Darashikoh, just in the door from his first college boxing practice, was surprised, and strangely unsettled.

CHAPTER 9

five

The ashtray's full, I haven't brushed my teeth, and there's no place for me to spit out the dry paste that's on my tongue.

My temples throb. Slow, sweaty throb-throbs. Joints have started giving me a headache rather than a buzz. Their smoke lingers in my sinuses, in my nasal cavities, air trapped in pockets between irritated membranes, drums reverberating with my heartbeat. I rub the ridges above my eyes with my fingers, the rooted hair of my eyebrows slipping over hard, impenetrable bone, swollen flesh over dead skull over incessant pain. Maybe I'm dehydrated. Maybe it's the heat. But I'm getting sick of sitting at home with nothing to do but wonder whom I can convince to lend me some more money.

It would be nice if Murad Badshah really were hard-core, if we really could take his gun and walk up to some rich little bastard, some nineteen-year-old in a Pajero with a mobile phone and nothing to do but order around men twice his age. A kid like that would have a few thousand in his wallet. Ten thousand, maybe. I could use some nice, new, thousand-rupee notes, like the notes

Mumtaz pulled out of her pocket at the party when she bought us the ex. But Murad Badshah's just a big talker. And when I think of the boy Ozi killed, of his flattened head like a half-cracked egg, the shell shattered but its shards still clinging together, keeping the wet stuff inside, I know I don't have what it takes to use a gun.

But you get no respect unless you have cash. The next time I meet someone who's heard I've been fired and he raises his chin that one extra degree which means he thinks he's better than me, I'm going to put my fist through his face.

I yell for Manucci.

"Yes, saab?" he says, coming in. His face has begun sprouting fluff like a caterpillar spinning a cocoon. I'd better teach him how to use a razor before he takes on the fundo look.

"I need to spit," I tell him.

He looks at me expectantly. When I don't say more, he ventures another "Yes, saab?"

"Bring me a tissue."

He goes off to the kitchen and reappears carrying a trash bin. "We're out of tissue, saab. You can spit here."

"Good thinking." I spit into the bin, scrape the paste off my tongue with my upper front teeth, and spit again. No more tissue. No more meat. Soon no more toilet paper, no more shampoo, no more deodorant. It'll be rock salt, soap, and a lota for me, like it is for Manucci.

Which reminds me, I haven't paid him this month.

A car honks outside, and after emptying the ashtray into the bin, Manucci goes to see who it is. I wipe the sweat from my face, dry my hand on my jeans, and run my fingers through my hair. The front door opens and Mumtaz steps in, wearing track pants, expensive-looking running shoes, a T-shirt, and big shades. She's followed by a very curious Manucci, grinning sheepishly.

It's been three weeks since the party, and I've thought of her every day. But I haven't wanted to meet Ozi, and I couldn't come up with a reasonable excuse for me to get in touch.

"Hi," she says. "I thought I'd drop by and say hello."

I stand up, flash my most charming smile, and almost step forward to give her a kiss, but think better of it, because my breath probably smells. "I'm glad you've come," I say, motioning for her to sit. "Can I offer you some lunch?"

"No thanks," she says, sitting down and lighting a cigarette. "I'm on my way to the gym. But I'd love a glass of water."

"Bring one for me as well," I tell Manucci.

Mumtaz takes off her shades and hangs them from the neck of her T-shirt, between her breasts. She has broad shoulders, not thick but wide, and she lounges in her exercise clothes with the relaxed physical confidence of an athlete. "It's hot in here," she says. "Load-shedding?"

I almost say yes, almost lie instead of saying that I'm out of cash and have no electricity and owe money to half the city. But I decide not to. I'm a bad liar. I don't have the memory for it. And I feel like telling her the truth.

"I'm broke," I say. "The power's been disconnected."

She smiles at me for a moment as though I'm making fun of her. Then she flicks the ash of her cigarette and says, "Really?"

I nod.

"Why don't you take some money from us?" she asks. "Ozi will give you as much as you need."

I shake my head. "I don't want any money from Ozi." The words come out more forcefully than I'd intended.

She raises her chin at my tone, but looks concerned rather than offended. "Why? Are you upset with him?"

I almost say, Because he killed a boy and doesn't give a shit and I don't want any of his corrupt cash. But instead I say, "I'm not upset with him. We had a little argument. Nothing important."

Manucci comes in, unable to meet Mumtaz's eye, giggling slightly as he hands us our water. When he leaves, Mumtaz leans forward and presses her glass against her cheek. "It sounds like there's more anger in you than you want to admit."

I shrug. "He's a good man." I'm shocked when I hear the words, not because I'm saying them, but because I don't believe them. "We'll be fine."

She takes a sip of her water and looks at me like she knows I'm lying. "We've been having problems," she says.

She strokes her glass with her cheek, and I keep my mouth shut and wait for her to go on. But she's quiet for a while, looking away, and when she looks at me again, I can see that she's decided to say no more about it for now. "I don't want to bore you," she says.

"You're not boring me," I tell her.

"I hate being so morbid all the time." She gives a little laugh that isn't at all happy. "I think part of my frustration is that I haven't been getting enough exercise. Do you work out?"

I let her change the subject. "Not really. I do some push-ups and sit-ups, or go for a run, but not regularly."

"What about boxing?"

"I hit a bag sometimes."

"Can you teach me?" she asks.

"What do you mean?"

"I need a good workout."

"Now?"

She gets up and raises her fists. She's grinning, but there's an intensity in her eyes that my coach would have liked to see.

"If you want," I say.

I go to my room for some equipment and take her to the back of the house, where my old heavy bag hangs from a rusty chain.

We sit down on a wooden bench, straddling it and facing each other.

"Show me your hand," I say.

She does.

I turn it over, a little hesitant when I touch her because I don't want to be rough but I'm afraid that if I'm too gentle it'll seem like a caress. "I'm going to wrap it," I tell her, slipping the loop of a rolled-up hand wrap over her thumb. I slide the cotton tape around her skin, encircling her wrist, slowly, so she can see how it's done, then curving the tape up and around her fingers.

"Take off your ring," I say.

She does. It's a solitaire diamond, simple and probably worth almost a year of my salary at the bank, when the bank paid me a salary. She puts it down on the bench behind her.

I keep wrapping, covering her knuckles, binding her long fingers together, then spiraling back down to her wrist. Finally I tie the two tassels at the end of the hand wrap. I tell her to make a fist and then let go, and I watch the blood rush back into her fingers.

"Do you want to do the other one yourself?" I ask her.

"I'll try," she says. She slips the loop over her thumb and starts to wrap, keeping about the right tension, neither too loose nor too tight. Sometimes I have to guide her hand with mine.

"Let me tie the end," I say when she's done.

"I want to try." She grabs one tassel with her teeth, pulls the other around her wrist with her fingers, and ties a knot. I've had these hand wraps for a long time, but seeing them on her skin, seeing her use her mouth to tie them, makes them seem less familiar.

Finally I show her my gloves, once bright red, now faded and scuffed with use. "These will be too big," I say, putting them on her. "But I want you to wear them, because I don't want you to hurt your hands."

She stands up, squares her shoulders, and raises the gloves. Her hair is pulled back, away from her face, and she looks beautiful. I reach out and take her shades off the neck of her T-shirt, conscious of my fingers touching the skin below her throat, and set them down on the bench near her ring.

I look at her stance. "Spread your legs slightly," I say. "And bend your knees. Stand on the balls of your feet." Her body moves exactly the way I want. "Perfect. Now bring your hands up. Higher. That's the basic on-guard position. After each punch, you want to come back to it."

She starts hopping up and down and making mean faces.

"Easy, champ," I tell her. "Let's learn a couple punches first. This," I say, tapping her left glove, "is your lead hand. And this"—I demonstrate—"is a jab." I throw another, much faster this time, just touching her glove with my bare hand. "Let's see it."

I talk her through a few basic punches, and she learns fast. Her movements are fluid, efficient, her attention focused on me when I'm explaining and on her own body when she's moving. I put my hands on her arms and shoulders from time to time to adjust her position, and I feel long muscles under soft flesh.

After she's warmed up and has the hang of it, we move to the heavy bag, and I start by demonstrating one punch at a time. She watches me, breathing steadily, her face shiny with sweat, a smile pulling at her lips. Reaching up, she shuts her eyes and wipes the sweat from her forehead with her arm. I want to touch her face, smooth the sweat out of her eyebrows with my fingers. Then she opens her eyes and sees me staring at her, and I turn and slam my hand into the bag with a ferocity that surprises me. Suddenly I'm going all out, punching hard, deep in my rhythm, coiling and exploding, again and again, dancing, my muscles full of blood, hitting on the move, slipping punches. The bag is jumping. My hands are brutal. I shake my head, smile violently, and hit it.

Then I stop, my breathing an easy pant, and look at Mumtaz. Our eyes meet and I feel the rhythm in my blood beating loud. I look down. Damn: my hands. I should have worn gloves, because now I've rubbed the skin off my knuckles.

Mumtaz steps up to the bag. She hits it hard, like she wants to punch right through it and trusts the strength of her wrist. The bag rocks slightly, and she hits it again, drawing power from her legs and twisting her body to put her shoulder behind the punch. She throws her punches at a slow, measured pace. Soon the bag is swinging. I hear a grunt of exertion, a sound almost like rage. She hits the bag like she's furious with it, like she wants to hurt it. And she keeps on hitting it, completely intent on the bag, and my surprise at her strength gives way to a new surprise at her endurance. Finally she stops, puts her arms around the bag, and presses her forehead into it.

I tap her on the shoulder and she turns. "I guess I needed that," she says, grinning.

"So who were you punching?" I ask her.

"Who were you punching?" she replies.

I smile. "I was just showing off, I suppose."

She hits her gloves together. "So was I."

"You have a lot of stamina for a smoker."

"I work out. Besides, I have an older brother, so I'm a fighter." Her T-shirt is dark around the throat and along the back of her shoulders, where her skin touches the wet fabric. "Are you ready to box?" she asks me.

I start to laugh. "You won't be able to hit me."

"Let me try."

I stand in front of her and let my hands dangle at my sides. "Punch me in the head," I say.

She puts her hands up and throws a punch. And she doesn't hold back. I watch the red glove coming and pull my head back at the last moment, grinning at her surprise. She keeps trying, but she can't hit me.

"Stop," I say finally.

She does, dropping her hands.

"I boxed for years," I tell her. "It'll take you a while before you can hit me." Then, just to tease her, I shut my eyes and lean forward, offering up my best "do it if you dare" face.

Hot sunlight glows orange through my eyelids.

I feel the punch coming and don't move, don't even open my eyes. I'm sure she's bluffing. Then my head snaps back as her punch hits me full in the face. "What the hell was that?" I say, shocked. I touch my mouth and my fingers come away with a streak of blood.

She's laughing, one glove in front of her mouth, her eyes wide with surprise. "I'm so sorry," she says, trying to look apologetic. "I didn't mean to hit you that hard. But I just couldn't resist."

I grab her by her wrists, just below her gloves, and pull her to me. She looks up, still smiling, and I can feel my mouth throbbing from her punch.

I'm intensely aware of every contact between my body and hers.

"I could knee you," she says. Her leg moves up slightly, between mine, and I realize how vulnerable I am. That would hurt.

I let her go.

"I wasn't actually going to knee you," she says.

"I didn't think you were going to punch me either." My lips feel a little puffy as I speak.

"I didn't think I'd be able to hit you."

I smile at her, feeling my lips stretch. "Very funny."

I help her out of the gloves, and she takes off the hand wraps, rolls them up, and gives them to me. Then we head back inside and finish off a pitcher of water. Mumtaz stays for lunch. The sweat has dried on her face and covered it with dirty streaks. I imagine licking one and almost taste the salt, but I try to get the thought out of my mind before she sees what I'm thinking. I don't eat very much, a little ashamed that there's no meat or even chicken. I just watch her serve herself and clean all the food off her plate, wishing there was some reason for me to reach out and touch her skin.

I look at my hands. Who would have thought that I would ever teach a woman to box and come out of it with a bloody mouth and torn knuckles?

"Let me see them," she says.

I reach across the table. She runs her fingers over my red knuckles, lightly, but doesn't say anything. Then she turns them over and strokes my palms with her thumbs.

"I went to see a palm reader the other day," she tells me.

Palm readers must be the new fad among the idle rich. "I would have thought you were too educated for that sort of thing."

"I've told you I'm superstitious." She lets go of my hands and lights a cigarette.

"And is this palm reader a well-connected young socialite?"

"Her name's Allima Mooltani. She's about sixty and she lives in Model Town."

"A well-connected old socialite, then," I say, taking one of her cigarettes. "How much did she charge?"

"Five hundred. But she spent an entire hour with me."

"I can't believe you paid that much." I do some quick arithmetic. Let's say she sees three people a day and works five days a week. That comes to seventy-five hundred a week, thirty thousand a month. That's more than what I made as a banker, before taxes. And she probably doesn't even pay taxes. Why am I sitting here, deeper and deeper in debt, when palm readers are making that much?

"What are you thinking?" Mumtaz asks me.

"Nothing," I say, noticing that the ash has grown on my cigarette. I flick it. "What makes you think this woman isn't a complete fake?"

"That's hard to explain. She doesn't try to tell you that your eighth kid's name will be Qudpuddin or anything. She just shows you yourself."

"For five hundred an hour I'd want to know my eighth kid's name, birthday, and favorite dessert."

"You have to go."

"No thanks. I can't afford it."

"My treat."

"I couldn't."

"You have to. I'll take you."

"When?"

"Tomorrow."

Manucci comes in with her ring and shades, which we forgot on the bench outside, and she takes them casually, not at all upset that she was so absentminded.

"Do you know what happens when you detonate a nuclear bomb under the desert?" she asks.

"No."

"The sand turns to glass."

"From the heat?"

She nods.

When she leaves, I present my cheek for her to kiss, but she kisses my lips instead, softly. I smile in surprise, and then I remember pulling her to me earlier, which makes my smile wider even though my mouth hurts. And she smiles back at me like she knows what I'm smiling about. Then she's gone, and I sit back down to lunch and finish off the food. Manucci clears the plates, giggling to himself, and although he's just being silly, he makes me laugh as well.

The celebrations begin not long after Mumtaz has left. How everyone knows I don't understand. The excited *trrring*ing of bicycle bells brings me to the gate, witness to the victory parade of a half-dozen gardeners, long shears tied to the backs of their Sohrabs, pedaling triumphantly, wobbling, clapping as often as balance and courage will allow.

Manucci brings the news with him at a run, doubled over with the effort, from the neighbor's servant quarters.

"What the hell is going on?" I ask him.

"We've done it," he pants.

"What?"

"We've exploded our bomb."

I feel something straighten my back, a strange excitement, the posture-correcting force of pride. Manucci looks up at me, his face sweaty, dirty, and grins. We shake hands like old comrades, two warriors home at last, and I'm about to say something, to launch into a little self-congratulatory speech, when a sound interrupts the flow of my elation.

From somewhere down the road we hear the first burst of celebratory gunfire, a hard-edged firecracker set to automatic, emptying its magazine into the sky. And I find myself thinking of my mother, beautiful, wasp-faced, with high cheekbones and hollow cheeks, her strict expression softened by sad eyes and a small, round smile. Never any jewelry, holes in her ears shriveled shut, still-black hair pulled into a bun. How young she always seemed, young enough to be mistaken for my sister the year she died. But not the day she was buried: bloodless, all color drained from her face, wrinkles visible in her pale skin like creases on a ball of paper.

Manucci puts his fingers in the air and launches into a spontaneous bhangra. The Kalashnikov spits again. I head inside.

That evening Raider comes to see me. He's wearing his power suspenders, the ones with a red polka dot on either side, which he calls the Rising Sun.

"Five each, baby," he says, giving me a hug.

"Five each."

We sit on the bonnet of his car and share a cigar. "It's a Havana," he tells me.

"I hate cigars. You can't inhale them."

He shakes his head and rolls up his shirtsleeves. Work is miles away, but Raider's still wearing his tie. His jacket hangs in the car, broad shoulders, no vents, very European, copied from GQ by a tailor on Beadon Road.

"Good parties tonight."

"Really?"

"Of course. People are feeling good. It's been a nervous couple of weeks."

"Armageddon parties?" I ask, trying to sound superior, mainly because I haven't been invited to any.

"Initiation parties. Welcome to the nuclear club, partner."

"Are you going?"

"I'm going to your buddy Ozi's."

"Maybe I'll see you there," I say, hiding my surprise. I didn't know Ozi was having a party.

Raider spits out a piece of tobacco and takes a few quick puffs. "I have to ask you a favor. I need some pot."

My stash is running low. "I can give you enough for a joint or two."

"I need more. I promised a couple of friends and all my sources are out."

"I can get you some in a few days."

"Before the weekend?"

"I think so." I should be able to track Murad Badshah down before then.

"Thanks, partner. I owe you, big-time."

Raider likes that phrase, big-time. He wants to make it, big-time. He owes you, big-time. He's going to party, big-time.

"No problem, yaar," I tell him, thinking I have nothing better to do. "How much do you want?"

He takes out a note and hands it to me. "Five hundred worth?"

"That's a lot of hash."

"I know. Do you think you can get it?"

I've never placed an order with Murad Badshah that he couldn't fill. "I think so."

"Great," Raider says.

I feel strange buying that much pot, especially since it isn't for me. It isn't even for Raider. It's for his friends. But Raider's an openhearted guy and there's no way I can turn him down. Besides, I might be able to keep a little for myself, a heartening thought given the sorry state of my supplies.

Once the cigar is finished, I invite him in to share a joint, but he tells me he has to run and drives off. Raider's always rushing. He's busy, big-time.

Mumtaz picks me up after lunch the next day for our date with Allima Mooltani, the palm reader. I know I shouldn't be doing this. But I am doing it, slouching a little in my seat as though it'll make me less visible if Ozi or someone we know happens to see us. Mumtaz seems completely unconcerned. I don't know what she's used to in Karachi, but here in Lahore going for a drive with a friend's wife when the friend doesn't know about it definitely qualifies as self-destructive behavior.

"I like your servant, Munnoo-ji," she says as we power down Main Gulberg Boulevard, cutting through traffic. We've decided to get a couple of paans since my appointment isn't for another half hour.

"He's called Manucci, not Munnoo-ji."

"Manucci? That's a strange name."

"I think it's Italian."

"But he's not Italian."

"No."

"Then why is he called Manucci?"

"I don't know."

"Where does he come from?"

"He tried to rob my mother."

"While he was working for you?" She takes the Liberty roundabout at high speed.

"Before. He's had a colorful past. Kind of like Kim."

"Kipling's Kim?"

I nod. "But not as romantic. Manucci's missing a kidney."

"What do you mean?"

"The kidney-theft racket. But he's lucky: they only took one of his, and they were nice enough to sew him back up."

We reach Main Market and pull into a space in front of Barkat's paan shop. A dozen runners surround the car, knocking on the windows, each claiming he saw us first. I realize that it was stupid of us to come here: Main Market's paan runners are Gulberg society's elite reconnaissance team. I point to my guy, Salim, and wave the rest of them away.

Once Salim's taken our order, the beggars move in. Most are genuinely crippled, or hooked on heroin, or insane, or too old to work, or dying from some debilitating disease, and I'd give them a rupee or two if it weren't for the few strong ones, perfectly healthy, waiting to take their cut when night falls. But Mumtaz is more softhearted than I am, and when our runner comes back with the paan, I have to tell him to clear them away. Give money to a few and the whole market wants some. I tip Salim very well, with a look that means keep your mouth shut, because he knows who I am and who Ozi is, and a leak from him could spark some vicious gossip.

Which reminds me of something I've been meaning to ask Mumtaz since I spoke to Raider. "How was your party?"

She looks embarrassed. "I'm so sorry he didn't invite you. But what a stupid reason to celebrate."

"Is he angry with me?" What I'm really asking is: Has he found out we've been spending time with each other?

"No, of course not. Why would he be?"

"You tell me."

"He isn't. I think he's just trying to meet new people. He's been away from Lahore for so long that he feels a little cut off."

Mumtaz honks until the driver of the car that pulled in behind us, blocking our exit, comes running out of a shop.

Then we're off to Model Town for our appointment. The palm reader lives in an old house with a crumbling boundary wall. I expect to be led inside, into a dark room with a crystal ball, perhaps, but Mumtaz takes me onto the lawn.

Allima Mooltani is sitting in the shade, on a cushion at the base of an enormous tree, smoking through a long ivory holder.

An extension cord snakes through the grass, providing electricity to a pair of pedestal fans. In front of each fan rests a slab of ice covered with motia flowers. Allima's long hair, mostly white but streaked with gray, moves like a tattered curtain in the wind.

"This looks like an abandoned ad for menthol cigarettes," I tell Mumtaz, but she elbows me. We say our salaams and sit down.

I have to admit that it's surprisingly pleasant out here, with the ice and fans and shade.

"I've been waiting for you, Darashikoh," she says.

"My God, you know my name!" I exclaim.

"Be serious, Daru," Mumtaz says.

"Give me your hands," Allima tells me.

I do, and she strokes them with her forearm, front and back. I break out in goosebumps. Her fingernails are long and unpolished.

"Shut your eyes."

I do it. She gives me an exquisite hand massage, following the bones of my fingers into my palms, tracing the scabs on my knuckles lightly with her nails.

"I have bad news for you," she says.

"What?"

But before she can answer a woman calls out from the house. "Telephone, Amma. It's Bilal."

"I'm so sorry," Allima says, jumping up. "My son. In Singapore."

And with that she's off at a trot. The door slams shut behind her like the distant retort of a howitzer, and I'm left looking at Mumtaz.

"The suspense is too much," she says.

"If she knows the future she should schedule these palm-reading sessions so they're not interrupted by phone calls."

Mumtaz shakes her head. "You have no faith."

I light a smoke, cupping my hands against the best efforts of the pedestal fans.

We hear the unmistakable *phirrr* of a kite at low altitude and look up. Sure enough, there it is: a red-and-black patang, slim-waisted, wasplike, wing tips curved back like the horns of the devil. On the rooftop, directly above the door that swallowed Allima Mooltani, the patang's young pilot acknowledges us with a jaunty salute.

Mumtaz waves to him.

And in the driveway, struggling to get aloft, we have the challenger: a battered machhar, its tail a white pom-pom, green-and-purple patches telling tales of battles past. And string in hand, jerking rapidly to capture altitude, is the machhar's commander, a barefoot servant boy a little taller than the bonnet of the car beside him.

We're in for a kite fight.

The patang, temporarily denied any more string, catches the wind and soars straight up.

The machhar flips about at tree level, displaying a tendency to circle in a counterclockwise direction. But its minuscule commander manages to use this imbalance to his advantage, timing his tugs to the moment the machhar's nose points in the direction he wants, finding maneuverability in capriciousness.

And slowly, the machhar climbs.

The patang paces back and forth far above.

Then suddenly, paper screaming in the wind, the patang dives at the machhar. The machhar makes an agile leap to one side, narrowly avoiding having its string hooked, and the patang spins and climbs again.

Mumtaz says a quiet "Olé."

"He's in trouble," I say. "The patang's not going to let him get high enough for it to be a fair contest."

Having lost some altitude, the machhar begins to jerk upward again, crisscrossing the sky warily.

Again the patang dives, and again the machhar dances off, too unsteady at this height to have any real chance of winning, but this time their strings entwine and the kite fight is joined.

The patang takes string like a sprinter, streaming away.

The machhar wobbles unsteadily.

Powdered glass on each kite's string cuts into the other's, but the patang's string is moving much more quickly, giving it more of a bite and less time to fray.

I follow the lines with my eyes, taut and straight from the roof, limp and curved from the driveway. The patang's posture is solid, strengthening. The machhar twitches weakly.

And with a final tug the machhar's string is cut, leaving it to flop onto its back and drift gracefully, more steady in death than it was in life, until it plunges onto a lawn several houses away.

A high-pitched victory cry from the rooftop: "Ai-bo!"

And in the driveway the servant boy sucks his finger, cut by the glass, as he gathers what string he can save with his other hand. There isn't much. He looks up at the patang, now a tiny dot in the distance, before trudging back to the servant quarters, defeated, kiteless.

Only then does it occur to Mumtaz and me that Allima still hasn't returned.

"What should we do?" I ask her.

"Let's ring the bell."

A woman answers the door, barefoot. She has beautiful feet. "I'm sorry, but Amma is meditating."

"Meditating?" Mumtaz gives me a look. "But she was just reading his palm."

The woman raises the big toe of her left foot. "She said she is done. You know all you need to know."

"But she was just beginning."

"I'm sorry."

Mumtaz is ready to continue protesting, but I take her elbow with a grin and lead her back to the car. "Forget it," I say.

She shakes her head. "How strange."

"Well, you know how these mystics can be."

She looks at me. "You're happy about this, aren't you? You thought she was a fake from the start."

"Amused, perhaps. And a little happy we can leave. I need a joint pretty badly."

"Where can we go?"

I think. I don't want to go back to my place. It's almost evening, not too hot now, and I'd like to be out in the open. "How about Jallo Park?" I suggest.

"I've never been there."

"They have a zoo."

"Really?"

"With peacocks."

"Let's go."

We drive down the canal, cross the Mall, and head out of town. I roll. Mumtaz prefers open windows to the AC, and the rush of air makes it difficult to keep the mixed tobacco and hash in my palm. But I manage. When I'm done, I ask her if I should light it and she says yes. I slide the car's ashtray out and hold it in my hand, underneath the joint, to catch any burning pieces that might fall as we smoke.

"Why Zulfikar Manto?" I ask her.

"Manto was my favorite short-story writer."

"And?"

"And he wrote about prostitutes, alcohol, sex, Lahore's underbelly."

"Zulfikar?"

"That you should have guessed: Manto's pen was his sword. So: Zulfikar."

I take a hit and cough through my nostrils, gently. "How have you managed to keep it a secret?"

"It isn't that hard. No one keeps tabs on where I am during the day. And I usually don't slip out to work at night unless Ozi's away."

"Don't the servants say anything?"

"They have, once or twice. Ozi asked me what I was up to and I told him I'd gone out for a get-together at somebody's place. That was that. Ozi isn't the untrusting type."

The joint's finished by the time we pull into the Jallo Park entrance. It's the middle of the week, so there aren't too many people here, and no one bothers us. We stroll around the caged animals, nicely buzzed.

"So how are things with Ozi?" I finally ask.

Mumtaz shrugs. "I don't know."

"You said you'd been having problems."

"We are."

We stop in front of the peacock area. A pair of albinos strut by, the male unfurling his white fan, making it shake by quivering his hips.

"That's a clear signal," I say. "Nature knows how to be direct."

Mumtaz laughs, her eyes on the peacock.

The peahen is less impressed. She walks away.

If there's ever an appropriate time to ask Mumtaz what's going on with us, it's now. I want to know what she thinks of me, of the time we're spending together, of where this is headed. And I'd like to tell her that I'm confused as hell. But my tail seems stuck and I can't unfurl it.

The moment passes.

We walk on, past other fences, other animals.

I ask her about Muazzam.

"He's fine," she says. "He seems to like Lahore."

"What does he do when you go out?"

"He has a nanny, Pilar. She's lovely. She cut the umbilical cord."

"In America?"

"No, here. Muazzam had me on a leash until she came along. But now I can disappear for the entire day and I don't have to worry about him. I could disappear forever, I suppose."

I grin. "That wouldn't be very motherly of you."

She turns, and I'm shocked to see anger in her eyes. For a moment I think she's about to punch me.

"What?" I ask softly.

"Who are you to judge me?"

"I wasn't judging you."

"Yes, you were."

"I'm sorry. I don't even know what I said."

She shakes her head and walks on, and I raise my face and squeeze my eyes shut, pissed at myself for being unable to understand. I follow a few steps behind her. We don't speak until we reach the car, but I don't want to get in without making amends somehow, so I take hold of her elbow and turn her around.

"Listen, Mumtaz, I'm sorry. Really. I've had a wonderful day with you. I think you're wonderful." I pause, aware that I'm being astoundingly inarticulate. "I don't want you to be angry with me."

Well, I'm clearly no poet. But what I said seems to work, because her face softens and she says, "Forget it. It has more to do with me than with you." That's it, no explanation, but at least my apology seems to be accepted.

Once, on the drive home, she holds my hand between gear shifts, between third and second, and I'm glad for the reassuring touch of her skin on mine. We talk, but we're talking about nothing, just reestablishing a comfortable space, and although our first fight hasn't been erased, I think it's safe to say we've survived.

When we get home we kiss, again on the lips, soft and tender and brief, like a kiss between friends, except that I always kiss my friends on the cheek.

I have to make two trips to Murad Badshah's rickshaw depot to get hold of him. That's usually how it works, because Murad Badshah's rarely in and there's no telephone number where he can be reached. I once told him he ought to get a pager and he said that pagers are an American idea and the only good thing America's ever given us is Aretha Franklin. Bizarre fellow, Murad is. Anyway, on my first trip I leave a message saying I'll be back at eight the following night. On my second I cruise down Ferozepur Road, past Ichra, hoping he'll be there, because the weekend's almost here and Raider's relying on me.

He's eating dinner, his drivers and mechanics gathered around him in a circle, their food on metal plates on the floor of the workshop.

"Hullo, old chap," he calls out as he sees me, surging to his feet. Or rather, he says something to that effect with his mouth full as one of the younger mechanics helps him get his bulk off the floor.

He offers his wrist for me to shake, because his hands are greasy.

"Will you do us the honor of joining us for dinner?" he asks. "Tonight we're having a special feast. Lakshmi Chowk's best."

I hadn't planned on it, but a free meal is a free meal, and I'm partial to Lakshmi myself. "I'd love to," I say.

A generous space is cleared for me next to Murad Badshah and I sit down, rolling up my sleeves as I grab a naan and get to work. I'm famished, and I can hold my own when it comes to eating, so

I match Murad Badshah bite for bite, until he pats his stomach, releases a resounding belch, and announces that he's stuffed.

A boy brings us mixed tea, milk and sugar already present in generous quantities, and Murad Badshah takes a dainty sip, the small finger of his left hand extended away from his teacup.

A driver wearing a Sindhi cap grabs the roll of flesh that circles his midsection and says, "I'm about to explode."

"I saw it last night on television, you know," says another, a drop of sweat hanging from his nose. "The explosion."

"What was it like?" asks a mechanic.

"They did it under a mountain," explains sweaty nose. "The mountain trembled like an earthquake. Dust flew into the sky. And the rock turned dark red, like the color of blood."

"How would you know?" asks Sindhi cap. "You only have a black-and-white television."

"But it's a very good one. You can almost see colors."

"Bloody fool. It's black-and-white."

"No, but you can sometimes tell what the real colors are. I swear."

"Nonsense."

Sweaty nose doesn't argue. "The blast was fantastic," he says to the mechanic.

"How fantastic could it be?" Murad Badshah asks. "It was underground."

"The shaking, the dust. It was too good."

Murad Badshah farts loudly. "There. Shaking. Dust. Was that too good as well?"

Sindhi cap pinches his nostrils shut. "That was a bad one, Murad bhai."

"My bad one won't double the price of petrol. It won't send tomatoes to a hundred rupees a kilo. But our bloody nuclear fart will."

"Let tomatoes go to two hundred," says Sindhi cap. "I hate tomatoes anyway. And if the price of petrol doubles, so what? We'll raise our prices. We've done it before."

"And who will pay?"

"The tomato farmers who are getting two hundred rupees a kilo."

This gets a laugh.

"Good one, yaar," says sweaty nose.

Murad Badshah shakes his head. "This nuclear race is no joke. Poor people are in trouble."

"Let us be in trouble," Sindhi cap says, to the approving nods of the group.

"The Christians have a bomb. The Jews have a bomb. The Hindus have a bomb."

"The Buddhists have a bomb," interjects sweaty nose.

"Right," continues Sindhi cap. "Everyone has a bomb. And now the Muslims have a bomb. Why should we be the only ones without it?"

"And when prices go up, and schools shut down, and hospitals run out of medicine, then?"

"Then we'll work twice as hard and eat half as much."

"We'll eat grass," says sweaty nose, quoting from one of the Prime Minister's speeches.

"And do you think people who eat grass will still go for rides on rickshaws?" asks an exasperated Murad Badshah.

"At least we'll be alive," Sindhi cap says.

"We would have been alive anyway. The entire world knew we had the bomb."

"I didn't know," says sweaty nose.

"Yes, and it's one thing to say you have it, and it's another to shake mountains," says Sindhi cap.

Murad Badshah snorts. "Shake mountains. We'll see who gives

a damn about shaking mountains when we can't pay for the rent of this depot and our rickshaws break down and the only things for sale at Lakshmi are boiled onions."

"We had to protect ourselves."

"My roof protects me," says Murad Badshah. "My full belly protects me. You boys think we've done a great thing. But you'll see. Difficult times are ahead."

Sindhi cap and sweaty nose exchange a look. But no more is said. The mechanics clear the food and the drivers head out to their rickshaws to begin their night rounds.

Murad Badshah and I remain seated.

When we're alone, I tell him I need five hundred rupees' worth of hash.

He strokes his jowls. "Five hundred, old boy? May I ask why such a large amount?"

"It's for some friends."

"Heavy smokers?"

"Clearly."

He gets up, opens a toolbox, rummages around inside, pulls out some hash, and plops it in my lap. It's about the size of my fist and wrapped in a transparent sheet of plastic.

"This is fine stuff. I'm giving it to you for five hundred, but you can easily sell it to people of means for two thousand or more."

"Why are you giving me so much?"

He laughs, his body shaking. "I help out my friends. And when a friend buys in bulk, he gets a fair price."

I grin. "Thanks."

He nods. Then he takes something out of his pocket. "See if they like this as well."

"What is it?"

"Heroin."

"No thanks."

"You never know. Your friends might be interested. It's not much. I'll throw it in for free with what you're buying."

I examine it. "It looks like hash to me."

"It's mixed with charas. But believe me, the heroin is there."

I slip it into my pocket and thank Murad Badshah, turning down his offer to smoke a joint, because I don't want to arrive at Raider's place too late. On my way I break off a healthy chunk of hash for myself. I'm almost out, after all, and five hundred for the rest is still a bargain.

Raider lives with his parents in a housing colony off the canal near the university. I ring the buzzer and he comes out of the house to see who it is.

"Partner," he says when he recognizes my face over the gate.

We shake hands. "I've got it," I tell him, handing it over.

"This is a hell of a lot of hash," he says. "Is it good?"

"Yes." Murad Badshah never fools around with inferior stuff.

"I can't take it from you for so little. Here, take another five hundred."

I wave his hand away. "It only cost five."

He pushes the note into my palm. "I'm not going to give it to them for less than fifteen hundred. If you don't take a cut I'll feel guilty."

So he is selling the stuff, after all. "Don't worry about it."

"I insist."

Pride tells me to give it back, but common sense tells pride to shut up, have a joint, and relax. I shrug and put the note into my wallet.

"Do you think you could do this again?" Raider asks.

"Get more pot?"

"This much for so little."

"I could, I suppose."

"There are definitely people who would buy from you. It might be good, you know, keep you liquid till you find some work."

"I'm liquid enough, thanks."

"Come on, yaar. Don't get defensive. What about the electricity? A little extra cash can't hurt."

"Enough, Raider."

"Okay. Sorry. Thanks for helping me out. I appreciate it."

We shake hands and I head off. In the car my wallet sits snugly between my rump and the seat, a folded note thicker than it was a little while before. I wait for regret and guilt to come, but they don't show up. The whole thing is between Raider and his friends. If he's selling and they're buying, it really has nothing to do with me. Just a little cash for my troubles, money that will make life easier for a few days. And it isn't another loan, another debt to Fatty Chacha, who can hardly afford to lend to me in the first place.

Besides, I've topped off my stash, and that's cause to celebrate.

When I get home I find Manucci staring at a candle on the mantelpiece for no apparent reason.

I walk over to him, my shadow dancing on a different wall from his.

"What is it?" I ask him.

"A moth in love, saab," Manucci says.

Sometimes I don't understand what he's talking about. But I do see a moth circling above our heads.

"Bring me the fly swatter," I tell him.

"No, saab."

I hit him across the top of his head, not too hard and with an open hand, but forcefully enough to let him know that I won't put up with any impertinence. "What do you mean, No, saab?"

"Please, saab," he says, cringing. "Watch."

The moth circles lower, bouncing like a drunk pilot in turbulence. I could clap him out of existence but I don't, because I'm getting a little curious myself.

The moth starts to make diving passes at the candle.

"He's an aggressive fellow, this moth," I say to Manucci.

"Love, saab," he replies.

"I never knew you were such a romantic."

He blushes. "The poets say some moths will do anything out of love for a flame."

"How do you know what the poets say?"

"I used to sneak into Pak Tea House to listen."

The moth stops swooping, enters a holding pattern about two feet above the candle, and then lands on the wall in front of us. It's gray with a black dot on its back that looks like an eye.

"That's an ugly moth," I say.

I wait for Manucci's response, but he says nothing.

The moth doesn't move.

"He's afraid," Manucci says.

"He should be. Love's a dangerous thing." I look carefully. Dark streaks run down the moth's folded wings. "Maybe he's burnt himself."

The moth takes off again, and we both step back, because he's circling at eye level now and seems to have lost rudder control, smacking into the wall on each round. He circles lower and lower, spinning around the candle in tighter revolutions, like a soap sud over an open drain. A few times he seems to touch the flame, but dances off unhurt.

Then he ignites like a ball of hair, curling into an oily puff of fumes with a hiss. The candle flame flickers and dims for a moment, then burns as bright as before.

Moth smoke lingers.

I lift the candle and look around the mantelpiece for the moth's body, but I can't find it.

For a moment I think I smell burning flesh, and even though I tell myself it must be my imagination, I put the candle down feeling more than a little disgusted.

The city plays host to a fundo convention the weekend after the kamikaze moth's last flight. The bearded boys are celebrating our latest firecracker with parades, marches, and speeches. The score is 6 to 5, and we're up. I suppose it's 6 all if you count their first one in '74, but that was arguably another match, and either way, we're certainly not behind, even if we're also not clearly ahead.

One night a very serious Ozi comes to see me.

He's here to talk, but it's too hot for him inside and I don't want to sit in his Pajero with the air conditioner on and the engine running, so we compromise by climbing up to the roof, where it's a bit cooler.

The last time Ozi and I were up here together was the night before he left for America, eleven years ago. That night I was the angry one, angry because he was leaving me behind, because Lahore was about to become lonely, because I'd done better than he at school, on the tests, and he was the one going abroad for college. I'd studied with the richest boys in the city, been invited to the homes of the best families. And money had never really felt like a chain until the summer they all left. Five of our class fellows were on Ozi's flight the next day. I remember their names. And dozens of other boys we knew were flying out over the next few weeks. Nadira would be in Lahore a little longer, until September. She was our biggest crush. Ozi joked I'd never have the guts to do anything by then, and afterwards he would be the one to get her because I'd be too far away. He was wrong: I kissed Nadira many years later, after she came back to Lahore, but before she launched her husband hunt, before she left me to pursue men with Pajeros.

I have no doubt why Ozi has come. He must have found out that I've been seeing Mumtaz behind his back. He probably wants to beat the hell out of me. I'd let him do it, because I know I deserve it, because I've betrayed him in my mind, even if little has actually happened. But Ozi knows I could thrash him if I wanted, and if he was going to beat me up he'd have come with some of his father's men. He's here alone because he's decided to hit me with guilt instead of hired fists.

He still hasn't spoken, so I ask, to make it easy for him, "Where's Mumtaz?"

"At home," he answers. "Muazzam has a fever. But I wanted to talk to you about the accident. Did you tell the police?"

"No," I say, surprised.

"Good. I wouldn't want to get my father involved." He looks at me. "So you haven't told anyone?"

Remembering that day, digging it out from under a month of charas and sweat, I start to get angry. "No," I answer.

"Thanks, yaar. I must admit, I've been pissed off with you. I didn't like the way you acted. It wasn't what I expected from a friend."

"Really" is all I can say.

"We're not the boys we were when we were seventeen," Ozi says. "But my view on friendship hasn't changed. Friends support each other no matter what. Do you agree?"

He's right. That's what friends do. I'm not sure if I have any now, but when I did, when I was younger and it was easier to have friends, that's how I thought of them. "I agree," I say.

"Good. I still consider you my friend. I'm ready to forget the way you acted after the accident."

"Thanks," I find myself saying, suddenly too sad to say anything else. "I'm sorry."

We shake hands and embrace. But for me, holding Ozi now, this moment marks an end. I hold him tight because I'll miss him. I already do. But he's a bastard, and I don't owe him a thing. And if his wife wants to see me without telling him, there'll be no pain in my guts over it.

I say so long to Ozi tonight, and I mean it.

As the five hundred rupees I made from the hash deal with Raider quickly disappear, I consider doing it again. It seems easy enough: buy the stuff cheap from Murad Badshah and sell it dear to acquaintances with money to burn. Most of the party crowd smokes, and so does the younger banking and business community. And everyone complains about being out of hash.

The problem is that selling hash seems sleazy somehow. Lower class. I still like to think of myself as a professional, not rich, but able to stand on my own, with a decent income and a job that doesn't involve bribing or being bribed, helping my friends with a little hash when they're out, getting a little booze from them when I am.

But I'm not a professional anymore. And I need the money. Temporarily.

I decide to do it again.

I buy another five hundred rupees' worth from Murad Badshah, split it into four little balls that I flatten into pancakes and wrap in plastic, and head out to a popular spot for business lunches near Mini Market. I recognize a dozen faces as soon as I come in, and a couple of people invite me to join their tables, but I turn them down because I see Akmal sitting by himself, sipping a soup while he chats on his mobile. He was one of my clients at the bank. His family sent him to Lahore a few years ago, when they thought they'd have to leave Karachi because of all the kidnappings, and he stayed, living off the income of a million-plus U.S. that he has sitting in his bank account. He does some small-time business ventures, but mainly he's a man of leisure, twice divorced and a big pot smoker.

I stand by the door, feeling a little embarrassed, and wait until Akmal hangs up.

"Sit," he says as we shake hands.

"Why not?" I take a seat and pick up a menu.

"My new account officer doesn't know the first thing about client relations," he says. "I offered him a Scotch when he came by my place and he said he doesn't drink."

I order some food, which is stupid, since a meal here costs much more than I can afford, but I need time to decide how to ask him if he needs some hash.

We talk general business talk for a while, and he listens closely to what I'm saying, because I know my stuff, I know the near-bankruptcies and defaults businessmen love to hear about, and my information may be dated, but it's still good.

When the bill comes, I reach for it, but he takes it from me over my objections, his manner slightly condescending, in the way the rich condescend to their hangers-on. I should pay, being the first to get my hands on it, but the total is four fifty-three and I only have a couple hundred on me.

"Drop by for a drink sometime," he tells me as he places a five hundred on the table, but I know the offer is insincere.

"I'd love to." Then I flex my abs and take the plunge. "You know, I got my hands on some good charas today."

"Really?"

I hope he'll say he wants to buy some, but he doesn't. "You don't need any, do you?" I ask after a while.

He grins. "I can always use some. I'll take whatever you can spare."

"I can give you about five hundred worth."

"Come by my place tonight."

"I have it here."

He looks at me, surprised. Then he starts to laugh. "I love it. You people have balls, yaar. Slip it to me under the table."

I don't like the "you people" comment but I do it anyway, startled to feel him place a note in my hand because I didn't see him take one out. But he's from a business family, so I suppose this is what he was bred for.

As he drives off he rolls down a window and says, "You didn't get fired for trying to sell dope to bank clients, did you?"

Laughing, he speeds away.

Maybe he doesn't think what he said was insulting, or that someone like me can even be insulted, really. But humiliation flushes my face.

And something inside me starts to snap.

I suck the spit through my teeth and nod to myself, rage building. Then I run to my car and pull out onto Alam Road behind him, my bald tires squealing. But even though I drive like a maniac, my Suzuki's no match for his Range Rover. I lose him near Hussein Chowk.

He probably didn't even know I was chasing him.

I circle the roundabout, five hundred rupees richer, and I think I'd be willing to pay all of it for the chance to hit him, just once, on his double chin. Making money this way isn't worth it. These rich slobs love to treat badly anyone they think depends on them, and if selling them dope makes them think I depend on them, I just won't do it.

But as I'm sitting at home I realize that I sold him a hundred and twenty-five rupees of drugs for five hundred. That makes me feel a little better. Not much, but definitely a little. I promise myself never to sell to any of these rich bastards unless I can rip them off. Let them think they're getting a fair deal. And if they're nasty enough, maybe I'll slip a little heroin into their hash, just to mess with them.

Making money this way isn't pleasant, but it's easy, and easy money is exactly what I need, even if there isn't enough of it to pay an electricity bill.

I spend most of my time smoking and thinking of Mumtaz. It's been a week since we went to Jallo Park and I miss her. I tried to reach her on her mobile once, but Ozi picked up and I had to ring off without saying anything. I wish she would come to see me.

Every time I roll a joint I keep it for a while, hoping she'll appear so I can share it with her. But she never does. And Manucci must be leaving the screen doors open, because there seem to be more moths in the house every evening, circling candles, whirring in the darkness. I kill them when I can catch them, until my fingers are slick with their silver powder. But most of the house is dark at night, and there's little I can do about the invasion. Sometimes, when Manucci's asleep and I have no one to talk to, I get stoned and take out my badminton racquet to smash a few. Occasionally the biggest ones make a pleasing little ping as I lob them into the ceiling, but more often they just explode silently into clouds of dust.

One night I'm doing this, sweating in the heat, my body lightly powdered with moth dust, when a car honks outside the gate.

It's Mumtaz. She says nothing when she sees me, shirtless and clutching a badminton racket. I take her up on the roof.

"Ozi's out of town," she says. "And Muazzam's crying like mad. I left him with Pilar. I had to get out for a while. I wanted to see you."

"Would you like a joint?"

"Please."

I have one rolled and waiting in my cigarette pack, so I light it and pass it over.

I watch her face in the glow of the burning hash and tobacco. She seems worried.

"What are you thinking about?" I ask.

She passes the joint back to me and watches me smoke it, but she doesn't answer. Then she reaches out and wipes sweat down my shoulder with the blade of her hand. "What were you doing?" she asks.

My fingers are trembling and I drop the joint so she won't notice. The tip breaks off, smoldering separately from the barrel between my feet. "I was killing moths," I say. My shoulder burns where she touched me.

"I want to kiss you," she tells me.

I can hear my breathing.

Her fingers curl through mine and I close my fist, holding them there. Our eyes meet and I look away, but she leans forward, leans until her forehead presses against mine and her hair falls around my face and her breath touches my lips.

She kisses me.

And we're touching and tasting, roving each other, and I'm overcome and afraid of her and willing all at once. We shiver, the hair on our bodies rising as the night heat bakes dry the sweat and saliva on our skin. I'm pushed down on the roof, worn brick pressing into my back. She takes a condom out of her handbag, one hand stroking my throat. Then we make love, and as my eyes follow the curve of her body above me, I see the moon, round, perfect, the color of rust, burning like a flame to her candle.

She takes me and keeps me.

It's like someone's died. I hold her tight, muscles tense, pulling away from the bone. And I know she knows what I'm feeling, because the tears on her face mix with mine.

Afterwards, when she leaves me lying there, I smell the moth dust mixed in with her sweat and my sweat on my body.

CHAPTER 10

the wife and mother (part one)

I'm sure we've already met, Lahore being such a small place and all, but let's reintroduce ourselves so there's no mistake. I'm Mumtaz Kashmiri. You're probably anxious to know about Daru and me, everyone else is, but you'll have to be patient, because I'm going to tell my story my way and Daru doesn't appear for a while.

Where to begin? Certainly before Muazzam was born. Definitely before I got married. Before I went to America? Hmm. No. We haven't the time to go that far back just now.

Let's start in New York City, my senior year in college. The scene is the East Village, a little before midnight, on the steps of a fourth-floor walk-up on Avenue A. The date is important: October 31. Halloween. I'm dressed as Mother Earth (rather ironic, as you'll come to see). My roommate, Egyptian, English major, is improvising around the Cleopatra theme again. This year there's a sun motif. Ra, you know. Last year it was more Leo.

So there I am, trudging up the steps, the wheat stalks on my head hitting the ceiling, when I see this cute desi guy in a white shirt and black trousers, looking ridiculously out of place but very comfortable at the same time. He catches my eye as I pass and says "Hi," but I ignore him, because the last thing I want to deal with tonight is some conservative boy from the homeland with nothing to say. I just hope we aren't related and don't know anyone in common.

The party is great. I down some excellent ex, low on zip but high on joy, if you know what I mean, and make out with one or two acquaintances. But at some point (you saw this coming) I find myself on the fire escape with the brown boy I'd seen before. We're dancing, just the two of us, and his name is Ozi and he's wickedly sexy, and what the hell, we spend the night together.

So that's how it all began. Nine months later we were married. My fault, of course. Because I should have known better. I should have known I wasn't the marrying sort, even then. But I didn't. Besides, I was in love.

Let me say a few more words in my defense. Ozi was magnificent. He was gorgeous, a fantastic lover, open-minded, smart, charming, funny. And he was, is, the most romantic man I've ever met. He feels love deeply and he's almost belligerent about showing it. Not that he isn't horrible to most of the planet, he is. But if Ozi loves you, you know it. You can swim in it, get a tan. Or rest in its shade, if you'd rather.

Still, I shouldn't have married him. He proposed during a snowstorm in March, looking cold as only a Pakistani man in America can. And I said yes. Because I was in love with him, and I had no idea what marriage really meant, and I didn't know myself, yet. And because of all the other wrong reasons, because of what every mother, aunt, sister, cousin, friend, every woman from home I'd ever known had always told me: that an unspeakable future awaits girls who don't wind up marrying, and marrying well (well being short for "wealthy Pakistani bachelor"). All of that advice, which New York had laughed out my window and into the Hudson, came rushing back to me, sopping wet, in that instant, and stupid or not, I said yes.

Before I knew it, I was showing him off at South Asian Student Association parties, enjoying the horrified jealousy on the faces of my prim and proper colleagues. Yes, Mumtaz, that slut, had bagged herself a prince, which meant there was one less out there for them. My friends adored him. My parents were thrilled. The summer after we graduated, he from law school and I from college, we were married in Karachi by the sea.

For a while, life was perfect. His parents bought us a beautiful one-bedroom with a view of Washington Square Park. I had a fabulous, virtually nonpaying editorial job at a magazine start-up. Ozi was doing sixty hours a week of trusts and estates for a big law firm and, surprisingly, loving it.

It's not hard to remember what things were like then, in that first year of our marriage, when we were so good together, even if my memories are a little colored now by what happened later. We went out all the time. We danced like crazy, both of us sweating and stripped by the end of the night. We had insane sex. Once, we were caught on Ozi's desk by his officemate, who later swore he hadn't seen anything and always blushed when I spoke to him at the firm's cocktail parties. But the best part of it was the talking. I was completely open with him. Almost, at least. More open than I've ever been with anyone else. I remember what it felt like to tell him how my father used to beat my mother, once so badly she lost her hearing in her left ear. How my brother never cried, not even when I almost died of pneumonia and he spent the entire night awake with me in the hospital. How upset I was when I finally got my period, at fifteen, because I'd accepted that it would never come. Ozi made me feel so known. He made love to my insides, filling desperate gaps and calming unbearably sensitive places.

And I brought his secrets out of him as well. I remember him trying to make a joke of the fact that he'd been molested by the owner of a tropical-fish store, who fondled Ozi through his track pants as my husband, then eight, tried to buy a pair of kissing gouramis. I became tender toward his obsession with cleanliness, his need to shower and wash his hands and brush his teeth many times a day.

We were growing together, and I was happy.

Then I got pregnant.

I'd always been a condom person, but since I was regular and we'd both tested negative, Ozi and I switched to the rhythm method. Which can be almost as reliable as the pill. Almost. I told Ozi about it sadly, because I'd decided to have an abortion. But he was ecstatic. I'd never seen him so happy. He told me I had to think about it for a week. And he did something I still haven't forgiven him for: he told his mother. She flew out to New York immediately, bringing gifts and advice. It's amazing what the gene pool will do to perpetuate itself. Anyway, when she left, I told Ozi I hadn't changed my mind. But I did have a tiny doubt, and he noticed. He asked me to wait another week, which I did, and he used the time to do everything he could to convince me to have the baby. None of it worked, really, not even his home screening of Disney's *Jungle Book*, which I love.

But I could see how much he wanted to have this baby, and it moved me. I decided to take another week to think about it. Then another week. And the more I thought about it, the less power I seemed to have to end it. I felt guilty. More than that, I felt selfish. I tried to convince myself that I wanted the child as well, that childbirth was an expression of female power, that it would make our bond even stronger. So the week turned into weeks. Eventually we had a sonogram done, and after that, the idea was a little person, growing, and it was too late to turn back.

I resigned myself to it. Or maybe I saw it as a kind of martyrdom. Sacrificing myself for something noble: for love, my man, the species. I don't think I realized how frightened I was until the third trimester, when the nightmares started. Nightmares inspired by the Discovery Channel. Visions of being eaten alive by larvae, like some poor animal stung by an insect and made into a host for its eggs. Ozi, my friends, even people at work asked me why I looked so upset. But I could hardly tell them. Most mothers glow when they're pregnant. I sweated.

Labor hurt like hell. I swore like a sailor the entire time. When they gave me the baby, I thought of *A Farewell to Arms*, because it did look like a skinned rabbit with a wrinkled old man's face. I asked if something was the matter with it and they said it was perfectly healthy and a boy.

The baby started sucking on my breast, and it seemed to know what it was doing, so I let it be. Ozi said, "You look like you're in shock," and I said, "So would you," and the nurse said it was only natural. Meanwhile, I kept feeling the cropped stump of the baby's umbilical cord pressing into me, and eventually I got so sick that I threw up. The next day they wheeled me out of the hospital like a cripple, but then I had to walk to a cab.

At first, the baby was like science class. I learned how to use new equipment, how to pump, sterilize, clean, burp, wrap, powder. And the experiment, my son, seemed to be going well. I stared at him for hours, because he was such an odd little thing, with his big head and eyes like slits and fat, slow hands. He was new, and he kept me busy, and for a while I didn't worry.

Ozi couldn't get enough sex in those first few months after

Muazzam was born. Which was fine with me, once I'd had a little recovery time, because my drive had always been more powerful than his. You learn a lot about your man when you become the mother of his child. Ozi began drinking my milk and talking like a little boy when we made love. Now, I'm no prude. I've done my fair share of role-playing, and I've sampled all kinds of kink. But this, coming from him, took me by surprise.

Not that I minded. What I did mind was that we had no time to talk about ourselves anymore. We just played with the baby and watched the baby and screwed, and then he went to work and I stayed home. When we did talk, it was almost always about Muazzam.

I started to get bored. And then I started to get frightened. Because when I looked at the little mass of flesh I'd produced, I didn't feel anything. My son, my baby, my little janoo, my one and only: I felt nothing for him. No wonder, no joy, no happiness. Nothing. My head was full of a crazy silence, the kind that makes you think you're hearing whispers and wonder whether you're going insane.

Meanwhile, Ozi was having a ball. He enjoyed building tax shelters in exotic places. His clients took an instant liking to him, and his golf game improved. His friends at the office said he might even make partner. And he loved his son. He would come home exhausted, much too exhausted for sex or a quiet conversation over a glass of wine, but not too exhausted to play with Muazzam until he went to bed.

I felt neglected, resentful at being the one left at home when I hadn't wanted to have a baby in the first place. Things came to a head when Muazzam was six months old. I decided I wanted to work full-time again. Ozi was shocked. He said Muazzam was too young. I said if he felt so strongly he could ask for paternity leave. But he won the argument. He won it with a low blow. He looked at me like I was a stranger and asked if I loved our son at all. The question destroyed me. I started sobbing and I couldn't stop.

I'd done everything I was supposed to. I'd played with Muazzam and read to him, even though he couldn't understand a word, and bought him clothes and fed him with my own body and cleaned his shit with my own hands. I felt so guilty. I knew there was something wrong with me. I was a monster. But I didn't want to be. Staying with my baby was the right thing to do, what everyone expected of me. My mother would agree with Ozi. Even my friends. So I gave in. I said I'd write freelance from home.

I didn't tell Ozi why I'd cried. He didn't ask. He just hugged me. And even though I needed him to, it felt empty. Ozi had found my weak spot. He may not have understood why, but he now knew he could make me do things I didn't want to do. And that's an awful power to give one person in a relationship. It killed our marriage. I think it would kill anyone's.

But it takes a long time for a good marriage to die, and even a dead marriage can pretend to be alive, with habit as respirator and heart machine. We stayed in America for another two years and people thought we were happy. We were invited everywhere. And we entertained lavishly. But we never could find a babysitter Ozi approved of. Every month or two he made me get a new one.

Sometimes I would explode at Ozi, and then he would take me seriously, almost become the Ozi I'd fallen in love with. But only for an hour or two. After a while I found that I was getting angry at him just for attention, which made me feel like such an infant that I stopped doing it. Ozi still came to me when he needed to be held and comforted, and I was so lonely that I was grateful for the opportunity. But my resentment grew. I had two selfish children on my hands, and they were making me miserable.

I started drinking Scotch, neat, during the day.

I didn't tell anyone how I really felt. Not my best friends. Not my mother. And certainly not my husband. It was a new experience for me. I'd never been ashamed of anything I'd done in my life. But this wasn't something I'd done. This was me. Not an act but an identity. I disappointed me, shamed me. So I hid my secret as well as I could. And to do that, I had to hide it from myself.

Perhaps the strangest thing of all was what I was writing. After trying my hand at a few edgy pieces and finding it a nightmare to get them published, I wrote an article on lullabies for a women's magazine. Really. I put an international spin on it, interviewing friends who came from all over the planet. Enough to put anyone to sleep, I thought. But I was wrong: it was a hit. The magazine was flooded with letters. And I was asked for more. So I did one on herbal remedies for diaper rash and vegetable balms for baby skin. Another winner.

I kept writing, glad for the distraction from the constant demands of my son. The income was important to me, as well. Between Ozi and his parents, we had everything we needed, but the idea of taking pocket money from my husband had begun to grate on me. So I managed to earn some financial independence writing about parenting, little hypocrite that I am. It was satisfying in a strange way, and in a not so strange way, too. The strange satisfaction came from at least being able to write about motherhood well. It helped me hide from myself. And the not so strange satisfaction came from learning that I was a good writer, feeling new muscles growing in my back, wing muscles, the kind that mean you're learning to fly.

But it wasn't the right season to lift off. Not yet. I sat in my apartment and looked out over the city, and I just didn't feel any passion to write about the place. I didn't give a damn about local politics, I wasn't moved by the issues. I missed home. And I was frustrated by people who actually thought the world had a center, and that center was here. "The world's a sphere, everyone," I wanted to say. "The center of a sphere doesn't lie on its surface. Look up the work 'superficial,' when you have a chance."

Slowly, even though I thought it would never happen, New York lost its charm for me. I remember arriving in the city for the first time, passing with my parents through the First World Club's bouncers at Immigration, getting into a massive cab that didn't have a moment to waste, and falling in love as soon as we shot onto the bridge and I saw Manhattan rise up through the looks of parental terror reflected in the window. I lost my virginity in New York, twice (the second one had wanted to believe he was the first so badly). I had my mind blown open by the combination of a liberal arts education and a drug-popping international crowd. I became tough. I had fun. I learned so much.

But now New York was starting to feel empty, a great party that had gone on too long and was showing no sign of ending soon. I had a headache, and I was tired. I'd danced enough. I wanted a quiet conversation with someone who knew what load-shedding was.

Then Ozi decided he'd had enough of being a well-paid small fish in Manhattan. His father needed him, and he wanted to go home. I agreed. I was desperate for a new start, too. So we took a deep breath and jumped and landed with a loud splash one summer in beautiful Lahore.

But Lahore wasn't the answer. I didn't know anyone, I had nothing to do, and I hated living with Ozi's parents.

At least Muazzam's new nanny was a blessing. For the first time since before he was born, he wasn't completely dependent on me, and that was liberating. I started thinking about what I wanted to do with my time, and then about what I wanted to do with my life. My twenty-sixth birthday reminded me that I was still young.

I tried to restart my marriage, to rediscover everything that had made me love Ozi in the first place. Honestly I did. But it didn't work, because I lost my respect for him. And once that happened, there was nothing more I could do.

How do you lose your respect for the person you love? It isn't easy. It takes—it took—a lot. It took his mother, for one thing. She'd spent half her life making her son into the man she'd wished she'd married, and now that he'd returned, she was back in business. She corrected his posture, critiqued his suits, made him self-conscious about his receding hairline by telling him again and again how a good haircut would hide it. And the effect she had on him was incredible. One look from her would transform the relaxed, charming, sexy man I'd married into an uncomfortable little schoolboy.

But it took more than his mother to utterly destroy my respect for Ozi. It took his father, too. No matter how much I wanted to believe otherwise, I quickly realized that the rumors about Ozi's father being corrupt were true. And when I finally, delicately, confronted Ozi, he seemed almost surprised that it bothered me. In fact, he said one of the main reasons he'd come back to Lahore was to help his father protect his assets, kickbacks from the good old days when Dad was a senior civil servant with the country at his feet.

Even then I might have stayed with my increasingly emasculated, amoral husband for quite some time. It took some serious miscalculations on his part to extinguish the last, lingering, stubborn spark of respect I had for him. It took one manipulative comment too many, one more comparison of myself to his perfect mother than I could take. I didn't confront him. I just gritted my teeth, took out a needle, and worked him out of my heart like a splinter.

But I still wasn't ready to leave him.

It might seem strange after everything I've said that Muazzam should prevent me from leaving my husband. But he did. I still wanted to believe that I loved my son, that I was a good mother, that I was a good person. I knew it would be wrong to abandon him. And I knew I couldn't take him with me. I couldn't bear it, having sole responsibility for the child. I didn't trust myself, and I didn't want to.

But a crack down my middle was splitting open, and I couldn't be just the good wife and mother anymore.

So how did I, after being faithful for four years of marriage, come to start having sex with my husband's best friend? It all began with writing under a pseudonym. A double life has to begin somewhere. There has to be a first lie, a first deception. And mine began when I decided to start working as an investigative journalist called Zulfikar Manto. It wasn't because Ozi would have objected that I didn't tell him. (He married a woman he slept with on the first night, remember that. He wasn't a close-minded man.) It was because I wanted to create a life that he knew nothing about.

But as soon as I began, wings that had been growing for years stretched and pushed and I found myself flying. I was home again, and there was so much I wanted to say. I found myself sitting up all night at the computer, writing with all of my soul, the window open and my wrists sweaty against the keyboard as Ozi slept under his blanket in the next room. I spoke with prostitutes and policemen who might have killed a girl and lawyers who gave safe haven to fugitive women from abusive marriages and an Accountability

Commission investigator with one arm and a grip so strong my hand hurt for days.

I wrote about things people didn't want seen, and my writing was noticed. Zulfikar Manto received death threats and awards. And the more I wrote, the more I loved home. I was back, I was finding myself again, and I was being honest about things I cared for passionately. Childbirth had hurt me inside, and I was finally starting to heal.

When I met Darashikoh Shezad, I didn't know whether I was going to sleep with him, but I knew I wanted to. He seemed the perfect partner for my first extramarital affair. He was smart and sexy, and since he was one of Ozi's best friends, I knew he'd keep his mouth shut.

It was fantastic. We had a delicious courtship, slow and exquisite, because we both felt so guilty. Sex was a revelation: being touched by another man, declaring my independence from the united state of marriage, remembering myself by being felt for the first time. We smoked joints and talked for hours and made each other laugh.

I once went to a coffee party where rich young wives sat around and moaned about being bored while their husbands were at work, and I laughed at them afterwards, because I knew that I had a lot to do. It wasn't until later that I realized they did, too. Affairs were the most popular form of entertainment around. And I know why. My affair with Daru was, at first at least, the most liberating experience I have ever had. I felt bad, of course. Selfish. But I also felt good.

The problem was that I started to get under his skin, and he, in a very different way, started to get under mine.

I'll tell you more later.

CHAPTER 11

six

I take the turn as fast as my car lets me, my road grip half a handshake away from letting go, from flipping my Suzuki onto its back, and cut through traffic with a smile on my face because I'm thinking of Mumtaz. The card in my shirt pocket presses into my chest, its corner painful, but I finish sucking the life out of my joint, curling my lips at the heat and smell of burnt filter when it's done, before I take the card out and put it on the seat next to me.

I'm going to a kiddie party.

The old chowkidar lets me in with no trouble, and I see maybe a dozen cars in a long driveway. I've shaved today and even treated myself to a haircut, my hairdresser taking it close to the scalp as he flirted with me, so I look as young as I can. But I'm definitely older than these kids, and they notice. This is the pre-college crowd, still in school and worried about the O levels and APs and SCs and SATs that stand between them and the States and Merry Old England, the only places they'd ever dream of going for an education.

One of them asks, um, excuse me, who I am.

"I'm a friend of Raider's."

"Raider?"

"Haider."

"Oh." He looks around to make sure we're not being watched. Naturally everyone's staring at us. "Do you have it?" he asks, lowering his voice.

"Aren't you going to offer me a drink?" I notice they only have Murree vodka. How cute. These kids are still learning to walk: they have the cash for Scotch but they don't yet have the contacts.

"Well, it's not really my party."

Come on, kid. Not you, too. At least try to pretend that I'm more than just a drug connection. I'm well dressed, hip. A little hospitality wouldn't hurt. "Whose party is it?"

"It's sort of all of ours. But it isn't my house."

"Are you saying you don't want me to stay?"

"No, I'm not saying that."

"Great. I'll have a drink, then."

He looks almost frightened.

I smile. "Just teasing, yaar. Don't worry, I won't steal any of your girlfriends. Take the stuff and I'm off."

"Do you mind if we go outside?"

"No." We head out onto the lawn, away from prying eyes. I hand him my fourth and last pancake of hash.

"How much?" he asks.

"A thousand."

He gives it to me without another word. This is incredible. He's buying it for eight times what it cost me, and he actually seems happy about it. I like this kid. "What's your name, by the way?"

"Shuja Rana. Yours?"

"Darashikoh Shezad. Call me if you ever need more."

"What's your number?"

I tell him, and he takes out the stub of a pencil and writes it down.

"I'm sorry you can't stay," he says. "I wouldn't mind at all. But some of these people are such snobs."

There you go, kid, putting your foot in your mouth. You can stand my stench even though your friends can't, is that it? You're lucky I need your money.

"That's too bad," I say, lighting a cigarette. "Run along. I'm going to have a smoke, and then I'm leaving."

It's a big lawn, and I stand in the middle, watching the house, wondering how many of these kids will grow up into Ozis. Quite a few, probably. Our poor country.

A couple walks out together, holding hands, but when they see me they turn around and go back inside, leaving me uncertain whether they think of me as a chaperon or a servant.

When I get home I'm still a little angry.

It's the wrong time for Manucci to ask for his pay.

"I don't have it," I say.

"Saab, you haven't paid me in two months."

I raise my hand and he flinches, but I don't hit him. "Enough. I'll pay you when I pay you. I don't want to hear another word about it."

He runs off, looking upset. I feel a little hard-hearted, but I tell myself I did the right thing. Servants have to be kept in line.

I go to my room with a candle and fish the heroin Murad Badshah gave me out of one of the drawers. Heroin and charas mixed. "I'll call you hairy," I say, pleased with the name. My curiosity has been killing me, but I haven't yet tried the stuff. Tonight I feel reckless, feel like having sex on the roof in the moonlight, except that Mumtaz hasn't called since that crazy night, and this hairy will have to do.

I roll a jay, or maybe I should call it an aitch, since I'm using hairy. It frightens me a little bit, so I use about half the amount I would if it were hash. I light up and puff delicately, but it doesn't taste so different from what I'm used to, and it doesn't seem to be any more harsh on my throat. I finish the aitch and sit back to see what it does to me.

The first feeling is jointy, a head throb from unfiltered nicotine in the tobacco. A light hash buzz slides in after that, nothing spectacular, just a medium-level high. I wait to see if anything else will follow, relaxing into the sofa and shutting my eyes. When I open them again, the candle has gone out and the moon is riding higher in the sky, its faint colorless light peeling off the wall opposite me. Long shadows. Should light another candle, but feel very comfortable, in no rush to move. My watch says an hour has passed. Skin itches, but in a good way, and hand slips under shirt to scratch it. Soon the moon's so high that I'm sitting in shadowless dark, but my eyes have adjusted and I can see well enough without a candle, so I stay put.

I would like a cigarette, though. Where are my cigarettes? I just made an aitch, so I must have some. Ah, here they are in my shirt pocket. How convenient. Now if I could find a lighter without getting up I would be so happy. Open the pack and there one is. Wonderful. Now the next question: aitch or cigarette? Aitch's too much work. But cigarette's boring. What the hell. Sit up. Roll one.

Light up.

Ahhhhh. World floats at body temperature. Very nice, very nice. I'm in a good mood. My head is clear. Thoughts are coming one at a time, nicely formed. I like this. Well, I might as well admit it: this hairy is damn pleasant. Damn pleasant, do you say? I do indeed, my dear sir, damn pleasant. Nice little interior dialogue, that.

What do you know? It's three o'clock. Well, Daru, time for you to give your bladder a release. Get up now, that's a good fellow. One, two, three. Up. There you go. Takes a lot of effort, and energy level seems low, but no problem with motor control here. Stroll over to the bathroom. Turn on the light. Oops, no electricity. What's this? A little nausea? Let it out, then. There. That wasn't bad at all. And again? No problem. Just let it come on up. Perfect. Now sit down, let your bladder relax, too. Great. Rinse your mouth and head back to the couch. Take a detour for a glass of water. Here's a glass. Here's the water.

Sit down on that couch and have some rest. You've earned it. What time is it? Four in the morning. That's a surprise. You should give Mumtaz a call. Can't: Ozi. But Ozi's out of town. Should you, then? Pick up the phone. *Ringringrrring*. Hang up. Don't want to wake her.

Well, you can chill out by yourself. This is nice. Must thank Murad Badshah. Look, the sky is getting lighter. Just slightly, from black to blue. Shocking. Time for bed. This couch is so comfortable. Pull your feet up and stretch out and exhale.

Hhhhhhhh.

I'm woken in the evening by Manucci shaking my arm. "Go away," I tell him, desperate to return to sleep.

"Your guest is here, Daru saab."

I feel a moment of panic. I don't want to face anyone at home, with no electricity and nothing to offer, unshaven because I don't have a job. "What guest?" I ask, opening an eye.

"Mumtaz baji," he says, looking down like a blushing bride.

Relief comes twice, a double release, because the guest is the one person I want to see, and because it's been a week with no contact since we made love and I was beginning to get anxious.

"Tell her I'm coming down."

I head into the bathroom and grip the sink. The sun is setting and it's getting dark, but I can make out the circles around my eyes and I can see the uneven stubble of my beard, the growth thickest above and below my mouth. I feel my gorge rising and spit once, but there's no real nausea, so I brush my teeth with a mangled toothbrush, white bristles spread and soft from too much use. I scrub my tongue and palate, unable to banish the bad taste I woke up with.

I need a shower, but haven't the time. I wash my face without soap, feeling as I rub them that my nose and eyelids are greasy. Then I throw on a pair of jeans and a white shirt, the only semi-ironed one I have, and head downstairs.

At least I had a haircut.

Mumtaz is sitting on the sofa, legs crossed, with Manucci squatting on the floor beside her. He's chatting away, which annoys me, because I don't like it when the boy forgets his place. It makes me look bad, as though I've fallen so far my servant thinks there's no longer any need for him to behave formally.

"It was hard to catch me, Mumtaz baji," he's saying. "I ran very fast. I knew all the hiding places."

"But when they did catch you?" she asks.

"Then sometimes they beat me."

"Is he telling you about his adventures?" I ask loudly, in the ringing tones of a master of the house making his presence known. Manucci falls silent. "He has the soul of a poet. It's hard to stop him once he gets started."

Mumtaz looks me in the eyes and smiles. "Hello, Daru saab," she says.

I feel awkward with Manucci in the room, uncertain whether I should give her a kiss on the cheek. I do my best to seem calm and in control, but I find myself confused, very conscious of her physical presence.

Mumtaz is perfectly at ease. "Quite the early riser, I see."

"Bring tea," I tell Manucci.

"Saab, there's no milk."

I open my wallet like a card player, as casually as I can but very careful to tilt it toward me so Mumtaz can't see how little it contains. "Run to the market and get some," I say, handing Manucci a fifty.

"Hi," Mumtaz says once he's gone.

"Hi." I feel silly sitting across from her. "How have you been?"

"Good. I'm working on a new article."

"About what?"

She lights a cigarette. "All the money that left the country before the government announced the freeze on foreign currency accounts."

"What's the story?"

"It depends on who you ask," she says, inhaling. "The version I like is that they knew they would have to freeze the accounts when they tested, because it was obvious everyone would be nervous about sanctions and start converting rupees into dollars, and our foreign exchange reserves would have been too low to keep up. But of course some of them had their own money in those accounts. So they tipped off a few insiders, and just hours before the accounts were frozen, millions of dollars left the country."

"And Zulfikar Manto is trying to discover whether this happened and who was involved?"

"Precisely, my dear Daru," she says.

"I should give you the names of some banker friends of mine who might tell you who pulled their money out." I think of my numerous c.v.'s dangling in the water with not even a nibble.

"Hopefully they'll be more helpful to you than they have been to me."

"What do you mean?"

"Nothing. My job hunt isn't going particularly well. It isn't going at all, actually. The economy is completely dead right now, with the rupee skyrocketing on the black market and bank accounts frozen."

"Have you ever thought of finishing your Ph.D.?"

"I can't afford to."

"I thought tuition was basically free."

"It is. But I can't afford not to work. I need an income."

"Did you finish your course work?"

I nod. "I was working on my dissertation. And I suppose I could do that part-time. Or full-time at the moment, since I have nothing better to do. But the whole thing is ridiculous."

"Your dissertation?"

"It was on development. What a joke."

"So you think nothing can be done?"

"I spoke to a lot of people. I think nothing will be done."

"I think you're wrong. A lot can be done. There's just a shortage of good people willing to do it."

"It's easy to be an idealist when you drive a Pajero."

"Ouch."

"Sorry. Let's change the subject." I glance at her, hoping she won't stay offended, and I see what I think is a willingness to let our disagreement go.

"You look exhausted," she says.

I consider telling her about the heroin and decide not to. "I couldn't sleep. It's so bloody hot."

Manucci returns with the milk and quickly serves up some tea. I sip slowly, feeling the heat rise from the cup and open pores on my face. I'm used to sweating all the time now, so it doesn't bother me. And Mumtaz doesn't seem to mind, either.

As it gets darker, Manucci starts lighting candles, and I pray that tonight we will have fewer visiting moths than normal, but here my luck leaves me. Mumtaz raises an eyebrow more than once at the whirring guests who join us for tea, bumping noisily into walls and windows.

Once Manucci's gone, Mumtaz puts her arms around me and pulls me close. We kiss, and she gives me a long lick, like a cat tending to its paw. I hug her, squeezing, and her ribs flex with the pressure. I feel my face flush with excitement, and at the same time I'm surprised by how comfortable this is, how new but also familiar.

"Sorry about the Pajero comment," I say.

"Don't worry."

We kiss again, harder this time.

"Why did you write that article about prostitutes?" I ask her.

"Manto often wrote about prostitutes."

"But why the fascination with Manto's subject matter?"

She pulls back slightly and looks at me. "A few years of marriage and motherhood, I suppose. Finding I don't quite fit into what's expected. I'm interested in things women do that aren't spoken about. Manto's stories let me breathe. They make me feel like less of a monster."

"You're not a monster."

"Don't be sure."

I massage the back of her neck, kneading with my thumb, pulling with my fingers, following the line of her spine. She has soft hair there, thin and smooth, and I feel the long cords of her muscles flaring gently as she moves her face forward to stroke my cheek with hers.

Unexpectedly, I find myself thinking of Ozi smiling at me on a rooftop many Basants ago, as I hold a red ball of string for his kite. The sun is behind him, hurting my eyes. I remember not paying attention for a moment, turning to watch some girls in the courtyard beneath us. My surprise as the ball jumps from my hand and falls, knocking over a tray being carried by a bearer far below. Ozi's yelp as his kite is pulled from his hands. Shouts from the girls. And the two of us staring at each other, wide-eyed, laughing, with our hands on our knees. We really were brothers, once. And now I'm kissing his wife, my arms encircling her possessively, our bodies pressing together.

But I also remember being angry with my mother for no reason, being upset after Khurram uncle's visits to our house, maybe because they reminded me of the permanent absence of a father I never knew but imagined vividly. I remember Khurram uncle's rough hands as he taught Ozi and me how to hold a bat, the slaps when we made mistakes, not hard but not gentle, either. I remember his hands touching my mother's elbow after giving me presents I needed but almost didn't want.

I stroke the side of Mumtaz's neck with my teeth, tracing two lines in her skin. Then I think of Manucci and take her upstairs. She turns to me in the darkness of my room and we make love like we're furious with each other, silently, brutally. And when we're spent I lie with my head on her chest and she strokes my hair and I fall slowly, slowly asleep. My dreams are so deep I wake with no idea of where I've been, and I don't know when she left me during the night.

Fatty Chacha has never given me a lecture before in his life, not really, so he keeps looking down as he speaks, as though he wants to apologize for what he's saying. And his embarrassment more than anything else makes it impossible for me to be annoyed with him.

"You know how proud we are of you, champ," he's saying, rubbing his hands together. They're big for his size, broad but not long, with strong fingers. Good boxer hands. Hard to break. "You've always done so well. You worked at a top bank. You went to a prestigious school. You have friends from the best families." His gaze drifts up from my feet to my chest, then sinks back down. He tries to laugh. "You probably made more money last year than I did."

I don't say anything. I've never made much, just a low-level banker's salary, and Fatty Chacha's remark, if he's right, is more of an insult to him than it is a compliment to me.

He goes on. "But now I'm a little worried by what I see. You've stopped looking for a job. You sit at home doing nothing."

"There aren't any jobs," I interrupt. "The rupee's at fifty-five. People are pulling their money out of banks to buy dollars, now that their foreign currency accounts are frozen. All the imported stuff is disappearing from the markets. There's no business to be done, and no one is hiring at banks or anywhere else, not unless they owe your father a favor."

"You need to keep trying. Maybe you'll have to accept a more junior position. Nothing will happen if you give up."

"I haven't given up. But I'm not going to work at a mindless job for ten a month."

"Ten a month is enough to feed yourself and have lights instead of candles."

"Ten a month is four bottles of Scotch. It isn't enough to turn on an air conditioner."

Fatty Chacha smiles and finally manages to look me in the eye. "You sound like your father. He would say something like that: four bottles of Scotch."

"I don't know how to live on ten a month."

"It's better than living on nothing a month, champ. You have rich habits, but we aren't rich. You can't afford to turn down work because it's beneath you."

"I haven't turned down anything. I don't think I could find a job that paid me ten a month even if I wanted one. There are a hundred guys for every opening, and the one who gets hired is the one with connections. I've given my c.v. to twenty companies. I've had twenty rejections. Only one even pretended to consider me seriously, and that was because he didn't want to offend you."

Fatty Chacha cracks his knuckles, one by one. "I know it's difficult. Especially for you. You've always succeeded so easily. But you must keep trying."

I don't say anything. It's strange to hear myself described as someone who's succeeded easily. But compared to Fatty Chacha I suppose it's true enough. He never really succeeded at all. He didn't marry until he was forty. And even now he barely manages to support his family.

I tell him I'll do my best, and he seems relieved, tapping a beat on his belly with his hands. This conversation was clearly difficult for him. And I think it gave him an appetite, because he looks at his watch and wonders aloud what might be waiting at home for dinner. When he asks me to join the family at his place, I lie and say I'm going out with friends.

A freshly bathed Manucci, his hair still wet, comes in just as Fatty Chacha is leaving. My servant is wearing an old kurta shalwar I gave him after one of my little cousins spilled a bottle of ink on it. But Manucci must have bleached it or something, because the stain is hardly visible, and although it isn't starched, it has been freshly ironed. I look from myself, in my dirty jeans and T-shirt, to Manucci, in his crisp white cotton, and feel a strange sense of unease.

"Well, well, Mr. Manucci," Fatty Chacha says. "Looking very smart this evening."

Manucci's face breaks into an enormous smile.

"Go clean my bathroom," I tell him. "And scrub behind the toilet. It's getting filthy."

I show Fatty Chacha out myself.

I think it's safe to say Mumtaz is already at least a tenth mine. At least. I saw her sixteen hours this week. I know, because I timed it. And even though a tenth of someone is a lot to have, she has more than a tenth of me. I'm always dreaming of her, or thinking of her, or fantasizing about her, or waiting for her to come or to call. Even when I'm with her I miss her.

And she cares about me.

"I tried heroin," I say, my lips touching the soft skin where her jaw meets her neck.

"Was it good?"

"Unbelievable."

"That's bad. Don't do it again."

I've already decided not to, but I say, "Why not?"

"Some things are too good. They make everything else worthless."

"Like you?"

"Say you won't do it again."

"I won't."

"You won't what?"

"I won't do it again."

Mumtaz has six moles. Two are black: behind her ear and on her hip, in the trough of the wave that crests at her pelvis. Three are the color of rust: knuckle, corner of jaw, behind knee. And one is red, fiery, at the base of her spine, where a tail might grow.

I touch them and know them because I watch her like a man in a field stares up at the stars, and I love her constellation because it contains her story and our story, and I wonder which mole is the beginning and which is the end.

I have no moles. Not even one. I didn't know that, but Mumtaz has looked and looked, and now she's given up.

Manucci adores her. He brings us tea without us asking for it and leaves it outside my bedroom when the door is shut. Mumtaz likes chatting with him. She says someday she wants to write an article on young pickpockets in the old city, and Manucci has promised to take her on a guided tour of his former haunts. Once, when I haven't seen Mumtaz for a couple of days and she wastes half an hour talking to Manucci before she comes upstairs to wake me, I get upset and tell her I don't understand why she would rather spend her time with him than with me. She says it's cute that I'm jealous. And I become angry, asking how she could even suggest I'm jealous of my own servant. She says she was only joking, and then I feel completely embarrassed, and when we make love I keep looking at her to see if she's laughing at me.

Then one night Mumtaz asks me if I've done heroin again, even though I haven't, and it turns out Manucci has told her I spend all my time sitting on the sofa, rolling joints and smoking. I decide enough is enough. I go to the servant quarters with a leather belt and tell him I'll thrash him if he talks about me behind my back. He pulls his bedsheet up around his eyes and stares at me. But he doesn't do it again.

The next day I see Mumtaz cry. Not just shed tears but cry, with furious gasps and shouts of pain. Her voice is always throaty, almost hoarse, but when she cries she chokes off her words, and it hurts me to watch.

When she stops trembling and sobbing and can speak, I ask her why.

"I'm a bad mother," she tells me.

"You're not." I stroke her hair.

"You don't know," she says, frighteningly serious, her eyes wide and sharp. "You don't know."

"Why do you say that?"

"Muazzam told me I don't love him."

"Why?"

"He wanted me to read him a story and I came here instead."

"Read him a story when you go back."

"I don't want to. That's the problem. I don't want to."

I don't understand Mumtaz's relationship with her son. Sometimes she does so much for him, too much, everything he asks, from the time he wakes until the time he goes to bed. But she never seems to do it because she wants to, only because it upsets her when he gets angry with her. And sometimes she won't do anything for him, leaving him at home with his nanny all day.

We think Ozi still doesn't know about us. Mumtaz rarely stays with me for more than a couple of hours at a time, unless he's in Switzerland or the Caymans. I'm surprised he doesn't smell me on her. Maybe he doesn't care, but I doubt it. Part of me wants him to know. Part of me is afraid. When we were small Ozi was a bully, but then he was just a boy, and if you were bigger than him he went away. Now he's not a boy. He's a man and his father's son, and what they want done can be done and done quietly.

Maybe I should ask Murad Badshah if I can borrow his revolver.

When I'm not with Mumtaz, I usually have nothing to do. When I'm not with Mumtaz and I do have something to do, I'm generally selling hash. It isn't much money. And even if it does buy me petrol and food, I don't like doing it. I don't like the way I think I look to other people when I'm doing it, and I don't like the way they treat me.

One day I catch Manucci taking a hundred-rupee note, washed out and red, from my wallet.

"What are you doing?" I ask him, coming into the living room.

He drops my wallet and the note onto my jeans and starts to back away. "It was to buy groceries for the house, saab," he says.

I take hold of him by the flesh of his upper arm and squeeze until he cries out. He's never been so eager to do the grocery shopping before that he couldn't wait until I woke up.

"You weren't stealing from me, were you?"

"No, saab."

"If you ever steal from me, I'll make you wish my mother never took you off the street."

"Please, saab."

I let go and he runs into the kitchen. I know I haven't paid him in a long time. But he isn't going hungry: he eats food from my kitchen and sleeps under my roof. Sometimes servants only want their pay so they can leave, and if that's his plan I won't make it easy for him. Not that he has anywhere else to go.

One day I'm at Main Market, picking up a paan and a pack of smokes from Salim, when I see Pickles get out of his Land Cruiser and walk over to a Pajero. He embraces someone I haven't met in a while, and I go to say hello with a big grin.

I tap Arif on the back. "Oh-ho," he exclaims, hugging me with enthusiasm. "This is turning into a reunion."

I like Arif. A bit slow, he was the butt of our section's jokes in senior school. Luckily for him, his family owns half of Sialkot.

Pickles and I shake hands. "Listen, boys," he says. "I'm having a little get-together for some of our batchmates at the Punjab Club this evening. You must come."

The "must" may be meant more for Arif than for me, but I smile anyway and say, "I'd be delighted." It's not every day I'm invited to the Punjab Club, after all.

"Batchmates only," Pickles says. "So no wives or financées. And jacket and tie, Daru."

That night, as I'm getting ready, Manucci reminds me he can't iron my shirt without electricity. "Boil some water and put it in the iron," I say. "Do the best you can."

I pull into the Punjab Club, curving around the tennis courts, and park in front of the bakery. The car next to mine is a Suzuki Khyber, which makes me feel good, because most of the spaces are filled by huge monsters.

A uniformed bearer greets me as I enter and directs me out the back to the swimming pool area, where I see thirty or so very familiar faces, rounder, of course, their flesh hanging more loosely from their bones, but still familiar.

Ozi waves me over. "How are you, yaar?" he asks, shaking my hand.

"How are you?" I respond, wanting to look friendly but aware that the smile on my face is forced. I hold on to him longer than is comfortable, trying and failing to think of anything to say, and I avert my eyes before letting go. I'm confused and a little out of breath, unsure whether what I'm feeling is fear or anger or guilt or dislike. Probably a bit of each. I force myself not to think about it as I drift about, chatting and embracing old buddies, but I'm deeply unsettled, and it's some time before I manage to relax.

Dinner is a delicious march through colonial culinary outposts like mulligatawny soup and roast beef and caramel custard. As I eat, I find myself starting to enjoy the evening, temporarily taken back to the days when I had a crew cut and a sportsman's colors on my blazer. It's amazing how quickly old school friends slip back into remembered relationships. For an hour I'm not the poorest person here by far, the only one without a job or any secure source of income, but a schoolboy good at academics, a solid athlete, and a heroic prankster with a legendary raid on our headmaster's house to my credit.

Then I meet Asim and reality slaps my beaming face.

Asim was our section's arm-wrestling champ. I haven't seen him in years, but it looks like he's taken up bodybuilding.

"Oye, Daru," he yells.

It's clear he's drunk, and I wonder where he's hidden his booze.

"Oye, Asim," I yell back.

"Is it true you're selling charas now?" He says it in a loud voice that I'm sure is overheard.

"Very funny," I say quietly.

"That's sad, yaar, sad." He shakes his head.

I've had enough. "What's your problem, sisterfucker?"

"Don't speak to me like that."

"Suck me."

He grabs me by my shirt, and I'm about to knock his teeth in when we're pulled apart and I hear Pickles cry, "No fighting, no fighting."

"Bloody charsi," Asim yells, struggling against the hands that restrain him.

"Ignore him," Ozi says, leading me away.

But I can't ignore him. The words have been said. I'm sure everyone wants to know what the scuffle was all about, and by the end of the evening they will.

Remember Daru? He's selling drugs now.

I pull away from Ozi and head for my car.

To hell with them all.

• • •

This time I buy a thousand worth from Murad Badshah. I've sold half of it when Shuja calls. He wants some more hash, so I tell him to come and get it.

He arrives later that night, in a car with a driver.

"How old are you?" I ask him as I take him inside. I'm stoned, as usual, and a little lonely because I haven't had anyone to talk to today.

"Sixteen."

I wonder whether sixteen's too young to be smoking hash. Then I decide it isn't. I wasn't much older than that when I started, and kids today are doing everything earlier than we did. It's the MTV effect.

Manucci watches as Shuja and I exchange the hash for a thousand, a disapproving look on his face. I give him a quick glare, and he ducks back into the kitchen.

"How long have you been a doper?" I ask Shuja.

"Oh, you know."

"I don't know. Six months? A year?"

He looks uncomfortable. "A month, maybe. A couple of my friends tried it before that, but we never had anyone to buy from."

Maybe I shouldn't sell it to him. But he pays a thousand when all my other customers pay five hundred. Besides, he's nothing to me.

"Don't do too much," I say.

"I won't. My father's strict. He'd thrash me if he found out."

I walk him out and stand in the driveway long after his car has disappeared, smoking a cigarette and trying hard to see even a single star through the night haze. I hear Manucci come up behind me. He doesn't say anything.

"What is it?" I ask.

"Saab."

Something in his voice makes me turn around. He's looking at the ground, and when he looks up I'm surprised because he's so afraid.

"What?"

"Don't do this."

I take a drag of my cigarette and then drop it onto the driveway, putting it out with my shoe. "Do what?"

"Sell charas."

I feel the anger coming, slow and dry, the air moving through my nostrils, the swelling in my torso. This will not happen. I won't permit it. My servant will not tell me what to do.

"What did you say?" I ask, my voice a warning.

"This is wrong, saab. You shouldn't sell charas."

I look at Manucci, this boy now almost my height, at the sparse, dirty curls of his newly arriving beard, the food stain beside his mouth, the slack hang of his lips. And I can't wait any longer.

I step forward and slap him across the face with all my strength.

His head snaps to one side and he stumbles, falling to the ground. He cries out softly, a low sound, rough at the end, and covers his mouth with his hands. Then he looks up at me, the fear gone from his expression, leaving only seriousness and a gleam in one watering eye.

My hand is numb. I walk into the house, rubbing it.

I wake up with my head pounding, sweating hard. Two blades of the ceiling fan come together in an insane grin, the whole contraption absurd as it hangs over my face, dead in the heat. I yell for Manucci, and the effort sends blood rushing into my skull.

Damn that boy. Where is he?

I yell again, so loud it hurts, and still he doesn't come. An uneasiness settles into my stomach. I drag myself into the bathroom and sit down, my thighs sweating against the plastic seat of the toilet. As a general rule, I'm not one to wake and bake. But today I feel like making an exception, so I hollow out a cigarette, repack it with some hash, and take a long hit just as a shaft of pain knifes through my rumbling bowels.

Liquid. Completely liquid. And acidic. The worst kind. Frothy and all that. I need some Immodium, a double dose double quick, or I'll be dehydrated by sunset.

I clean myself, wash my hands in the hot tap water with a sliver of soap, take my bedsheet, wrap it around my waist, and trudge out of my room in search of Manucci. The house is quiet, dead moths on the floor and sooty marks on the ceiling above candles that burned themselves into puddles of wax overnight. Not only has the boy forgotten to sweep, he's wasted perfectly good candles by not blowing them out. He's in for it when I find him.

But I can't find him. I'm smiling now, the kind of smile that stretches over clenched teeth. When I step outside, gripping my bedsheet with one hand, and see the gate open, both metal doors flung outward, I tilt my face up to the sun and cover my eyes with my fists. Then I stand there, naked, the taste of blood in my mouth, holding the first knuckle of my fist with my teeth. A woman walks by the gate, leading a little boy with a balloon of hunger in his belly and hair bleached by malnutrition. Neither of them sees me.

I shut the gate, stare up and down the street from behind it. Somehow I know that he won't come back. Manucci is gone. My own servant has left me, left because of one little slap. That boy had better pray I never see him again. To think that I fed him, sheltered him, for all these years, and this is his loyalty, his gratitude.

I can feel the heat radiating from the metal of the gate.

I head back inside, and my stomach is so bad that I vomit before I can make it to the bathroom. Then I curl up on my bed, exhausted. When the sun goes down, I get up again, take a cloth and bucket, and clean up the mess I've made, gagging from the smell. Even when I'm done, the stench lingers in the house. I head out to the medical store to stock up on Immodium and rehydration salts. I also pick up a packet of biscuits, but when I try to eat them, I can't.

I wake up the next morning feeling weak, but I haven't had any vomiting episodes or bowel movements during the night, so I know that I'm not in danger of dehydration. Besides, I've finished off several packets of salts, taken three times the recommended amount of Immodium, and downed a full two-liter bottle of water. Excessive, I know, but I hate being sick.

The only person I see for the next two days is Mumtaz. She buys canned soup and heats it for me, saying I shouldn't have high expectations because she's a horrible cook. I tell her about Manucci, and she gets angry with me. She seems to think it's my fault. I'm too tired to argue, and I don't want her to know I've been selling charas, so I sip my soup and keep my mouth shut.

After she leaves I'm alone, all by myself in the house. Alone even when I feel better.

Until the phone rings.

"Um, hello?"

"Who is this?" I ask.

"Shuja."

"How are you?"

"Okay. Do you think I could get some more hash?"

I laugh. "You can't already have finished what I gave you."

"No, I didn't. But it's all gone. I, um, gave some to my friends."

He sounds tense. "Is everything all right?" I ask.

"Yes. So can you sell me some more?"

"Of course. Come by this evening."

"Do you think you could come here?"

I wouldn't mind getting out of the house, but something in the tone of his voice makes me uneasy. Then again, he overpays like no one else I know. "Where do you live?"

He tells me.

"I'll be over in half an hour," I say.

"Do you think you could come a little later. Like in two hours?"

Again I feel suspicious. "Why?"

"My, um, my father's home. But he'll be gone by then."

"Are you sure you don't want to come here?"

"Yes. I can't."

"Fine. I'll be there in two hours."

When I arrive at Shuja's family's compound, I notice the boundary wall is topped with jagged glass that glints in the sunlight. I read the name above the house number and recognize it. So Shuja's from a big feudal family. Who would have thought it? He seems so Westernized.

Instead of uniformed security guards at the gate there are a bunch of men with serious mustaches and shotguns slung over their shoulders. They look enough like village thugs to make me nervous. And there seem to be quite a few of them. But they open the gate without any questions and I walk in. The house itself is gaudy, huge and white, with massive columns and pediments and domes and even a fake minaret, as if it's uncertain whether it wants to be the Taj Mahal or the Acropolis when it grows up.

The gate swings shut behind me with a loud clang, and some of the men with shotguns start walking in my direction. Palm trees line the driveway. I hear them rustle in the hot, dry wind.

I walk up to the house and ring the bell.

The door opens to reveal Shuja and a stern older man I somehow know is his father. I guess Shuja was wrong about his going out, and I'm about to pretend I've come to the wrong house when Shuja's father says, "Is this him?"

I don't like the way he says it.

Shuja nods. He looks scared.

His father gestures, and two men grab hold of my arms from behind.

I'm frightened and my heart is pounding hard. "What is this?" I say, but my voice sounds weak.

"You sold drugs to my son?" Shuja's father asks me.

"No."

One of the men holding me slaps the back of my head, and suddenly it all makes sense. They're going to kill me. Shuja's dad is a sick bastard whose son does pot, and I'm going to pay for it.

My mind disappears behind desperate terror.

Surging forward, I break loose from one of the men and slam my fist into the face of the other, feeling his nose crunch. And then I'm free, running. But there are too many of them, and I'm swinging, hitting hard, but the world spins, my legs slip out from under me, and I curl into a ball as they kick me, waiting for them to stomp on my head, screaming until I lose my breath.

I pass out once or twice, briefly. When my eyes open, Shuja's father is standing over me, saying something. He's pointing a shotgun at my head, and I can only whimper, blood and foam spraying from my lips. Then he kicks me in the face.

I come to on the bonnet of my car outside the gate. They've smashed all the windows. The gunmen are watching me. I try to stand, but I collapse and lie next to the road, slipping in and out of consciousness. Cars pass, so many cars, but no one stops. I sit up and crawl into my Suzuki, throwing up on myself from the effort and the nausea that comes when I see my hand. I slump in the seat. They wait for me to start the car, but I can't. One of the gunmen finally drives me to the hospital, and he tells me that Shuja's father will have me killed if I say anything to the police.

Later the doctor tells me how lucky I am. I only have a concussion, a dent in my skull, a broken nose, a broken rib, a compound fracture of my left forearm, cuts totaling seventy-one stitches on both legs, one arm, my neck, my shoulder, my eyebrow, and the spot where I bit through my lip. I'm missing one of my front teeth. The small finger of my left hand was partly torn off, but it's been reattached and I may be able to use it again with time. There's no internal bleeding, my brain seems to be working even though I'm groggy, and my eyes may look bad but the retinas are still attached.

"Who did this to you?" the doctor asks.

"Auto accident," I say.

He shakes his head.

CHAPTER 12

the best friend

I'm Aurangzeb. Ozi to my wife, my friends, and even those of my friends who sleep with my wife. But mostly I'm Aurangzeb. And regardless of what you've heard, I'm not a bad guy.

You see, the problem is, I make people jealous. Which is understandable. I'm wealthy, well connected, successful. My father's an important person. In all likelihood, I'll be an important person. Lahore's a tough place if you're not an important person. Too tough for my best friend, apparently.

Some say my dad's corrupt and I'm his money launderer. Well, it's true enough. People are robbing the country blind, and if the choice is between being held up at gunpoint or holding the gun, only a madman would choose to hand over his wallet rather than fill it with someone else's cash. Why do you think my father got into it? He was a soldier. He served in '71. He saw what was going on. And he decided that he wasn't going to wait around to get shot in the back while people divided up the country. He wanted his piece. And I want mine.

What's the alternative? You have to have money these days.

The roads are falling apart, so you need a Pajero or a Land Cruiser. The phone lines are erratic, so you need a mobile. The colleges are overrun with fundos who have no interest in getting an education, so you have to go abroad. And that's ten lakhs a year, mind you. Thanks to electricity theft there will always be shortages, so you have to have a generator. The police are corrupt and ineffective, so you need private security guards. It goes on and on. People are pulling their pieces out of the pie, and the pie is getting smaller, so if you love your family, you'd better take your piece now, while there's still some left. That's what I'm doing. And if anyone isn't doing it, it's because they're locked out of the kitchen.

Guilt isn't a problem, by the way. Once you've started, there's no way to stop, so there's nothing to be guilty about. Ask yourself this: If you're me, what do you do now? Turn yourself in to the police, so some sadistic, bare-chested Neanderthal can beat you to a pulp while you await trial? Publish a full-page apology in the newspapers? Take the Karakoram Highway up to Tibet and become a monk, never to be heard from again? Right: you accept that you can't change the system, shrug, create lots of little shell companies, and open dollar accounts on sunny islands far, far away.

I'm really not that bad. A victim of jealousy from time to time. But definitely no hypocrite.

Speaking of hypocrites, let me tell you a thing or two about good old Daru.

Daru's an educated fellow. No foreign degrees, it's true, but he went to the most prestigious school in the city. A very exclusive school, mind you. A school that's difficult to get into. The sort of school unlikely to admit a boy if he comes from a no-name middle-class background, if his father's main distinction is being dead.

So how did Daru get in?

My father got him in, that's how.

You see, my father knows something about loyalty. Captain Shezad (that's Daru's dad) died of a rotting shrapnel wound in East Pakistan. But before he died he went to the military academy with my father, served for a time in the same regiment, got married the same December, had a son the same age. My father and Captain Shezad were like brothers, and my dad treated Daru like his son. He sent us to the same school and paid both of our tuitions. My father gave Daru his pedigree.

You didn't know that, did you? I didn't think so.

But you did know my father got him his precious bank job? Well then, you must admit Daru has some nerve calling himself a self-made man, whining that he's the victim of the system, that he never took advantage of anyone, that he was wronged, and wronged by us, by me of all people.

He's full of it.

Now, I'm a money launderer, right? Money launderers are bad, right? Bad because they take dirty money and make it look clean. Bad like Pol and Idi and Adolf and Harry and the rest of the twentieth century's great butchers of unarmed humanity. Oh, not quite that bad? Thanks, you're too kind.

Well, what about the guys who give out the Nobel Prize? What are they? They're money launderers. They take the fortunes made out of dynamite, out of blowing people into bits, and make the family name of Nobel noble. The Rhodes Scholarship folks? They do the same thing: dry-clean our memories of one of the great white colonialists, of the men who didn't let niggers like us into their clubs or their parliaments, who gunned us down in gardens when we tried to protest.

And what about the bankers of the world? What about family fortunes held in accounts that make more in interest than the income of every villager in the Punjab put together? Where did all that money come from? How much of it was dirty once, how much came from killing union leaders and making slaves pick cotton and invading countries that wanted control over their natural resources? Would you like your money starched, sir? Box or hanger? Thanks for using GloboBank.

Luckily for the downtrodden, in the midst of all this money laundering, of transforming ill-gotten gain into prestigious titles and luxurious mansions, we have a Champion of the Good. Tan-ta-ta-ran! It's Darashikoh Shezad. But wait a minute. What does he do? He's a banker. An account manager, as a matter of fact. And whose accounts does he manage, what clients does he please, whose asses, if you'll pardon the expression, does he kiss? Men like my father's. So enough of this nonsense about me being the big bad money launderer and Daru being hung out in the wash. We're all in this together.

And let me tell you something else about Daru. Just before she left me, Mumtaz hired a houseboy. A very hardworking kid. Good-natured. Sweet. Cooks. Cleans. And I was glad to have him, because, jokes aside, it's difficult finding good servants these days. Anyway, the boy's name was Manucci, and it turned out he used to work, if you can call slave labor work, for Daru. For the man of the people himself. Why did he run away? Because Daru beat him, humiliated him, and didn't pay him, sometimes for months. That's right: self-righteous Daru is a hypocrite and a menace. Ask Manucci. As soon as his knees stop knocking together, he'll tell you.

So take another look at us, Daru and me. I may clean dirty cash, but I don't beat defenseless children and I don't screw my friends' wives and I stand by my father when push comes to shove.

• • •

Not convinced? Still think I'm the bad guy? Then do me a favor and try to put yourself in my shoes. Just for a moment. Don't think you can? Well, let me tell you a story.

Once upon a time there were two boys. Let's call them Hero and Villain, or Ro and Lain for short. Ro's a pudgy little kid, quiet, studious, with a runny nose. He has no real friends. You know, one of those social misfits you had in your junior school class who hung out together because they were ostracized by everyone else.

Anyway, this kid, Ro, drives to school every morning with another kid, Lain. They're driven by Lain's dad's driver in Lain's dad's car. Lain sits in the front and Ro sits in the back, and they hardly exchange a word, because Lain's ashamed of Ro. Lain, you see, is a stud, even at age five. He's not the fastest sprinter in the class, the best batsman, the most brilliant student, the scrappiest fighter, or the cheekiest prankster. But he can run fast, he is good with a bat, he does get solid marks, he will stand up to bullies, and he isn't scared of getting caned if a joke is funny enough. And most important of all, people like him. He can make friends with a grin, and he knows it.

Yes, I won't deny it, Lain's a little asshole.

Lain isn't mean to Ro. Not exactly. He just ignores him. But the more he does, the more Ro looks up to him with puppy-dog affection, ready and eager to do Lain's homework whenever Lain will let him.

Anyway, this pathetic state of affairs lasts until the end of junior school. Until the arrival of Ataris in Lahore, to be precise. Lain is the first kid in the class to get one, and his father forces him to invite Ro over to use it, which Lain does rather ungraciously.

The funny thing is, fat little Ro is actually good at it. Combat,

Adventure, Space Invaders: by the end of a day he's teaching Lain new tricks. And a friendship begins to form between the two, not much of a friendship, it's true, but something. They start playing every weekend. Ro spends a night once. Twice. Then sleepovers become more regular. And because Lain's parents force them to go to bed when they're still wide awake, the two boys find themselves chatting until they fall asleep. Neither has a brother, so each is getting to know another boy really well for the first time in his life.

Lain has a wild imagination. He's always liked to pretend that he's stranded on a desert island, or fighting in a war, or whatever. And the boys are now getting to an age where make-believe is uncool. But to Ro, everything Lain does is cool, so Lain feels comfortable playing games with Ro he wouldn't play with his other friends, and telling him things he'd never tell anyone else. And Ro, for his part, turns out to be the most loyal friend imaginable.

Well, things might have stayed like that, Ro remaining Lain's loving pet forever, but Defender came to town. By now, many boys in school have Ataris, and they decide to have a competition at somebody's house, a video-game battle to find out who really is the best of the best and who's just talk. And naturally, the game for the competition is Defender.

The week before, Lain practices every day. And by the time the weekend rolls around, he's ready. When the dust has settled and all twenty-eight boys have taken their turn, it's official: the highest score goes to Lain. He's the champ. And Ro, the video-game wunderkind, is number two.

Ro has probably never been second at anything in his life. All the boys are impressed that he's done so well. But I guess he wanted more. He wanted to win, to be the best, just this once. So when Lain goes up to his friend to congratulate him, Ro says, "If I had an Atari at my house, I could have scored double what you did."

Lain, shocked at this display of bad sportsmanship, says without thinking, "You might as well take mine, then. You'll never have one unless my family gives it to you."

And right there, as twenty-six of their classmates look on, oohing and aahing, Ro turns red as a tomato and starts to cry.

The other boys laugh at him.

And Lain, for probably the first time in his young life, realizes what an asshole he is.

Ro won't talk to Lain for a long time after that. They still drive to and from school together every day, but Ro won't say a word. Lain, surprisingly enough, is miserable. So one day he goes to Ro's house and breaks down in front of Ro's mother and starts sobbing and tells her how sorry he is. She calls Ro into the room and Ro forgives Lain. And after that the two become best friends.

Ro still looks up to Lain because he's cool and popular. Lain gives Ro his first cigarette, his first blue video, his first joint. He sets Ro up on his first date. Helps him pick out his first leather jacket. Teaches him how to use gel and pull a one-eighty.

And Lain, for his part, respects Ro for his honesty and decency.

Meanwhile, both boys are going through some changes. In particular, fat little Ro isn't quite so fat or little anymore. His uncle is teaching him how to box, he's exercising like a maniac, and he's becoming stronger by the day. He isn't a pretty boy by any stretch of the imagination, but girls are beginning to notice him. Together, Lain and Ro share the adventures that are the plus side of developing a bad reputation.

By the time they enter senior school, they're in love. No, no, nothing like that. Do I really have to spell it out for you? Many boys, probably most boys, have a first love before they fall in love with a woman. It begins the moment two boys realize they'd die for one another, that each cares more for the other than he does for himself, and it lasts usually until a second love comes on the scene, because most hearts aren't big enough to love more than one person like that.

Ro and Lain realize they're in love one evening on Ro's roof, as they lie on their backs sharing a joint and holding the string of a battered patang, undefeated after five kite fights. "I love you," Lain says suddenly. And Ro, who's probably surprised, even more so when he realizes that he's been longing to hear those words for some time, says, "I love you, too." And they don't look at each other, they're too embarrassed, but all in all, they feel pretty good.

Then SAT season arrives and Lain does well and Ro does better. They apply to the same eight colleges. Lain gets into three and Ro doesn't get into any, because he's asking for financial aid and it's hard to get when you're a foreign student. So Lain jets off to the States and Ro enrolls in GC. After that, they see each other only during vacations, but their lives are following different paths. Lain loves college abroad. Ro hates GC. And even though he makes the boxing team year after year, he's never good enough to win a title for himself.

On the rare occasions when they meet, Ro is angry and Lain is sad, because both sense that one of them is going nowhere.

Then Ro's mother dies and Lain goes to law school and gets married, and the two hardly see one another for years. And when Lain returns to Pakistan, wife and son in tow, Ro seems more frustrated than ever by his situation. But Lain reaches out to him, tries to broaden his social circle, asks his father to find Ro a new job.

Lain still loves Ro. He's still his best friend. And if Lain doesn't invite Ro to every dinner and get-together he has at his place, it's only because he knows Ro wouldn't like the superficial people Lain now socializes with.

But Ro is jealous of Lain. His resentment, dormant since

childhood, has begun to rumble. Lain can see it (he isn't blind), but he knows Ro well and trusts him completely. He's certain Ro's anger will pass.

Then one day there is a reunion of sorts at the Punjab Club, and the same twenty-eight boys, more or less, who gathered for that Atari competition long ago are reunited. And again Ro is humiliated: this time he's called a drug dealer and mocked because he has no job. So the next evening Lain goes over to console him.

And there, from the driveway, through an open window, the curtains spread wide, Lain sees his best friend on top of his wife, moving. Moving.

Now put yourself in Lain's shoes.

What would that do to you?

Maybe I should have suspected it. After all, Mumtaz and Daru hit it off from the very beginning, and there were certainly enough hints. But hindsight is twenty-twenty, and besides, I trusted him.

I trusted her, too. I knew Mumtaz was up to something, wandering all over town, telling me she'd been to places I later learned she hadn't, getting defensive whenever I'd ask what she did while I was away. But I didn't mind, because I'd found out about Zulfikar Manto. I discovered his first article in the computer's trash folder. And I let myself preview his later work, files hidden on an unmarked floppy disk in her handbag. I could see that she was passionate about it, so I let her keep up the pretense for as long as she wanted, certain she'd eventually tell me. I once gave her a book of Manto's short stories in translation, a gentle hint, to see if she'd open up. And I was a little hurt when she kept her secret. But what could I say? I adored my wife. And I was thrilled that she was having adventures.

I just had no idea that journalism was only half of it, that Mumtaz and Daru were having an affair.

Once we were eating mangoes, the three of us together. I said, Sindhris are my favorite. Daru said, You can't juice Sindhris, you can only cut them. I said, So what, cutting is more civilized. He said, It lacks passion, Chaunsas are my favorite, because they're the best for sucking. I looked at Mumtaz and smiled and said, I like fruit from Sindh. She said, Both cutting and juicing have their merits. Then she said, I like Anwar Ratores, because they're small and you can have two or three at a time. She said Daru and I were overly preoccupied with size.

I wonder if they were making fun of me, even then.

But I'm not going to treat you to a look inside the mind of the cuckold, a view into the near crack-up that accompanies the realization that your best friend is sleeping with your wife. I don't want your pity, thanks. And even if I did want it, I couldn't put what I endured into words. There's a reason prophets perform miracles: language lacks the power to describe faith. And you have to land on faith before you can even begin to hike around to its flip side, betrayal.

So what did I decide to do?

Nothing.

I couldn't confront Daru. You haven't seen him when he's angry: he can be a scary guy. If he'd become twisted enough to sleep with my wife, who knows what he might have done to me. I could have had him killed, I suppose. Shot like a favorite dog gone rabid. But I didn't.

I told you, I'm not a bad guy.

And I couldn't bring myself to confront Mumtaz either. Because I didn't want to lose her. You see, I knew things hadn't been going well in our marriage for some time. And even though I wasn't sure if I could ever forgive her, I still loved her and I didn't want her to leave me. Can you understand that? If you can't, you've never been in love, not really.

But she left me anyway. And even though she denies it, I know she left me for Daru. My one consolation is that they won't be seeing each other for a while.

So: no, I'm not sad to hear he killed the boy. I won't lie to you. But I certainly didn't frame him for it. I'm not the sort.

He was my best friend, after all.

CHAPTER 13

seven

My cocoon is too tight. Uncontained by my broken body, blood and wet flesh combine with cloth, bonding me to my bandages. Eyes shut by swelling see only orange, translucent light.

Wrapped inside my painkillers and the shell of my scars and bruises like a slow-growing larva, I wait.

She comes in with her palms pressed together, fingers touching lips, wide eyes above a prayer or a shush so forceful it requires both hands.

"What happened to you?"

"Don't ask." The words whistle through the gap in my teeth, tickling the raw hole in my gum.

She takes my good hand in both of hers and strokes it with her cheek, runs her fingers over my face, over my bruises, my cuts, the train tracks of my stitches.

"Who did this?"

I shut my eyes and reenter the dizziness that spins inside my head like two drinks too many too fast too strong. I can't vomit it out. I've tried. I can only hold on to myself in the whirlwind, staring up at Shuja's father, crying, begging. The barrel of his shotgun pressing against my abdomen like a needle, suddenly sharp. Gasping as my skin rips, as the needle slides into my body, pushing muscle and tissue aside, tearing through me, snapping my back, pinning me to the ground, mounting me like an insect on a board. And the nausea grows stronger, pulling me into itself, twisting me, wrenching at my guts, becoming unbearable.

I open my eyes. I want to kill him.

She sits down on the bed beside me.

I protect my rib cage with my arm.

"Where's your family?" she asks.

"I haven't told them." I don't want to explain, don't want to see them until I've recovered and there's no reason for questions. But that won't happen, not in a lifetime, not with a dead finger and a crushed nose and a smile that can't hide the darkness inside my head.

"How will you pay for this?"

"I don't know."

She slips her arm around my shoulders and cradles my head against her breast.

We breathe together. Slowly.

Time passes, flowing, a long, less and less painful sigh. And I shut my eyes.

Pain becomes only physical again.

Fear recedes.

Anger flickers for a moment longer, gas in the pipes after the stove has been turned off.

She says, "I'll take care of you."

And I feel gratitude and happiness rise up inside me: old friends, long-forgotten and yet much missed.

. . .

When the doctors tell me I can leave, she drives me home in my car. Its windows have been smashed, even the little triangles above the rear doors, but when the engine comes to life I smile, feeling unfamiliar muscles in my face flex.

In my room she lays me down on my bed, pulls the curtains shut, and undresses me.

Then she finds a bucket of cool water and a soft cloth and a bar of Pears soap. And she bathes me.

She begins with my eyes, stroking them shut. She follows my throat down to my collarbone, to the inside of my arm, to the skin between my fingers. To my chest, avoiding my broken rib, to my stomach, the bones of my pelvis. My feet, my shins. My thighs.

Then I feel her mouth and I exhale, slowly.

And after, she takes off her clothes and bathes herself. Touches herself. And then she lies beside me and watches me sleep.

When she leaves I'm alone. Completely alone. I'd hoped Manucci might be there, but he hasn't come back. It frightens me to look at myself, and it frightens me even more to run my good hand along the broken rib curving around my soft innards, a gap in my body's protection more shocking than the gap in my teeth.

That night I lie on my bed with my badminton racquet, tapping moths ineffectively, because it hurts too much when I move fast enough to kill them.

It's more difficult to bear the pain when I'm alone. I know it's good for me, a sign of life reasserting itself after the damage I've sustained, but it's hard to put up with when there's no one watching, no reference point, no sign that the struggle will lead anywhere but to more struggle. I can smile as a doctor sews stitches into my skin or a nurse slides a needle into my rump, but who can smile at a headache as he lies in bed in an empty house? I can't. I haven't that much strength.

The pain gets worse as the night goes on. The painkillers help, and the joints help as well, but what helps most is the heroin.

I find the stuff in my bedside table drawer, where it's been lying untouched since the night of my first try, and I know from the second I see it that I want some. It's wonderful. It doesn't kill the pain exactly, but after an aitch the pain doesn't seem to matter. Pain without hurt, as though I don't understand what my nerves are telling me. Or don't believe them.

I tell myself not to use it again, unless I really need the release. Hairy's serious, after all. Wouldn't want to get in the habit.

Mumtaz comes in the morning with halva poori for breakfast. Feeds me with her own hands, the halva still hot. Kisses the crumbs from my lips. And she brings me lunch and dinner: omelets and parathas, wrapped in greasy newspaper. Also candles. Matches. Mangos. Toothpaste.

I don't tell her about the hairy.

When I look in the mirror, when I see what's been done to me, rage lifts my eyelids and twists my reflection. I cherish the anger, center myself in it, draw power from it, strength for my healing. Because I will heal. And then it'll be my turn at the crease. And I won't be gentle with my bat.

She understands how I feel. Knows how to calm me.

When I tell her how my body was broken, fury comes, and I start screaming until I exhaust myself, panting from the pain in my rib cage. She wipes the spit from my chin and cradles my head, somehow corking my anger, bottling it up. And after a while I do feel better. Bottled, starved for air, even anger can't burn.

The longer she stays, the more I hate it when she leaves.

One evening she says, "You look less monstrous every day."

"So do you."

"How do you feel?"

"Stronger."

"Good, because Ozi's back. I won't be able to come as often."

I'm silent.

"You look disappointed," she says.

"I am."

"Well, I can't blame you. I wouldn't mind being fed and bathed by you every day, either."

"It's not that. I want to see you."

"I'm here."

"I want to see you as much as Ozi sees you."

"I'm best in small doses, believe me."

My rib twinges, but she slides her hand under my shirt and onto my chest, and then I must breathe more softly, because I can't feel the pain.

We lie naked in bed, a small chocolate cake with a red-and-white sparkling candle balanced between my nipples, fizzing and smoking merrily. Two weeks out of hospital. Two months without electricity. Three months since I lost my job. Twenty-nine years since my first smack on the bottom, the first time I cried.

Today is my birthday. My family has already been by, honking at the gate until the neighbors started shouting and they had to go away. I'm not ready to face them yet. And I wanted to be alone with Mumtaz. She tells me to make a wish. I wish for work and money and air-conditioning and a healed rib and a new tooth and ten good fingers and my ex–best friend's wife. Then I blow out the candle. It takes two tries, and makes me wince.

"Don't tell me what you wished for," she says.

"It would take too long," I say. And I grin, because at this moment, with her beside me and an undisturbed afternoon ahead, I feel almost happy.

She takes the plate off my chest and strokes my hair.

I shut my eyes. "What would you wish for?" I ask.

She thinks. "Perfect foresight, a little courage, and a time machine."

I smile. I like the slow rasp of her voice, the way she draws out her words. "Why?"

"So I could go four years back into the past, realize what was going to happen if I married Ozi, and say no when he asked."

My head begins to throb, full of blood, stuffed by the excited pumping of my heart. I open my eyes. "So it was a mistake?"

She turns onto her side. Her breast brushes my shoulder. "I have no clothes on. I'm with you. You're not my husband. I've clearly made a mistake somewhere."

"Did you ever love him?"

She nods. "I loved him. Did you?"

"I think so."

"So what happened?"

Something is caught between my teeth. I pull it out: a hair. Maybe an eyelash. "I don't know. A million things. There were problems even when we were kids. He was vicious, full of himself. And when he left, we drifted apart. Maybe I just realized what he was all along: not a good guy. A bastard, really. A self-centered, two-faced, spoiled little bastard . . ."

"Stop."

The sharpness of her tone makes me realize I'm getting carried away, and I bite down on my words. But I feel myself choking on all I'm leaving unsaid.

"Don't," she says. "I don't want to lie here and attack Ozi. It isn't right."

"You said it was a mistake to marry him."

"For me, yes. But which one of us is the problem? Ozi's a good father. He's sweet. He's generous. He's smart . . ."

I feel the muscles in my chest contract. "He's rich. He's got everything he wants. He's perfect."

She pulls back. "Why are you so bitter?"

"He's a bastard."

"There's no reason for you to be jealous."

My mouth is wet with unswallowed spit. "If you think he's so wonderful, maybe you shouldn't be here."

She watches me, her eyebrows rising, wrinkling her forehead. "Are you serious?"

I realize she's getting angry. And I don't want to fight. "No," I say. And when she doesn't respond, I add, "I'm sorry."

She's quiet for a moment. "I don't think I should be married to Ozi. But not because of him. Because of me. I'm really not all that nice. I don't think I'm the sort who should marry at all."

"That isn't true."

She smiles. "You don't know me that well. I'm a bad wife. And I'm a worse mother."

I put my arm around her and she presses against my side. "You're just stuck in a bad situation."

She shakes her head. "I chose my situation. No, it's deeper than that."

"What is?"

"Where am I right now?"

I stroke her back. "With me."

"And what about my son? He's at home. He misses me. But I leave him with Pilar as much as I can. I can't help it. I'm flawed. A bad design."

"It's normal. Everyone gets tired of their children sometimes."

"I'm not talking about getting tired sometimes. I don't know. I don't think I can explain it."

"My mother didn't spend every minute with me."

"No?" Her belly swells against my side with her breathing.

"Of course not. She worked, for one thing. And I went to school during the day, sports in the afternoons. And at night I went out with my friends."

"But when you were home together?"

I think of my mother and feel myself starting to slip, a sudden weightlessness, the dip in my stomach as a car crests a hill, fast, the uncertainty that entered my life the day she died. I pull Mumtaz to me. "We used to talk. We were close."

"You see. I hear it in your voice. Muazzam is never going to speak of me that way."

"You don't know that." I kiss her, softly. "You're wonderful. You make me feel completely cared for."

She stops breathing and stares at me for a moment, almost a glare. I pause. Then it passes. Her body relaxes, her waist sinking deeper into the bed, the curve from her shoulder to her hip becoming more pronounced.

"Maybe that's why I'm here," she says. She doesn't smile, but she kisses me back, and both of us shut our eyes.

Sometimes when Mumtaz is with me, moving about the house, I watch her. I'm mesmerized by her posture. She stands with strength and poise and supple flexibility, like a village woman balancing a pitcher of water on her head as she walks home from the well. Shoulder blades pulled back. Chin up.

The muscles of her neck flare, taut when she turns, when she inhales before speaking.

She has the long torso of Sadequain's imagination. And solid, strong legs. One half slender, one half less so. A mermaid.

Her breasts are small and wonderfully round. One hangs half a rib lower.

Her fingers are thin. Nails short, unpolished. Veins raise the smooth skin of her hands before subsiding into her forearms. Roots feeding blood to her grip.

She curls and uncurls her toes without thinking when she sits.

And her mouth is wide and alive.

I commit her to memory.

When I'm alone, I feel a strange yearning, the hunger of a man fasting not because he believes but because he's ashamed. Not the cleansing hunger of the devout, but the feverish hunger of the hypocrite. I let her go every evening only because there's nothing I can do to stop her.

And I ask myself what it is about me that makes this wonderful, beautiful woman return. Is it just because I'm pathetic, helpless in my current state, completely dependent on her? Or is it my sense of humor, my willingness to tease her, to joke my way into painful, secret places? Do I help her understand herself? Do I make her happy? Do I do something for her that her husband and son can't do?

Has she fallen in love with me?

As the days pass and I continue to heal, my body knitting itself back together, I begin to allow myself to think that maybe she has.

And one day, after many joints, as we lie replete in bed, as I play with her hair and she kisses my hand, I realize that she watches me. That she touches me not just with tenderness but with fascination.

And my mind starts to whirl.

Suddenly I think I'm about to understand.

She's drawn to me just as I'm drawn to her. She can't keep

away. She circles, forced to keep her distance, afraid of abandoning her husband and, even more, her son for too long. But she keeps coming, like a moth to my candle, staying longer than she should, leaving late for dinners and birthday parties, singeing her wings. She's risking her marriage for me, her family, her reputation.

And I, the moth circling her candle, realize that she's not just a candle. She's a moth as well, circling me. I look at her and see myself reflected, my feelings, my desires. And she, looking at me, must see herself. And which of us is moth and which is candle hardly seems to matter. We're both the same.

That's the secret.

What moths never tell us as they whirl in their dances.

What Manucci learned at Pak Tea House.

What sufis veil in verse.

I turn her around and look into her eyes and see the wonder in them that must be in mine as well, the wonder I first saw on our night of ecstasy, and I feel myself explode, expand, fill the universe, then collapse, implode like a detonation under water, become tiny, disappear.

I'm hardly aware of myself, of her, when I open my mouth. There is just us, and I speak for us when I speak, and I must be trembling and crying, but I don't even know if I am or what I'm doing.

I just say it.

"I love you."

And I lose myself in her eyes and we kiss and I feel myself becoming part of something new, something larger, something I never knew could be.

Union.

There are no words.

• • •

But after.

"Don't say that," she says.

And faintly, the smell of something burning.

When I wake, it seems a little less hot than usual, so I'm worried I have a fever until light flashes behind the curtains and the sound of a detonation rolls in with a force that makes the windows rattle. As I step outside with a plastic bag over my cast, a stiff breeze pulls my hair away from my face, and I see the pregnant clouds of the monsoon hanging low over the city.

The rains have finally decided to come.

I sit down on the lawn, resting my back against the wall of the house, and light an aitch I've waited a long time to smoke. Suddenly the air is still and the trees are silent, and I can hear laughter from my neighbor's servant quarters. A bicycle bell sounds in the street, reminding me of the green Sohrab I had as a child. Then the wind returns, bringing the smell of wet soil and a pair of orange parrots that swoop down to take shelter in the lower branches of the banyan tree, where they glow in the shadows.

A raindrop strikes the lawn, sending up a tiny plume of dust. Others follow, a barrage of dusty explosions bursting all around me. The leaves of the banyan tree rebound from their impact. The parrots disappear from sight. In the distance, the clouds seem to reach down to touch the earth. And then a curtain of water falls quietly and shatters across the city with a terrifying roar, drenching me instantly. I hear the hot concrete of the driveway hissing, turning rain back into steam, and I smell the dead grass that lies under the dirt of the lawn.

I fill my mouth with water, gritty at first, then pure and clean, and roll into a ball with my face pressed against my knees, sucking on a hailstone, shivering as wet cloth sticks to my body.

Heavy drops beat their beat on my back and I rock slowly, my thoughts silenced by the violence of the storm, gasping in the sudden, unexpected cold.

The parrots the monsoon brought to my banyan tree have decided to stay awhile. There's been a break in the downpour today, and I can see them from my window, swimming in and out of the green reef of the canopy like tropical fish, blazing with color when the sun winks at them through the occasional gap between storm clouds.

Along with parrots, the rains have brought flooding to the Punjab and a crime wave to Lahore. Heists and holdups and the odd bombing compete with aerial food drops and humanitarian heroics for headline space on the front pages of the newspapers. Looking out on the soggy city, I pretend to move my hand through a table-tennis shot, but I'm really reenacting the slap that sent Manucci away, wondering how a little twist of the wrist could have such enormous consequences.

What am I going to do? I don't know how to cook or clean or do the wash. And I'll be damned if I'm going to learn. The only people in my neighborhood who don't have servants are servants themselves. Except for me. And I refuse to serve. I'm done with giving. Giving service to bank clients, giving respect to people who haven't earned it, giving hash and getting punished. I'm ready to take.

"What are you looking at?" she asks me.

"Parrots," I tell her.

She gets out of bed, picks up my jeans, and puts them on, rolling the waistband down so they don't fall off her hips. "Do you have a shirt I can wear?" she asks me.

"Nothing clean," I answer.

"It doesn't matter."

I take a white undershirt out of my closet and sniff it. Smells neutral enough. She puts it on and walks out of the room, her bare feet avoiding the dead moths and the puddles near the windows.

"You need a replacement for Manucci," she says.

"I can't afford one," I reply, following her.

She sees what she's looking for, a box of matches, and lights her cigarette. Then she sits down on the couch and pulls her legs under her. "I'm going to give you some money until you find work."

I sit down next to her and shake my head. "I don't want any more of Ozi's money, thanks."

She kisses me. "Well, once you've started having an affair with his wife, taking his money doesn't seem like such a big step."

I rub the corner of her jaw with my chin, feel my stubble scratch her skin, turn it red. "I don't want to be having an affair with his wife."

She smiles. "Tired of me so soon?"

"I'm serious."

She shakes her head and looks away. Her hair covers the patch of redness. "Don't do this."

"What?"

"Don't make this into something it isn't."

"What isn't this?"

"This isn't a courtship."

I tug at the bottom of her undershirt. My undershirt, on her. It's old, the cotton very soft, fraying slightly around the collar. "This isn't just sex."

She turns and looks at me. One hand covers mine, stops my tugging. "Nothing is just sex. I care about you. I need this right now."

"I love you."

"Stop saying that."

I pull on her shirt again, gently. "Do you think you can go back to Ozi as though nothing ever happened?"

"Daru, I don't have to go back to him. I'm married to him. I'd have to leave him to go back to him."

"But you started this."

She takes my hand off her shirt. "You didn't exactly resist."

"But you're the one who made it happen."

"I just got over my guilt first."

"So why hold back now?"

"Daru, I'm married. I have a son. I'm not looking to mate. I'm looking to be with a man for me, because it makes me happy."

"And I don't make you happy?"

"You do."

"But you don't care about my happiness."

"Of course I do. That's why I'm being honest with you. If you're looking for a wife, you need to look somewhere else. I'm an awful wife. And I'm already married."

I walk over to a cabinet and take out the hairy. I haven't told Mumtaz I've been smoking the stuff. But suddenly I see no reason to hide. Let her be angry.

Then again, maybe she won't even care. I'm just her lover, after all.

I light up and she asks for a puff.

"No," I say.

She stays seated, hugging her knees on the sofa. "Why not?"

I pull the smoke into my lungs, growing calm before the aitch has even begun to work: the relaxation of anticipation. "You don't want it."

"Are you angry?" Her tone is neutral, neither cold, accusatory, nor warm, inviting reconciliation.

"It's an aitch."

"Aitch?"

"Aitch. Hairy. Heroin. Bad for your health."

She's quiet. I don't feel any need to say more. I like this, the sense that she's trying to communicate with me while I hold back, waiting.

"You're more stupid than you look," she says.

I ignore her. The aitch is almost gone. I hold it between thumb and forefinger, fill my chest with a last puff.

"Are you such a coward?" she snaps. "Have you really just given up on everything?"

"Don't overreact. I've had some occasionally. Twice or thrice." I'm acting cool, but inwardly I'm overjoyed by her reaction. She's furious. Which means she's concerned.

She glares at me. "You have to stop it."

"Why?"

"Don't be an idiot. It's heroin. It isn't hash or ex. It isn't a nice little recreational drug."

"It depends on how much you have. I'm a recreational user."

"Do you think you can quit?"

"I'm not hooked. How about you?"

She's touching her chin with her finger. "How about me?"

"Do you think you can quit?"

She shakes her head and gives me a frustrated smile. "I don't smoke heroin, you maniac."

"Quit Ozi. He's bad for you. You're unhappy."

She looks at me, still shaking her head. Then she lights a cigarette. "Let's not confuse things. Your doing heroin has nothing to do with my marriage."

"You're here every day. Why don't you leave him?"

"I have a son, in case you've forgotten."

With the heroin comes clarity. And a certain cruelty, a calm disregard for consequences. "You don't give a shit about your son."

She stops smoking. "Don't say that," she says in a low voice.

"You don't love him. Stop pretending."

She drops her cigarette on the floor. "I'm leaving."

"You run away from him every chance you get. Do you think it's good for him that you stay? He's going to grow up wondering why his mother never really talks to him, why she's always so distant. And do you know what that's going to do to him? He'll be miserable."

She stares at me, eyes wet, face hard. "You're a bastard."

"Quit them," I say. "It's for the best."

She stands, wipes her tears.

I reach out, but she slaps my hand away. Pain slices up from my finger.

"I don't love you," she says. "And the reason you're so desperate to think you're in love with me is because your life is going nowhere and you know it."

With the pain in my hand comes unexpected, ferocious anger. But even more than anger, I feel triumph straighten my back and flush my face, triumph because I know I'm right about her, because she'd never be so vicious if I were wrong.

She holds out a note. "Here's a thousand. You'll need it."

"I don't want it."

She walks into the bedroom, strips naked, puts on her clothes, and leaves without another word.

When she's gone I pick up the clothes she was wearing and put them on. I can smell her in them, and I'm suddenly filled with the longing to speak with her.

Then I find the thousand-rupee note in my wallet.

I'm at once furious and ashamed, furious because people give money after sex to prostitutes and ashamed because I'm so hungry that I have to take it. But I make a decision. To hell with handouts. I'm ready for a little justice.

. . .

I'm driving slowly to Murad Badshah's workshop, trying not to splash pedestrians wading through the flooded streets with their shoes in their hands and their shalwars pulled up their thighs, when I'm overtaken by a Land Cruiser that sprays muddy water in its wake like a speedboat and wets me through my open window. Bastard. I dry my face on my sleeve and clear the windshield with the wipers.

All my life the arrival of the monsoon has been a happy occasion, ending the heat of high summer and making Lahore green again. But this year I see it as a time of festering, not rebirth. Without air-conditioning, temperatures are still high enough for me to sweat as I lie on my bed trying to sleep, but now the sweat doesn't evaporate. Instead, it coagulates like blood into peeled scabs of dampness that cover my itching body. Unrefrigerated, the food in my house spoils overnight, consumed by colored molds that spread like cancer. Overripe fruit bursts open, unhealthy flesh oozing out of ruptures in sickly skin. And the larvae already wriggling in dark pools of water will soon erupt into swarms of mosquitoes.

The entire city is uneasy. Sometimes, when monsoon lightning slips a bright explosion under the clouds, there is a pause in conversations. Teacups halt, steaming, in front of extended lips. Lightning's echo comes as thunder. And the city waits for thunder's echo, for a wall of heat that burns Lahore with the energy of a thousand summers, a million partitions, a billion atomic souls split in half.

Only after light's echo has come as sound, after it is clear sound's echo will fail to come as heat, do lips and teacups make contact, and even then minds and taste buds remain far apart.

It is, after all, our first nuclear monsoon. And I'm looking for a fat man.

I follow Ferozepur Road as it curves past Ichra, hoping as the water gets deeper that my car won't stall. But soon I reach a point where most of the traffic is turning around and only the Bedford trucks and four-wheel drives are continuing on. Ahead, a few cars have foundered, their exhaust pipes submerged, and I doubt mine will do any better, so I park my car beside the road on a raised slope in front of a shop that sells toilet seats and bathroom tiles. With my shoes tied together by the laces and hanging from my neck, and my jeans rolled up to my knees, I head out on foot.

It takes me the better part of an hour to wade the mile or so to Murad Badshah's workshop. He's chatting with a mechanic, and their hands are stained with motor oil. "Hullo, old chap," he booms when he sees me. "This is a pleasant surprise."

"I thought we had an appointment," I reply, shaking his hand.

"Yes, but I assumed it was canceled, force majeure and all that." He gestures in the direction of the street. "How did you make it here, by ship? I'm losing money every hour because this damned water has two of my rickshaws stranded." He tells the mechanic to take a break and offers me a stool next to a rickshaw lying on its side. "I tried to call you from the shop next door to tell you not to come, old boy, but no one answered at your end."

"My phone is dead," I tell him. "It must be the rains." Either that or I've finally been disconnected.

He smiles and strokes his chin, his stained fingers leaving streaks. "No job, no electricity, no telephone. Perhaps you ought to reconsider joining me in the entrepreneurial venture I mentioned before."

I have reconsidered. That's why I'm here. I only hope I'm not about to be disappointed. "I'm in no mood to be laughed at," I warn him.

His puffy eyes open wide. "I'm being serious."

"Tell me."

Murad Badshah lights a cigarette and leans back on his stool like a child on a wooden horse. "A mechanic in my employ has a dimwitted cousin who managed to secure a position as a guard at a storage depot on Raiwind Road. In April of last year, during the flour shortage, a hungry mob attacked the depot. The guards shot three people dead. People were dying for their hunger, old boy, dying for their hunger. But there was no need for them to go hungry. My mechanic's cousin told me, and I heard this with my own ears, mind you, that there was over a hundred tons of flour in that warehouse alone. Stockpiled, hoarded to keep up the prices."

"May I have a cigarette?" I ask. "Mine seem to be soaked."

"There you are." He offers his pack and lights one for me.

"So what does all this have to do with your plan?"

"Just laying the intellectual foundation, old boy," Murad Badshah tells me. "This is how I see things. People are fed up with subsisting on the droppings of the rich. The time is ripe for a revolution. The rich use Kalashnikovs to persuade tenant farmers and factory laborers and the rest of us to stay in line." He reaches under his kurta and pulls out the revolver I've seen once before. "But we, too, can be persuasive."

"Let me see it," I say, and he hands it to me. It feels cool against my cheek, soothing, like a wet compress on a feverish forehead. I sight along the barrel, pleased that I hold it rock steady, without the slightest trembling. "What's your plan?"

He takes the gun back from me and tucks it away. "Boutiques. I want to rob high-end, high-fashion, exclusive boutiques."

Is he mocking me? "Why boutiques?"

Murad Badshah starts rocking back and forth with excitement

as he ticks off the reasons on his fingers. "Built on main roads with easy access, rarely more than one guard, good cash-to-patron ratio, small size, risk-averse clientele, high-profile hostage possibilities, little competition. And, as an added bonus, symbolism: they represent the soft underbelly of the upper crust, the ultimate hypocrisy in a country with flour shortages. Boutiques are, in a word, perfect."

"It can't be that easy or someone else would be doing it."

Murad Badshah smiles. "Entrepreneurs tend to ignore that argument."

I look at him, at his good-natured face, his chin streaked with motor oil. "Don't take this the wrong way, but do you know what you're talking about? Have you done this sort of thing before?"

He looks offended. "You doubt my qualifications?"

"It's a reasonable question. Don't look at me like I've demanded a copy of your c.v."

He pulls up his kurta, revealing the long, slow roll of his belly. Dead center, a scar the size and shape of a large bird dropping on a car window.

"Polio vaccination?" I ask.

He turns around and bends forward, revealing another, larger scar. "Polio vaccinations don't leave exit wounds."

I'm relieved. Impressed, even. Exaggerated or not, there's obviously some truth behind his stories. But one thing still bothers me. Why does Murad Badshah need me if his plan is so good? "I don't know anything about robbing boutiques. I don't even know how to use a gun."

"You can walk into a boutique without arousing suspicion," Murad Badshah says. "If someone like my mechanics, or my drivers, or even myself showed up, the guard would watch him like a hawk. No offense, but you blend in with those boutique-going types. When you walk in and act like a customer, no one will look at you twice. Then you put a gun against the guard's head, I come in, we generate some revenue and implement our exit strategy. No violence, no profanity, suitable for viewing by young children, and potentially extremely lucrative."

"Let's do it," I say, extending my hand.

We shake. Surprisingly, I don't feel the slightest tremor of doubt or worry. Must be the hairy. Which reminds me. "Do you have any more heroin?"

He's quiet for a moment, looking at the rickshaw lying on its side. "My supplies have been cut off by the rain. The Jamrod-Lahore trucking circuit has been disrupted."

Just my luck. "That's bad news. I'm completely out."

"Don't do any more. I'm being very serious now, old chap."

"How do you know I've done any?"

"You look awful. Besides, I can see you're on it right now."

"What do you mean?"

"Your eyes. And you keep scratching yourself."

I have to remember not to do that. "Are you sure you don't have any?"

"I have a little. But I'm not going to give it to you."

"I don't need your protection."

He looks at me, surprised at the tone in my voice. Then he shakes his head.

As I wade back to my car, excitement builds inside me. I'm finally taking control of my life. I keep waiting for the fear to come, but it doesn't. In fact, I'm walking taller, grinning, empowered by the knowledge that I've become dangerous, that I can do anything I want.

I get behind the wheel and point my finger at a passing Pajero.

Bang bang.

• • •

In the morning, the smell of something burning brings me out of the house and onto the street in search of its source. Neat mounds of rubbish in front of the neighbors' houses smolder, trash smoke rising only to be beaten down by the rain.

I walk closer.

Definitely an odd smell. Maybe there's plastic in the heaps. Or maybe the rain does something to the way they burn.

I kick one. Sodden refuse, half-burnt, flies off. Underneath it's more dry, but I see no fire, no embers even. Just smoke coming out of fissures in the black heart of a trash pile, like steam from the cooled crust of lava.

The stench released is unbearable.

Like burning skin.

I walk inside. But the smell stays with me. On my shoes maybe, on my clothes. It lingers even after I shower.

Even after I dump my clothes in a tub of soapy water

It clings to me. Wafts over the wall. Makes me want to retch.

I wish Murad Badshah would give me some more hairy. But we're partners now, and I need him, so I never ask him for any when he comes by. Wouldn't want to worry the old boy. Instead, we discuss strategy: the boutiques he's scoped out, the gun he's going to buy for me (the cost will be deducted from my share of our eventual take), when we're going to do target practice, et cetera. I want to get on with it, but he keeps telling me to be patient, saying that planning is nine-tenths of the work.

"I'm running out of things to sell," I tell him. "Yesterday some-one bought my television."

He adjusts himself inside the folds of his shalwar. "I wish I could help, old chap, but the rickshaw business has been dead since the tests. My customers are worried about food prices. They prefer to walk."

Luckily, I have another idea where I can get some hairy. I've seen fellow aficionados chilling out in the old city near Badshahi Mosque.

I wait until late at night. The last prayer of the day has been prayed, and there isn't much traffic in the area except for revelers and diners on their way to Heera Mandi. I park my car and walk down the street, the walls and minarets of the mosque towering up to my left. Scattered beneath them, sitting or staggering about in their moon shadows, are the very people I was hoping to meet: junkies.

I know I'm in the right place by the smell, and by the faces floating in the great womb of the drug, content to stay there until they die. Which shouldn't be long, by the looks of some of them.

I hunt for someone to buy from, but he finds me before I find him.

"Heroin?" he asks from behind me.

I turn. He has awful teeth, a rotting smile. But he's clean, unlike the addicts. Without waiting for an answer he puts out his hand and says, "One hundred."

I give it to him, and he passes me something that I slip into my pocket.

"How do you know I'm not a policeman?" I ask him.

"It doesn't matter if you are. Same price, same price."

I grin, but he seems to find nothing funny in what he's said and wanders off, prowling around the addicts like a shepherd tending to his flock.

At home I'm apprehensive until I try the stuff, wondering if he's sold me rat poison, but it turns out to be fine. I spend much of the night smoking and wake up exhausted the next evening. The curtains are wide open. A murder of crows flaps around the gray sky, coming to land one by one on power lines across the street. Somewhere a dog offers up a token bark, but they ignore him and go about their business in silence.

I know I need a meal, even if my stomach isn't bothering to say it's hungry, so I fry myself a couple of eggs and toast some bread over the gas flame. Sometimes hairy kills my appetite.

The other thing hairy kills is time, and that's good, because when Murad Badshah isn't visiting, which is most of the day, I have nothing to do. My only fear is that some relative or unwanted visitor will drop by and see me and my house in the state we're in, which is filthy. So I keep the gate locked and don't answer unless I hear the right open sesame: beep beep bee-bee-beep.

I'm getting good at moth badminton. I now play sitting down, and I try to be unpredictable so the moths will never know when it's safe. Sometimes they whir by my face or even land on me and I leave them alone. At other times they fly at full velocity several feet away and I slam them with an extended forehand.

Here are my rules. I play left hand versus right hand, squash-style. That is, I switch hands whenever I try to hit a moth and fail to connect. At first, I gave a hand a point just for hitting a moth. Then I made it more difficult by adding the "ping" test. According to the "ping" test, a hand scores only when the moth makes a "ping" as it's struck by the racquet. If I hit a moth but there's no "ping," it's a let and the hand must "ping" a moth on its next attempt, or the racquet switches to the opposing hand. Three factors come into play here: moth size (small moths rarely "ping"), stroke speed (only delicate swings produce "pings"), and racquet position (most "pings" come from the racquet's sweet spot). My racquet is made of wood, and I've managed to misplace its racquet press, so it's beginning to warp in the humid monsoon air. As a result, finding the sweet spot and successfully "pinging" becomes increasingly difficult. Scores drop rapidly, until a good evening ends with a tally of left four versus right two, or something like that. I'm right-handed, but my left seems to win more often than not, which pleases me, because I tend to sympathize with underdogs.

I often find myself smiling when I'm playing moth badminton. What amuses me is the power I've discovered in myself, the power to kill moths when I feel like it, the power to walk up to someone and take their money and still put a bullet in them, anyway, just for the hell of it, if that's what I want to do. And I'm amazed that it took me so long to come to this realization, that I spent all this time feeling helpless. Self-pity is pathetic. Hear that, little moth? Ping!

Murad Badshah drops by at night. I try to interest him in some moth badminton, without success. He's decided on a boutique, a shop in Defense near LUMS.

The thing is getting serious. For two days we take turns staking out the boutique, recording what time police patrols pass and guards change. Sometimes I smoke hairy and doze off on my shifts, napping in my car right in front of the place we're supposed to rob. As a result, my reports are impressionistic rather than empirically accurate.

Even though I've stopped scratching myself, I can tell Murad Badshah still wonders if I'm on hairy. The doubt makes him angry. When he gets angry I can see why people might be afraid of him. But I deny it, and he never hits me. Which is good for him, and for me, too, because I don't want to break up our partnership. Besides, he has thick bones, the kind that can hurt your hand if you aren't wearing a glove.

Always remember to lock, I tell myself. The gate, the front door. There isn't much of value in the house that's light enough to be carried away, just a powerless AC and fridge, really, so sometimes I get careless. And when Dadi comes in, waddling as she has since she broke her hip, and Fatty Chacha follows behind her, then I shut my eyes for an instant, at once desperate to disappear and furious with myself for letting this happen, before I get to my feet and greet them.

A half-filled aitch-in-progress crumples in the fist of my left hand. A smattering of tobacco peppered with hairy falls quietly from my right. It's dark inside and sunny out, a rare bright afternoon, and I'm hoping their eyes haven't adjusted enough to make out what I was up to.

"I've been trying to call you since your birthday, but there was no answer." Fatty Chacha's voice trails off. Dadi is staring at me.

"I'm so happy you've come," I say, gesturing to the sofa. "Please."

They don't move. Finally, Dadi speaks. "What happened to you, child?"

I force a laugh. "This?" I say, raising my cast-encased forearm. "It's nothing. A car accident."

Dadi's eyes are watery but still keen. She touches my face. "You've been hurt badly." Her horrified expression makes me want to recoil. She strokes my scars, her shriveled finger remarkably soft.

"But when did this happen?" Fatty Chacha asks.

I want to lie, but I'm afraid they won't believe me. "A month ago," I admit.

"Why didn't you tell us?"

"I didn't want you to worry."

"Foolish boy," Dadi says, sitting down.

Fatty Chacha remains standing. "What's happened to the house? It's a mess."

"Manucci left."

"Impossible."

"He walked out on me."

"But why?"

"He wanted more pay." I can see that Fatty Chacha is doubtful, and I'm about to say more when Dadi calls me over to sit beside her and pats me on the cheek.

"Do you know," she says, trying to reassure herself, "your father never told me when he broke his nose at the military academy. Just like you."

"He was far away," Fatty Chacha points out, sitting down. "There was nothing we could have done to help."

"But I'm fine," I protest.

"You don't look fine, champ," Fatty Chacha says. "Is there some kind of infection? You seem ill."

"No infection. It was a bad accident."

"You must have lost twenty pounds."

I force a grin. "I'm back in my weight class."

Dadi takes a proprietary hold on my upper lip and pulls it back. "You've lost a tooth."

"So have you," I say cheekily.

She chuckles, but I can see she's still shaken. She asks how the accident happened, and I invent a story, claiming I don't remember many details because of the shock. Dadi strokes my good hand as I speak and Fatty Chacha keeps shaking his head, whether in sympathy or out of disbelief it's hard to say.

To change the subject, I ask about Jamal's business.

"He's doing well," Fatty Chacha says. "They have two new clients, with no discount this time."

Dadi offers to move in with me and stay until I'm better, but I manage to convince her not to. She tells me I must promise to visit her every day or she will worry. When they ask if I have tea I admit that I'm out of milk.

As they leave, visibly reluctant to go, Fatty Chacha insists on giving me five hundred rupees. Taking hold of my upper arm, he says quietly, "Come to see me tomorrow. I'm serious, Daru. I'm very worried about you."

And with that, I'm alone again. I lock the gate and the front door. Then I retrieve the battered aitch from my pocket and see what I can salvage.

The day I go to the hospital and have my cast cut off and emerge from the last of my cocoon, the day I can again see the muscles in my forearm when I flex my hand into a fist, is also the day Murad Badshah finally takes me out of the city for some target practice. He's bought me my gun: a 9-millimeter automatic, black, used, Chinese. Just a tool, really, like a stapler. A stapler that can punch through a person. Pin them. Drive blunt metal through flesh and bone.

I've always had steady hands, so I'm surprised to discover that I'm a bad shot. Horrific, really. At twenty paces, I can hit a tin can about one time in five. As for moving targets, I have no hope. Walking from left to right, I don't hit it even once in fifteen minutes of shooting. Murad Badshah tells me not to worry. There will only be one guard, and with my gun pressed against his head there should be no reason to actually shoot, and no way to miss if I do. At the end of half an hour of practice we start running low on ammunition, and we can't afford any more. So that's it: our prep work is over and we now have no reason to procrastinate. Time to move on to the real thing.

At home I keep playing with the gun, unloading and reloading the magazine, chambering rounds, popping them out. It's strange that pistols are such inaccurate devices. If I designed something with the power to kill people, I'd want it to give the user a little more control. But I'm not complaining. There's something appealing about it, something wonderfully casual in the knowledge that when you squeeze the trigger you might kill someone or miss them completely. I like that. After all, moth badminton would be less fun if my racquet wasn't so warped.

My father gets off his motorcycle and runs his hands through his short hair, cropped close in accordance with military academy regulations. He gives his olive suit a once-over, making sure that nothing is amiss, and heads inside. For three coins the white-gloved attendant at the ticket box gives him a seat, not in the most expensive section, but not in the least expensive one, either.

He chooses a well-upholstered couch behind a group of young ladies, students at Kinnaird College who pretend not to notice him, and lights a cigarette. Refined conversation fills the enormous cinema with a gentle murmur. Once all have risen for the national anthem and then sat down again, once the lights have dimmed and the projector has whirled to life, only then does my father reach forward and squeeze the hand my mother extends back to him.

At intermission they eat cucumber sandwiches and sip tea, standing next to each other like strangers. Although he does bow slightly to her as he passes a plate, and her friends cannot help smiling with their eyes.

The Regal Cinema did at one time deserve its name.

Now I sit on a broken seat at the very back, a seat, not a couch, with a crack that pinches my bottom when I move, munching on a greasy bag of chips, trying to ignore the shouting of the men next to me as Chow Yun-Fat kicks his way to another victory for the common man, for good over evil, for hope over tyranny. I love kung fu flicks from Hong Kong. They're the only movies I go to see in the cinema anymore. Everything else is better on a VCR, without the smells and sounds of the audience. But not kung fu.

A fight breaks out somewhere in the middle rows, with much yelling and hooting. People surge up and at each other as Chow flashes a six-foot grin over the scene. One of the men to my left throws a packet of chips into the scuffle. There are no women to be seen here, except on screen, and when those appear, the men in the audience go wild, whistling joyously. Maybe the real ones are in private boxes. Maybe they know better than to come to see Chow Yun-Fat on opening night. Or to go to the cinema at all. No woman I know goes unless the entire cinema has been reserved in advance. Reserved for the right sort of people, that is.

I sit for a while after the movie is over, watching the unruly audience make its way out, sad at what's happened to this place since my parents were my age. Look at us now: we can't even watch a film together in peace. I cover my face with my hands and it feels hot, my entire head feels hot. I'm on edge. I think I need some hairy.

The cinema is almost empty when I realize someone is watching me. I stare at him, and he hesitates for a moment before walking over, motorcycle helmet in hand. Thick black beard. Intelligent eyes. Looks about my age. Salaams.

I return the greeting.

"Have we met before?" he asks me. Calm voice.

"I don't think so."

"Were you at GC?"

"I was, as a matter of fact."

"I remember. You were a boxer."

I nod, surprised.

"So was I," he says.

I extend my hand. "Darashikoh Shezad."

He shakes it firmly. "Mujahid Alam. I was a year junior to you. Middleweight."

"Now I remember. The beard is new."

He looks around the deserted theater. "I came over because you looked upset."

"I'm fine," I say, a little taken aback.

"Did you find today's spectacle disturbing?"

"What do you mean?"

"All the shouting, the fighting, the disorderliness. Our brothers have no discipline. They've lost their self-respect."

"One can hardly blame them."

He lowers his voice and continues in a tone both conspiratorial and friendly. "Exactly. Our political system's at fault. Men like us have no control over our own destinies. We're at the mercy of the powerful."

Normally a speech like this from a virtual stranger would seem odd. But something in the way he says it makes me comfortable, drawing me in. I lean forward to hear him better.

"We need a system," he goes on, and it sounds like he's quoting something, "where a man can rely on the law for justice, where he's given basic dignity as a human being and the opportunity to prosper regardless of his status at birth."

"I agree."

"Then come to our meeting tomorrow."

"What meeting?"

"A gathering of like-minded people, brothers who believe as you and I do that the time has come for change."

I'm not surprised. I could tell he was a fundo from the moment I saw him. But at the same time, I've taken a liking to him and I'm reluctant to let him down. I say gently, "I'm not a very good brother, brother. I don't think I'm the sort you're trying to recruit."

He smiles. "I'm not recruiting you. I just keep my eyes open for like-minded men. Besides, no believer is a bad believer."

"And what if I'm not a believer at all?"

"You should still come. None of us can change things acting on our own. And to act together we need direction. What else is belief but direction? A common direction toward a better end?"

I smile. "We could be hiding enormous differences."

"If differences can be hidden, perhaps they aren't differences at all. Maybe you're more of a believer than you think."

I look at him. He seems like such a nice, earnest guy. "Tell me where the meeting is."

He writes it for me on a piece of paper, and as we part ways he shakes my hand with both of his. "I hope we'll meet again."

"As God wills," I reply.

He accepts that with a nod.

In the car I take an aitch out of the glove compartment. Prerolled. I thought I might need one after the movie. I light up, thinking about Mujahid. What a nice guy. I hope he doesn't get himself killed trying to make things better for the rest of us. I guess there are all kinds of fundos these days. And they're obviously well organized if they even have a sales pitch for people like me.

I can't say that I entirely disagree with their complaints, either.

But I'm definitely not going to that meeting. I roll the paper Mujahid gave me into a ball and toss it out the window.

I need a drink.

I watch a lizard strut along a wall, its shoulders and hips moving in a sensuous swagger. I can't tell if it's dark brown or dark green in the candlelight, but I can see that it's missing half its tail. Lizards look obscene without their tails, naked somehow. But tails grow back eventually, if the lizard is lucky and lives long enough. And this lizard is already only partly naked, partly tailless. Partly bald, like Ozi. Or partly damaged, like me, with my nine good fingers.

I like its eyes: two black dots, nonreflective light-trappers. Utterly determined eyes, doubt-free, unselfconscious. Frightening eyes if they happen to be looking at you and you're small enough to be dinner. The same eyes a man probably sees on an alligator before it drags him down and shakes the air out of his lungs and leaves him to rot a little in the murk, to be tenderized properly before he becomes a meal.

The lizard dashes forward and stops. Two feet away, on the wall above a candle, taking a much-deserved breather from hectic lovemaking, sits one of my shuttlecocks in waiting: a moth the perfect size for pinging. Black dots eye dinner. And dinner, exhausted from a rather strenuous dance with the candle, pants with its wings folded in an aerodynamic delta, more sleekly angled at rest than in flight.

The lizard steps forward. Two steps. Two more. Then four. Stops. Dinner doesn't move. Black dots come closer, close enough to blow moth dust off dinner if the lizard should happen to sneeze. But dinner doesn't seem to think of itself as dinner. No, dinner is completely caught up in its own fantasy, a romantic Majnoon, antennae unkempt, warming itself in the updraft of heat from the flame of much-loved Laila.

Slowly, with no hurry at all, the lizard takes the moth into its mouth and squeezes. Only now does dinner realize it is dinner, one wing trembling frantically until it breaks off and falls like a flower petal, twirling. The lizard swallows, pulling the moth deeper into its mouth, then swallows again. And that's that.

I clap loudly, my legs crossed at the knee, smiling at the lizard. Thanks for the entertainment. Clapclapclap.

Echoes bounce back from the walls.

• • •

Mumtaz comes. She doesn't want to go inside. So even though a light rain is falling, we stand by her car.

"I missed you," I say, reaching for her.

She steps back and looks down without saying anything.

Her silence frightens me. I say, to make her speak, "What have you been up to?"

"I've been writing."

"Zulfikar Manto?"

She nods. "A piece on corruption."

How convenient. "You can do all the research without leaving your house."

She looks at me, and the sadness in her face makes me want to hold her. "Daru, it's over."

Has she left him? "What?" I ask, wanting to make sure.

"This. I'm not going to be coming to see you anymore."

Confusion. What is she saying? Stay calm. Try to sort out what's happening.

"You can't just walk away from this," I say.

She reaches out and hugs me, pulls my head down to her shoulder. "I can. I'm sorry, Daru. We can't be lovers anymore."

"Why are you saying this?" I whisper.

"I was never going to leave Ozi for you. I told you that from the beginning."

I step back, disengaging myself from her embrace. "Do you know he killed a boy?"

"What are you talking about?"

"I was there. I saw him. He ran him over."

"Stop it."

"He didn't even bother to stop. He just drove off."

"Don't do this."

"But he's a murderer. Doesn't that mean anything to you? How can you stay with him?"

"I'm leaving."

Suddenly I understand. I grab her arm. "Has he threatened you?" I'm screaming. "I'll kill him! I'll kill the bastard!"

She tries to pull away, but I hold her by the wrist, tight.

"Let go of me."

"I have a gun. If he hurts you, I'll kill him."

She twists violently and pulls her arm free. "He hasn't threatened me," she says, backing away.

"Wait. Don't go."

She stops at the door of her car. "Daru, please do something about yourself. Tell your family. You need help. You shouldn't be alone." She looks at me for a moment, then slams the door shut and drives off.

I wait for her in the driveway, but she doesn't come back. Then I go inside and sit down and wipe my face, but no matter how much I wipe, it seems to stay wet.

And everyone on my street must be incinerating their garbage, because the stench of burning flesh is so strong I can't sleep. Once, in the darkness, I even imagine that I'm on fire, smoke rising from my body, and leap out of bed.

But it's nothing. Just a moth fluttering by my eyes.

I lie awake and think.

And the more I think, the clearer it becomes. Ozi hasn't threatened her. It's Muazzam. Muazzam is the problem.

I never won a championship when I boxed for GC. Our coach used to say that the guys who win championships are the ones who decide they aren't going down, no matter what. I was one of the best boxers on the team, and I worked hard, but he still disliked me. He told me I wasn't a real boxer, because there was only so much pain I was prepared to fight through. My last fight was for the All-Punjab. I was TKO'd in two rounds with a bad cut above my left eye. The coach said I was a coward.

But I've decided that I'm not going to lose Mumtaz. I'm not going down this time.

In the morning I find myself heading out for a drive. I've taken my gun with me. First I pass by my bank, slowing down to watch the customers slipping inside. Then I drive to Shuja's house. The gunman outside doesn't recognize me, even though my Suzuki must be distinctive with its smashed windows. I stop and stare at him, my gun on my lap. He looks uncomfortable and goes behind the gate. And that makes me feel good.

Eventually I find myself where I knew I'd end up: parked near Ozi's house. I think Mumtaz told me he was out of town, in Macau or something, but I don't care if he is here, if he does drive up and see me. I'll tell him I'm having an affair with his wife. What can he do about it?

But I don't see him, and I don't see Mumtaz either, which is fine with me. Because I'm hoping to see someone else. And early in the afternoon, when the sun comes out and the gray clouds part to reveal a beautiful blue sky, I do see him: little Muazzam, in a black Lancer with his nanny and a driver.

I slip into first and follow. Muazzam is what stands between Mumtaz and me. She feels so guilty about leaving him that she's willing to stay in a meaningless marriage. I wonder what would happen if Muazzam got into a car accident, if he died suddenly. Mumtaz might be upset for a while. But eventually it would be better for her. She would be free, happy again, able to come to me. What adventures the two of us could have. We would be unstoppable.

The Lancer takes a left, heading toward FC College. Dirty water stretches across the road, hiding potholes, and the driver slows down. I get closer. I can see the driver's eyes in his rearview mirror. Then he accelerates, the Lancer pulling away, and I have to floor my Suzuki to keep up. But he isn't trying to lose me. He slows down again at a roundabout, takes a right. I'm very close. Muazzam disappears. Then he stands up again on the rear seat, his curly head visible through the window, just ten feet away from me.

The Lancer gives a left indicator and turns into the driveway of a house I remember, Ozi's grandfather's place. We used to play there sometimes, when we were younger.

Dark clouds with red bellies, lit from below by the electric city or a last gasp of light from the drowning sun, and a smoky breeze that stinks of burning flesh from the trash pile down the street. A joint in my mouth, heavy on the hairy, and a 9-millimeter automatic tucked into my jeans, pressed into my hipbone, bruising my flesh painlessly because of the numbness. Crows flap against the wind, sitting on a telephone line, quiet, watching the outnumbered parrots in my banyan tree.

Finally, fear stronger than the hairy can hide.

I'm so scared that I feel like throwing up. I'd force my finger down my throat and make myself gag if it would make me a little less dizzy. But I'm not drunk, I'm frightened, and I don't think vomiting would be much help.

Murad Badshah arrives and parks his rickshaw, and we head out in my car. We don't speak much. For once, even Murad Badshah doesn't have anything to say. He keeps adjusting himself under his shalwar, or maybe he's trying to find a comfortable position for his revolver.

The hand brake makes a loud sound when I pull it up. Light pours out of the big glass windows of the boutique. Mannequins cast shadows on our car. Murad Badshah reminds me what I have to do, and even though I'm listening, I don't understand a word he's saying. My college boxing coach once had to slap me before a fight to get me to attend to his instructions.

I get out, feeling self-conscious. Then I turn and walk into the boutique. The guard stares at me and my heart starts pounding in my head, hard. I stare back at the guard like I'm a rude patron. I realize I'll kill him if I have to. He's a young guy, balding, with dark skin and glistening temples and a mole like a fly on his left nostril. He's sitting on a stool with a short-barreled pump-action shotgun across his thighs, and I'm standing beside him so its barrel is pointing at my knees. If he squeezes the trigger he'll blow my legs off.

I walk out of his line of fire and his eyes don't follow me. An ugly kid who looks like Muazzam is crying and pulling on his mother's arm, and the sound is so unnerving that I want to shoot him to prevent myself from panicking.

Get hold of yourself.

Walk around, avoiding eye contact, touching fabrics, seeing who's here. No men except the guard and one of the salespeople, who looks harmless. The other salesperson is a fierce-faced woman with arms bigger than mine. Keep my distance from both of them, because my mouth is dry and I'm zoned on hairy, so I don't know how well I can talk. If they ask me what I'm looking for, I might shoot them. I think shooting something might calm me down. I feel hysterical. That damn kid keeps crying and tugging on his mother.

I walk up to the guard and pull the automatic out of my jeans and put it in his face. His shotgun isn't pointing at me. I notice that my finger's on the trigger guard instead of the trigger, so I slip it into the right place. I click off the safety. The guard watches me. Above his head I can see my reflection in the window, and I look just as calm as he does, but I'm not calm at all and I don't think he is either. He's raising his hands, which is good. They're not near the shotgun.

I can't believe I forgot to take my automatic off safety before I came in. He could have killed me. Thinking that makes me want to kill someone just to calm down.

Murad Badshah's here. He's taking control. Good. The salespeople are giving him a lot of money. The customers are taking off their jewelry, their purses. The guard is lying on his face, his shotgun out of reach, and I realize I'm standing on his right hand, but I don't move. I look around me, feeling embarrassed, but no one seems to notice.

A police mobile drives by on the street outside without stopping. I watch it. If they stop I'm dead, and the first thing I'm going to do is start shooting. Shooting anyone and anything. But the police keep on going.

I take my foot off the guard's hand, but this makes me nervous.

The woman with the kid yells something, and I look and see the boy running for the door. I don't move. Little ugly boy who looks like Muazzam. Runs right by me and reaches the door. No one gets out, that's the rule. No one gets out.

My hand. Hand's rising. Hand with the gun in it. Leveling off at Muazzam's head. He's not going to make it to Mumtaz. He's not going to ruin this.

The sound of an explosion and the glass of the door becomes opaque with cracks but doesn't shatter.

Was that me?

CHAPTER 14

judgment (after intermission)

The gavel weighs heavily in your hand. Suppressing a yawn, you use the handle to scratch yourself beneath your robe.

The actors sit upright in these, the final moments of the trial. Murad Badshah perspires comfortably, his wet face beatific as it catches the light. Any thought, no thought, could be passing through his mind.

Tension animates Aurangzeb's handsome features, a streak of cruelty visible in his expression of uncertain triumph. It suits him. Women (and not a few men) cast admiring glances his way.

Mumtaz carries herself with the equestrian elegance of a woman who looks good in hats, leaning forward as she prepares for a jump. Her eyes glitter. She watches Daru.

And the accused, Darashikoh Shezad, coils without moving, explosive, motionless, barely contained. His smile is predatory. He stares at you.

The prosecutor is closing his closing.

"The accused would have you believe, Milord," he is saying, "that our trials are on trial here, that our judgments are being judged. The accused would have you believe that a crime is in progress in this courtroom. The accused would accuse those who accuse him. Hooked by the line of truth, thrashing against the current of evidence, the accused would have you believe, Milord, that the fish is reeling in the fisherman.

"But what are you to make of the testimony of the witnesses who saw the accused kill the boy, of the witnesses who recall the make, model, and registration of a car the accused concedes to be his, fleeing the scene of the crime? What are you to make of the testimony of the police officers who conducted this most thorough and professional investigation, of the confession the accused made in their custody?

"Nothing. You are to make nothing of the testimony you have heard. You are to make nothing of the evidence you have seen. You are instead to put your faith in the promises of the accused, in his fantasy that he is being framed by interests powerful enough to corrupt the professionalism of the police, wealthy enough to bribe these legions of witnesses, and malicious enough to destroy the life of a man who is as innocent of this crime as the innocent can be.

"But the accused has been unable to demonstrate the existence of foul play, unable to find an alibi, a single witness, an atom of evidence that might corroborate his version of events. The accused has been described as untrustworthy by a former employer, as a peddler of drugs by a father whose son he corrupted. He has been seen consorting with known outlaws. Illegal narcotics and an unlicensed firearm were found in his home. The words of such a man must be given little weight, Milord, if indeed they are to be given any weight at all.

"It is true another voice has joined the accused in crying that he is the victim of a shadowy conspiracy. But surely, Milord, if the rule of law demands anything, it demands you ignore the voice of his adulterous lover, distraught at the thought that prison bars may do what the sacred contract of marriage could not: stand in the way of her carnal relations."

The prosecutor licks his lips like a victorious mongoose.

"Enough of this nonsense, Milord," he says. "Do justice."

There is a pregnant pause, and one by one the other actors in this drama turn to you. The audience awaits. The director bites his nails. Critics and producers will judge your decision.

Here comes your cue.

"Come on," someone hisses from offstage. "What's it to be? Guilty or not?"

CHAPTER 15

eight

I hear over the sound of the car's engine the ringing of a gunshot fired close to my ears. It diminishes in volume without subsiding into silence, becoming more and more irritating, too quiet not to be imaginary, stealing my attention from the road.

Murad Badshah doesn't speak. He holds his gun in his lap, the barrel pointed at my kidneys, and although he faces straight ahead, I know he's watching me out of the corner of his eye.

At home I wait in the car as he gets out, so we don't have to look at each other or talk. He stands for some time in the driveway, thinking, then climbs into his rickshaw and drives off. It's raining. He forgot to give me my half of our night's take, and I forgot to ask.

I can't sleep. I stand in the open door of my house, a candle behind me, light glittering off raindrops until the instant they pass into my shadow, smoking a cigarette, straight up, no hash, no hairy, snapping out smoke rings the monsoon washes away. When it's done I go back inside and sit down, the badminton racket beside me. But I can't bring myself to touch it, and I hardly notice the moths as they pass.

I worry a thumbnail, trying to make the edge smooth, until I peel a long sliver still embedded in flesh and the pain makes me suck my thumb. Then I start to squeeze with my canines, harder and harder, covering one pain with another, and when I take my thumb out of my mouth it's almost numb, sensation-free except for the throb of my pulse deep inside the flesh.

The morning comes gradually, with color in the sky, the deepest blue not black. Shadows appear. I know what day this is. I know Zulfikar Manto checks his mail today, and I know where. But I don't know when, so I'm in my car, outside the post office, waiting well before it opens.

Across the street, the flow of people from bank branch to money changer's stall builds steadily, rupees shifting into dollars in the wake of the nuclear sanctions, the exchange rate ticking into the high fifties, the low sixties. Some families ride with gunmen to protect the contents of safe-deposit boxes they intend to take home. In a car beside me four men with beards jot down license-plate numbers. A ripple in the city's crime wave.

I wait for Mumtaz.

A letter writer near the post office entrance starts to eat a paratha. Oil mixes with the ink stains on his fingers. When he wipes them on a greasy newspaper, they leave blue streaks.

I didn't see Mumtaz enter the post office, but I see her now, emerging, and my first thought is to leave, to slip the car into reverse and slide back onto the street. The wind and rain have made a solid mass of her hair and it hangs in clumps beside her face, curling, thick. The way it does when she sweats, after boxing, after sex on a hot day. I know what it must smell like.

I'm startled by her walk, how familiar it is: shoulders back, chin up. For all the world invulnerable, perfect, until she stumbles on the uneven pavement in front of the post office, a quick trip followed by an even quicker smile, a smile I've seen countless times, what her mouth and eyes do when her guard slips and she laughs at herself.

I don't know what I can say to her. I don't know why I thought she would be different. I wish the sight of Mumtaz had brought my memory of her into even the slightest doubt. Because this, seeing her as she was, makes me want to run away.

I don't run, though. I get out of my car. Wet dust on cement, smooth like paper, like silt, retains my footprint. I take two steps and wait. She stops. Then she walks over. We stand for a moment, watching each other. She doesn't speak.

Something hot rises inside me, like a sob on fire, demanding release, and I tilt my head back and shut my eyes, my mouth in line with my throat, my face flat to the rain. And gravity pulls me down, overcoming exhausted muscles, an unfed, unslept body, bending weak legs, bringing me to the earth, leaving me on my knees. The air lacerates my lungs as I breathe, the world turning against me, existence an agony.

Then a shock as I feel her hands. She strokes my hair gently, cradles the back of my head with long fingers, pulls me to her, buries my face in her loins. And I lean against her legs, upright only with her support, my arms at my sides, my chest against her thighs, as she caresses me from above. It lasts until I've stopped waiting for her to let go. When she walks away my body remains erect. And when I open my eyes I find I have the strength to stand.

The police come for me that afternoon. I hadn't expected them, but I go quietly. In the back of their mobile unit, one asks me why I did it. I don't answer him.

"Why were you in such a hurry?" he asks.

"What do you mean?"

"The boy you killed because you couldn't be bothered to stop for a red light. What was so important you couldn't wait for him to cross the road?"

I look at him, not understanding.

"He was probably rushing to meet a woman," another says.

They laugh.

And as I look out the open back of the mobile unit at the intersection falling behind and people on firm ground receding as though carried away by the earth's spin, I begin to remember and to understand. I feel something, wild anger and confusion perhaps, but I'm so tired I can't place the emotion, and it, too, slips away as I shut my eyes.

CHAPTER 16

the wife and mother (part two)

It's me again: Mumtaz. Now commonly called "the monster." Sometimes even to my face. Which makes my story, I suppose, a kind of monster story. With Daru among my victims.

I wonder what would have happened if I'd met him a few months earlier, when he still had his job. Or maybe even years earlier, before his mother died, before I'd gotten married and had Muazzam. We probably would have had an insane affair, a couple weeks of wild sex, and that would have been that. I wonder, because that's what should have happened. But when I met Daru his life was falling apart, and our relationship became something else.

Even though I told him not to, Daru fell in love with me. Maybe "love" isn't the right term. He became obsessed with me. And I guess you could say that it was, at least in part, my fault. I stayed with him past the first warning signs. I don't know if that was wrong of me. All I know is that it made me feel good to take care of him. I was desperate to prove to myself that I wasn't a bad person, that I wasn't selfish and uncaring, that I could be giving and good. That it wasn't my fault I didn't love my son.

As soon as I heard Daru had been arrested for killing a boy in a car accident, I told Ozi. And Ozi smiled.

That's when I realized Ozi knew about our affair. He'd never said anything, didn't say anything even then. But something in his expression left no doubt in my mind. I felt sick. Disgusted by what Daru had done, disgusted by my husband's glee, disgusted at myself for having the affair in the first place, for ending it so abruptly. I felt sorry for all of us.

And then I made up my mind. I decided that I couldn't stay in this house any longer, that I needed to abandon my family to save myself.

I thought about Muazzam growing up without a mother. I told myself that he would still have Ozi, his grandparents, his nanny. That they would take care of him. That he'd be emotionally disturbed if he grew up with a mother like me. That already I was spoiling him to make up for the love I didn't feel. But as much as I tried, I never convinced myself I wasn't hurting my son by leaving him behind. I just knew I had to. And I felt strong enough to live with it.

So one day I transferred half the money in our joint account to one I'd opened for myself, took my jewelry out of the safe-deposit box, and packed two suitcases. I felt almost as determined as I had the day I told Ozi I'd marry him. But when I told Ozi I was leaving, when I saw him register the shock and pain, then I felt sad, too. For both of us. And for Muazzam.

Ozi didn't get angry. He was quiet for a long time. And when he spoke, softly, he just said he'd see to it that Daru wouldn't get out of prison for a long time.

I didn't lie, didn't pretend I hadn't had an affair. I just said, "You killed the boy, didn't you?"

Ozi didn't answer. Which was his answer. I felt like crying.

He didn't speak again until the servants were carrying out my suitcases. Then he said, "Please stay. I'll forgive you."

And who will forgive you?

I thought I would go home to Karachi, but I haven't. Something keeps me here. Zulfikar Manto, maybe. My parents' complete inability to understand. A reluctance to run from where I've been, what I was.

I think about Muazzam more than anything else. I remember his long eyes, eyes that are neither mine nor Ozi's but his own, uninherited, original. He isn't a strong boy. He tires easily, cries more than most three-year-olds. But he likes my voice, likes me to read to him. It puts him to sleep.

Muazzam called me "Amma." And not softly, but insistently, desperately, even when he was barely awake. I wonder if he always knew I would leave him. Maybe all children do, maybe that's where nightmares come from, nature telling them their parents will be gone one day. But I wonder if mine suspected his would leave sooner than she should.

I don't think I will ever be able to explain to him why his mother couldn't stay.

One thing he will definitely know is that his mother was a very bad woman. Everyone's talking about this trial, and more than anything else they seem fascinated by the question of whether or not Daru and I were having an affair. I say "the question," but it isn't, really. I don't think many people are giving me the benefit of the doubt.

Or Daru, for that matter.

But Zulfikar Manto's been writing an article that tells things from Daru's perspective, or what I imagine his perspective to be

—I haven't spoken with him since he was locked up. I've interviewed people who are willing to say, anonymously, of course, that a Pajero and not a Suzuki killed the boy. And certain members of the Accountability Commission, while refusing to be quoted, have pointed out that it would be extremely inconvenient for Khurram Shah, himself under investigation, if his son were to be accused of this crime.

Manucci's been a big help tracking down witnesses. When I left Ozi he left with me. I've discovered he's a brilliant investigator. I might make a journalist out of him, once I've taught him how to read properly.

I doubt the article will do much good, but at least Daru will have some defenders. Which is more than I have. But I'm finding I can live with myself, which shocks me more than anything.

Maybe I am a monster, after all.

CHAPTER 17

nine

In the cell a man moves and I watch him, his shadow in the shadows, as he looks past the bars at the light, itself so pale the hot yellow of its filament fails to fill evenly the glass of the bulb. An ember unable to catch fire.

The envelope glows in my hands. It reminds me of things I'd rather not remember, a smell like burning flesh, a hazy world seen through smoke. Mumtaz's face, the faces of many boys blurred together. A ringing sound. Places I will not let my mind go.

I want to tear it up. But I can't. So I pull my knees to my chest and open it. Across the top of the page, Mumtaz has written, "The Trial, by Zulfikar Manto."

It is the story of my innocence.

A half-story.

I read it over and over again, until I notice the paper getting wet, the ink blurring into little flowers.